THE
HIGH SCHOOL
EXPERIMENT

ABHYUDHAYA VENKAT

WRITERS REPUBLIC L.L.C.
515 Summit Ave. Unit R1
Union City, NJ 07087, USA

Website: *www.writersrepublic.com*
Hotline: *1-877-656-6838*
Email: *info@writersrepublic.com*

Ordering Information:
Quantity sales. Special discounts are available on quantity purchases by corporations, associations, and others. For details, contact the publisher at the address above.

Library of Congress Control Number: 2019952024
ISBN-13:   978-1-64620-088-7   [Paperback Edition]
                  978-1-64620-089-4   [Digital Edition]

Rev. date: 10/28/2019

CHAPTER 1

DISAPPOINTMENT

I've never really understood why people hate Mondays so much. Maybe it's because I've never been to a school before so I don't understand the horrors of waking up on a Monday morning after the weekend is over. Or maybe it's because my weekends are just like any other day for me, my time spent studying for my classes and delving further into my research into string theory. This Monday was different though. Waking up with the dread of what was to come made me realize for the first time how people usually felt on Monday mornings, despite it being for a different reason. After all, today was the day MIT acceptance letters went out, and I was now filled with the dread of not getting into the school I had all but been forced to aim for since the day of my birth 13 years ago. Exactly 13 years ago today. Just my luck that what possibly could be the worst day of my life also happens to be my 13th birthday - not that I care for birthdays at all, I find them a useless thing to celebrate. Of course, I expected today would be a life-changing moment, as most college decisions are, but I most definitely was not expecting it to change my life in the way it did ...

Even though today was an important day for me, I wasn't going to let that change my schedule. Ever since I was ten years old, I have woken up at 5:30 AM every day to take my usual 90 minutes run around the neighborhood. My Appa, who could have been a professional cricket player back in India if his parents hadn't wanted him to focus on his studies and become a Computer Engineer, had instilled in me that physical exercise is important for people to get the brain flowing and your body in good shape. When I got back home, I ate breakfast with

1

my two sisters, before they went off to school. Unlike me, they are not homeschooled, with my older sister, Rakshini, in her junior year and my younger sister, Lakshmi, in 4th grade. While they were at school, I continued my research, as Amma hadn't scheduled any of my classes for today, which was usual for a Monday. It was hard to focus today as my mind kept going back to worrying about the decision, and I made no progress today. By the time I had called it a day, it was 6 PM. That meant I only had 28 minutes before the decision came out. On a normal day I would have spent this time reading, or maybe taking a walk outside, and I was tempted as the mid-March weather was fairly nice. Instead, however, I opened up the admissions portal and waited for the moment I had been dreading all day to finally approach.

I stared at the screen in shock. Even though somewhere in my head I knew that they couldn't deny me, I had mostly been expecting a rejection. It had never crossed my mind that I would be accepted into MIT, despite all of my credentials. I then started screaming, which was uncharacteristic of me, bringing the rest of my family into my room to congratulate me. However, I then noticed my parents quickly glance at each other, as if they had something troubling to say.

"Amma? Appa? What's wrong?"

"Devadas, I know you might not like what we are about to say, but your mother and I think it is for the best," I was confused. What bad news would my parents have for me, on what had become the best day of my life? It must be serious, since Appa seldom calls me by my full name.

"What happened?"

"I know that you were excited to go to MIT next year, after all, we were the ones pushing for it for the last 18 months..." Were my parents going to stop me from pursuing my future? I was panicking inside, my parents couldn't possibly be thinking of ruining this day for me! "... but after observing you the last few weeks, we feel like we have failed you as parents." How could they have failed me? If it weren't for their support and homeschooling me, this never would have happened.

"What do you mean?"

"Don't get us wrong, we are extremely proud of everything you have achieved so far, but we don't think you are ready to go to college. After watching you interact with people the last few months, we realized that despite how gifted academically you are, you can't even hold a conversation with anyone. You scare people your age, why do you think your sisters always have to go to their friends' houses instead of inviting them over?" This was making no sense! I mean, I will be the first to admit that I might not be the most social person in the world - far from it- and that I tend to intimidate people because of my brilliance, but that shouldn't be stopping me from pursuing my education, right?

"I don't understand, what does this have to do with college?"

"Deva…" now Amma was speaking, "you might be able to take care of yourself when you stay away for nine months, but we feel like being surrounded by kids five to ten years older than you would only further isolate you in this world. You already have no friends, but in college when you don't have the constant companionship of your family, we think it would only be detrimental to your mental health." Before I could respond, Appa continued,

"Not only that, they will feel intimidated by your presence on campus, and go out of their way to make sure that you won't feel like you belong there. We already have talked to the MIT Admissions Office, and they agreed with us. However, they were happy to still keep your acceptance, and we made a deal with them that you will be entering their campus two years from now, after you have completed two years of high school. This decision is final." How could they!? Forcing me to go to a high school, and take classes I had finished five years earlier? This was an outrage. I knew that they were just afraid to see me gone, and weren't ready to let their only son leave the house. I stormed out of the room and left the house to take a walk. I needed to regroup and come to terms with this awful and disappointing decision my parents had made for me.

CHAPTER 2

PREPARATIONS

Three months. That's how long I've had to digest the fact that I will not be going to college in the fall. And I'm still not over it. I had been planning this for almost two years, and now because my parents think I'm incapable of mingling with others, these plans have been postponed for two years. I mean, I understand where they are coming from, but at the same time, I don't think this is enough to hinder my potential future by delaying college until after I am done with two years of high school. Things aren't getting any better either. Today is my new student orientation event, where I will be joining some other incoming freshmen in a tour of the school. I'll also be meeting the principal and my counselor, as apparently my situation is unique and they want to talk to my parents and me about my high school education. A high school education for a kid that could be going to MIT in the fall.

High schoolers are weird. Pep assemblies make no sense. This is a waste of my time. Those were the three thoughts going through my head after the orientation. I knew high school was bad, but if this was just an introduction, I'm not sure if I can brace myself for an entire two years in this place. The upperclassmen who gave us a tour were so phony, as well. If they didn't want to be there, why were they here? The last few months I've been preparing myself by reading all about the types of things that happen in high schools to smart kids - getting shoved in your locker, swirlies, and of course, doing the jocks homework so I don't get beat up - but I must have missed the part where you need earplugs because the band and cheerleaders try to make you go deaf during assemblies. I already know I'm going to hate my time in this school, and all the hope

I have left is that they will at least tailor their resources to my needs. After all, I did all of the materials they teach in this school five years ago. Hopefully, the meeting with the principal goes a bit better than this torture.

"Mr. and Mrs. Shanmugan, you don't know how much of a pleasure it is to have your son Devadas attend our school!" Well, it looks like the principal is just as fake as those upperclassmen who had led the tour.

"Seeing as my older sister goes here, it shouldn't have been that much of a surprise that I am going here, Mr. Davidson." I'm not sure why I was being so snarky; sure I was in a bad mood, but usually, I would have just remained silent.

"Dev, be respectful!"

"Sorry, Appa"

"Anyway, your son is truly a gifted student; we have never seen someone score so highly on the aptitude tests," That was the counselor, Mrs. Thompson. "He is more advanced than what our curriculums are geared for." Before anyone could say anything, a new man entered the room, he looked to be in his late 30s, with a black goatee that made his face instantly memorable.

"Mr. Shanmugan! I've read all your papers on String Theory. The theories you have suggested are truly remarkable. I'm Mr. Turner, the physics teacher." I liked this man already. Not only because he recognized my work, he just had that aura around him that just made you feel good. "Sorry Mr. Davidson, Mrs. Thompson, but I just had to meet this kid. It's a shame you don't allow freshmen to take physics, he could probably teach the course already."

"We wanted to talk to you about that. Because of Dev's extracurricular studies, we had thought that we could have him take independent math as well as a study hall, to give him three periods, if we include his lunch, that will allow him to pursue his research." Maybe I had underestimated the school, they had come prepared for this meeting and how to deal with my 'unique situation', as Appa had put it. "Now that you're here, however, maybe we can have his study hall be with you during a free period, it would make more sense, after all, to have him with you instead of in the general study hall classroom." Ok, maybe high school won't be so bad after all. I'll still have close to three hours a day to work on my research, and that's not counting the downtime I will have in my other classes since I most definitely won't need to pay full attention in those.

The rest of the meeting went fairly well, as my parents, the principal, and the counselor continued to discuss what classes I would be taking. It ended up being a nice mix between free periods for me to do my research, as well as classes where I will have a chance to meet new people, which of course was the reason why I was stuck in high school in the first place. I still wasn't sold on high school though, the kids seemed a little too rambunctious, and outside of my research periods, I would be wasting my time in classes that I had no business being in. Oh, and I had to take gym. While I was fit enough to not get murdered by other kids, I wasn't too sure how much I was looking forward to a class where the kids couldn't be filtered to be academically talented, like the other classes I was taking.

The next few months passed by in a hurry, and soon it was August 14th, the day before school started. In the last five months, my life had taken a complete 180 turn, but I was ready. I would go to high school, and prove that I can mingle with kids my age, and show my parents that I was ready to go to college.

"Deva?" Amma was standing at the door to my room.

"Yeah?"

"Are you ready for school tomorrow?" She already knew the answer, of course, she was just easing herself into whatever she wanted to talk about next.

"As ready as someone who was forced to go to school against his will can be."

"Well, before you went off to high school, I wanted to talk to you about what we are expecting from you."

"Yes, I know, I need to be friendly to other people, make some friends, the whole nine yards."

"We have some rules still," This was new. I wonder what she was expecting. "I know that peer pressure is a strong force, and you shouldn't fall for that. You should also remember your culture. You are an Indian boy, no white man will ever accept you as American, and if you turn your back on our ways, you will begin to no longer be Indian either. The worst outcome in life is a man that has no culture." Well, this was getting a bit weird. Not that I haven't heard this lecture before, but I still couldn't see where she was going with this. "Firstly, we expect you to maintain top-notch grades. We may be sending you to high school to learn social skills, but that doesn't mean we will be okay with your grades slipping. You have a reputation to uphold, as well as the reputation of your father and me." As if I was going to be distracted enough to not ace all my classes. "We also do not want you on social media. We know the temptation will be strong, but bad things have happened to kids on those websites like snapgram and instabook, we don't want you digging a hole for yourself through these websites." I nodded my head, I already knew how much of a distraction these could be to my research. "And finally, the most important rule. White people may be okay with their kids dating, and being distracted by girls, but they also come from a culture where they believe in 'love marriages' and divorces after a couple of years when you get bored with your current wife. We Indians have standards, and as your mom, I do not want you getting distracted foolishly by girls when you should be focusing on studies. Of course, if you do happen to meet a girl that you know is good for you, I would be happy to talk to her parents about a possible arranged marriage after your college education." Wait. Amma was afraid of me getting distracted by girls? She must be truly paranoid. I was going to high school to learn social skills, not to get familiar with the female anatomy, after all. She must have been reading a novel about teenage romance, or something, that had put this thought in her head.

"Of course, I would never think of harming my studies."

"Good. Just remember that if a girl is interested in you, she does not have good intentions. She's either after your brains, your future success, or your looks… " Ok, I need to end this now before it becomes embarrassing.

"Goodnight!"

CHAPTER 3

DISASTER

The first day of school. The day where you make your first impression on your classmates. As the only reason I'm even going to high school is to make friends, and interact with kids my age, I should probably be making a good impression. According to the research I've done, the first way to make a good impression is to dress nicely. I'm not usually one to care about my clothes but today is an important exception. I need to prove my parents wrong and show them that I can make friends.

"You know you're going to a high school, not a business meeting right?" Rakshini was frowning when I entered the kitchen to eat breakfast. I'm not too sure why though, isn't it normal for people to wear a tuxedo on their first day of school? Especially when they want to make a good impression.

"I need to make a good impression, my research has told me that dressing nicely leads to good impressions."

"Well, if you get beat up, you'll know why." Always so negative. That's one of the things about my older sister that can be annoying at times. Why assume that I will get beat up? It's more likely that kids will flock to me because of my tuxedo and I will easily make friends, and prove my parents wrong.

"ARE YOU OUT OF YOUR MIND?" That would be Lakshmi. Looks like she's also of the opinion that my clothing choice isn't appropriate. I still disagree with them, but I'm starting to have second thoughts now. Alas, it's too late to change into something else, so I will have to go with the tux anyway.

Okay, maybe they were right. I haven't been in this school for even five minutes and I'm already getting strange looks. I'm sure people are snickering behind my back as well. I start to walk a bit quicker, hoping that the faster I reach my English classroom, the more quickly this humiliation will end. I couldn't have been more wrong.

"What are you running away from?" Well, maybe running in the halls wasn't the best idea. I'm now face to face with this giant of a human being. The amount of facial hair he has makes me wonder if he isn't actually an animal. "I wonder why a puny kid like you is all dressed up like this? Did you think you were going to a wedding?" I'm starting to think that this kid isn't a nice guy either.

"I'm just trying to get to class on time." I could feel my voice go quiet as I finished the sentence. Suddenly my feet aren't on the ground. So I did the only logical thing a person in my situation would do. Flail my legs and hope it hits him.

"Let him go!" Sadly I knew that voice. The last thing I needed was for people to think I needed my older sister to save me from difficult situations.

"And why should I?"

"Because anyone that wants to hurt my little brother will have to deal with me." The giant let me go. I'm not sure why he looked scared though, Rakshini isn't that scary. I turned around to begrudgingly thank her, and saw the real reason he was scared. A teacher was walking towards us, and the crowd that had gathered quickly dispersed.

"You two go onto class, Luke, come with me, looks like we have a meeting in the disciplinary office immediately." So the giant was named Luke. I'll have to keep that in mind in case I come across him again. I think I might also be asking my parents to be enrolling me in Karate, so I can defend myself.

"Now what did I tell you about being beaten up because of the suit?" Leave it to my sister to rub my unfortunate predicament in my face.

"Yes, you were right, congratulations do you want a sticker?"

"You're impossible." She starts walking off, and I decide to head onto my first period English class. It's amazing that I will manage to be on time even after nearly getting beaten up.

Most of the seats were already taken when I reached my English classroom. I managed to find one near the back of the classroom, which was perfect since I was most likely not going to be paying attention anyway. I had better and more important things to do, after all.

"Hi! What's your name? I'm Summer, nice to meet you!" The voice was coming from my left at the desk next to mine. I turned to see a girl, a little over five feet tall, with wavy, auburn colored hair going past her shoulders, waving at me with a bright smile. Well, I guess it was time to show that I can actually interact with other humans without getting beaten up.

"The name is Shanmugan. Devadas Shanmugan. But you can call me Dev, like if it was short for David." Ok, maybe relying on pop culture references to talk to people comes out a bit awkward.

"I'm guessing you like James Bond movies? Is that why you're wearing a suit, trying to look like a secret agent? I think it's brave that you would try and get attention to yourself on the first day of school as a freshman." How does one respond to this? I haven't even watched a James Bond movie, I've just heard the quote! Brave? I didn't even know that wearing a suit was a faux pas, I just wanted to make a good impression. Wait, she's staring at me strangely. Oh yeah, I need to respond.

"I actually haven't seen any James Bond movies. And the suit is the result of a prank by my older sister." Well, if she doesn't know my sister, then putting the blame on her won't do me any harm. "She thought it would be funny to have her brother make a fool of himself on his first ever attempt at public school."

"What do you mean?"

"I was homeschooled until this year, both my sisters have been in the public school system since kindergarten, though." Her bright green eyes filled with surprise, but before she could reply, the bell rang, and our teacher, Mr. Bakerman, was calling for our attention.

"Welcome to Freshman Honors English! As today is the first period of the first day of high school for y'all, I thought we would have a little fun, to kick off a great four years of high school!" Fun? I thought people came to school to learn... and to make friends. Having fun in classes makes no sense at all when you're supposed to be learning. "Now I know some of you will know each other from middle school, but you also will most likely not know everyone in this room, just like I don't either. So to help us out, we will be playing a little name game, so I can put a face to the names on my attendance sheet, as well as give you a chance to get to know your classmates a bit." Okay, this makes more sense, after all, the teacher needs to know our names in order to grade us. "Let's start with you here to my right in the front row, I want you to tell us your name, and three interesting facts about you that you want people to know!"

"Uhh, hi? I am Ethan, and I play the violin, my favorite food is lasagna and I lived in California until I was ten years old." This continued on, while I got to learn that Hazel is an artist, Jake likes to hike, and a bunch of other random facts about people until we got to…

"Umm, I'm Summer, I have four older brothers, I play chess, and was homeschooled until this year, so this is actually my first day of any kind of school." Oh. So that's why she looked surprised when I mentioned I was homeschooled. Why is everyone staring at me? This is a little uncomfortable.

"Why is everyone staring at me?"

"It's your turn to share something about yourself." Oh yeah, it's my turn in this game.

"Well uh, I'm Dev, I have an eidetic memory, which makes this whole facts thing kind of pointless for me to remember your names, my parents sent me to high school so I could learn to talk to people, and in a weird coincidence, I was actually homeschooled as well. Oh and the suit was not my idea, my older sister tricked me. And my favorite color is yellow, I hate cats, I wanted a pet frog but my parents said no…"

"That was more than three, thank you for sharing so much about yourself Dev." High school is horrible. I've now made a fool of myself in front of a large crowd two times today, and we are only ten minutes into the first period. How will I ever survive the next seven periods?

"I'm guessing you're not good with people then?" Summer whispered to me.

"Why do you think my parents forced me to go to high school instead of MIT?" Oops. I shouldn't have said that.

"MIT?"

"Can you forget I ever said that? I'm not supposed to be flaunting it or anything, and if it gets out it will be harder for me to make friends, and my parents will be proven right, and they'd also be disappointed in me for trying to flaunt my 170 IQ and trying to buy friends with my genius and the fact that…" Oh no. I'm rambling again and letting out way too much information. What a disaster.

"Your secrets are safe with me, I guess? You know you really shouldn't be trusting someone you met ten minutes ago with your deepest secrets." Was that sarcasm? Or was she implying that she was going to betray me? I don't even know whats going on anymore, I think I need to go home, I have a headache, and I wish I never acquiesced to this stupid high school experiment. My breathing started to quicken, and I'm sure my heartbeat could be heard from across the room. "Are you okay? You're becoming pale." This is horrible, now even the closest person I have to a friend is being weirded out by me. "Mr.Bakerman! Dev needs to go to the nurse, I think he's about to faint!"

"Then go with him to the Nurse! If someone's about to faint you don't need to ask just get them to the Nurse as quickly as possible." Summer took my hand and dragged me out of the classroom. However, the moment we were out of sight of the classroom, she stopped and put me against the wall.

"Dev? You need to calm down, you're hyperventilating." In and out. In, one… two… three… and out, one…two… three… I do this for 30 seconds and begin to breathe normally again.

"I think I'm okay now. Thanks, I guess."

"No problem, but do you want to explain to me why you had a panic attack?"

"It's actually an anxiety attack, panic attacks are uncontrollable and unpredictable, while anxiety attacks are a response to a stressor. In this case, it looks like my stressor is large groups of people, or maybe it's talking to large groups, either way, it led to me freaking out, I guess."

"So what was that all about MIT, a high IQ, and using your genius to buy friends?"

"Can you not repeat that to anyone else? I'm trying to just blend in as a normal high school student, and not be known as some sort of prodigal son or something. My parents wanted me to have a semblance of a normal education so I could learn to interact with other humans. As you can see, this isn't working out so well."

"My lips are sealed. Let me make a deal with you. You help me through classes, and I help you get over your people anxiety."

"Sure, I guess that would be mutually beneficial to both of us."

"Can I see your schedule? To see if we have any other classes together?" We swapped schedules, and compared. "Looks like we only have 8th-period Biology together other than this class." She actually looked a bit disappointed. Is it possible she would actually want to be my friend? Only one way to find out I guess.

"Want to go to the library after school then? We can talk about the classes that you think you will need help on, and you can give me some tips on how to not make a fool of myself tomorrow."

"If we are going to meet up outside of classes, then I think we will need to be friends."

"I think that I can live with that." And that was how I managed to make my first friend in high school. Pretty smooth, if I can say so myself.

CHAPTER 4

SURVIVAL

My next few periods were less eventful, as most of my free periods are in the morning. So after going to my independent math class and my library study hall, it was time to face the newest horror of my day. The lunchroom. I walked slowly towards the lunchroom, trying to figure out what I was going to do. I don't think I know anyone I could sit at a lunch table with, but I also don't want to be that one kid that just nervously walks around the lunchroom trying to find a place to sit. Hopefully I will be able to find an empty table in a secluded area, to keep the attention away from me and maybe get some work done.

As I entered the lunchroom, I quickly spotted an empty table and made a beeline for it. I could feel the stares of people as they noticed my suit, but I ignored them and headed straight for the table. As I was eating my sandwich, I pulled out my notebook to continue some of the calculations I had been doing during my two earlier free periods. I could feel the stares die down, and finally was able to get some peace after what had been a pretty tumultuous morning. After about ten minutes however, I noticed two other kids looking nervous as they were walking around the lunchroom. They were both Indian, one relatively tall and skinny, with an athletic build, dressed in a t-shirt and shorts, while the other was shorter, wore glasses, and was dressed in a formal shirt and khakis. The taller one had black hair which seemed messy, but at the same time fit his appearance, while the shorter one had neatly combed hair and an overall more well-groomed appearance. He also was quite skinny, but his body language was not as confident as his tall friend, as he seemed timider as he walked with him, barely making eye contact with anyone. It didn't seem that important at the time, so I went back to my work, trying to solve the current problem at hand. After a few more minutes though, I was interrupted yet again.

"Can we sit here?" I looked up and saw the two kids I had seen before standing next to me. I thought about this for a moment as I knew this was a good opportunity to try and make some new friends, but at the same time, my research was calling me. I looked back up at the two kids and once again was met with blank stares - something I had been getting accustomed to. Right, I needed to answer them.

"Sure, there are seven empty seats here, so you can take your pick." After all, I only came to this school to meet new kids, so I might as well make an effort.

"Thanks! I'm Sachin, and this is my friend Surya, we are both freshmen." The tall kid was named Sachin it looked like, while the shorter one named Surya.

"The name is Shanmugan. Devadas Shanmugan. But you can call me Dev, like if it was short for David." The line had worked so well with Summer, so I don't see the harm in repeating it. "I'm also a freshman."

"Is that why you're wearing a suit? To look like James Bond?" The other kid, Surya asked this time. Maybe this intro isn't the best, I'll have to ask Summer that later when she's giving me tips. And why does everyone assume I want to look like James Bond? Can't a kid just use good introduction lines they have heard from movies they haven't even watched?

"No, the suit was a prank by my older sister, and I haven't watched a James Bond movie, I just know the line."

"So what middle school did you go to before this? We went to Lakes. We've actually been friends since first grade." Is this like the name game in English? Where I have to learn random facts about the people I meet? Surya was staring at me now. "So...?" Right, I need to answer.

"Oh, I was homeschooled. My two sisters were never homeschooled, but my parents thought it was the best for me. Until this year, since they decided that I needed to go to a real school for my high school education." I guess I better be used to saying this, since people seemed to keep questioning me about my homeschooling history. "So what is your schedule, maybe we have some classes together?" I handed my schedule over to them while they gave theirs to mine so we could look.

"Looks like we have Biology 8th period together, and lunch of course." Sachin said after a minute. Wow, so I know three people in my Biology class now? Too bad it's not even a real science class or I might actually have enjoyed that period.

"I have World History and Biology with you, but what is your math class? It just says independent study on your schedule." Surya nervously glanced up to me, a little confused. Now I was in a conundrum. What do I say about my math class without revealing that I'm way ahead?

"Independent study? Isn't that the math class that's for kids that have already finished Multivariable Calculus?" Sachin answered for me. Looks like I had to say something now.

"Yeah, I kind of got ahead when I was homeschooled. I want to keep it on the down-low though, so can you not go around sharing that information? And we all have Bio together? I have another friend in that class as well, so despite it not being a real science, that class might be pretty fun." I was now fully embracing the 'school can be fun' ideology that Mr. Bakerman had mentioned in English. It makes sense as well, that you might as well have fun when you don't have to try too hard in your classes. "Do you guys have anyone you know in Bio? Or in any of your other classes?"

"Actually, not many kids from Lakes Middle School go to Northshore, most of them actually go to the high school across town, Northwest. So we don't know many kids either." So they were in a similar boat as I am regarding people they knew.

"So tell me more about yourselves then, I think we may become good friends."

"Well, I'd like to start by pointing out that Surya has a, how should I phrase this, unusual fascination with people, like, he stares at random characteristics and…"

"Anyway, yeah we're not geniuses like you are, I'm just in Algebra 2, and Sachin is in Trig/Calc A, but we are also fairly good students and outside of academics, I play tennis, and I also enjoy playing chess so I'm thinking of joining Chess Club."

"That's funny actually, my other friend, the one in our Bio class also plays chess. I'm not sure if she's joining the Chess Club though, we didn't talk about that."

"Oh really? Maybe you guys could come with me so I have company, because I don't think Sachin knows how the pieces move and he's only coming because I promised him a bag of chips from the vending machine."

"I actually don't know how to play chess, but with two of my three friends being chess players, I guess I will have to learn, so I can give you some competition at chess club. And Sachin, what do you do outside of school?"

"I'm really into sports, especially cricket, so I'm either watching or playing something, and I'm trying out for the soccer team, and other than that I just like hanging out, maybe playing Xbox, and beating Surya at everything we do. Also, I do happen to know how chess pieces move."

"So Dev, what about you?"

"Well, I guess I have two sisters, Rakshini is a senior here, and Lakshmi is a 5th grader. I have a 'unique situation' as my dad has coined it, so my parents have had me homeschooled for all of my life. However, they reconsidered their options and thought it would be best if I did high school in an actual high school instead of at home. Apparently, they thought my homeschooling was stunting my social skills, so I'm out here to prove to them that I can actually talk to kids my age."

"So did they like, keep you indoors 24/7 and finally realize that kids shouldn't be living under a rock?" Sachin asked.

"No actually, I wanted to go to college, but they thought I wasn't ready. Just don't tell anyone else, but I was actually accepted into MIT, but my parents thought that I needed to be more socially aware, or something like that, before I could leave them to live halfway across the country as a young teenager. It's also why I have three free periods, it was an agreement reached with the principal when talking about my schedule, to allow me to continue my independent studies."

"Woah, so you're like the next Albert Einstein or something?" Surya looked at me incredulously.

"No, I just have some above average intelligence, and being homeschooled just allowed me to be a little further ahead than most kids my age." People around us started to get up from their tables and towards the cafeteria doors. I looked at my watch and saw the time. "Well, looks like we only have two more minutes of lunch. I'll walk with Surya to History I guess, and I'll see you in Bio, Sachin?"

"You really need to work on saying goodbye." Sachin replied as the bell rang, and Sachin went towards his next class, while Surya and I walked towards History. Despite how horribly this day had started, I think that it is starting to look up. What can you expect after all, I'm a survivor, so I can definitely handle high school.

I sat next to Surya in history, but the class was mostly uneventful. It went more along the lines of English, in which we got to learn people's names, and of course, had to deal with people staring at the stupid suit. I still can't believe how badly Google had misled me with that bit of advice. After my study hall with Mr. Turner, and a forgettable period of gym, where we basically just got locks, a locker, and then sat on the bleachers for 40 minutes, it was finally 8th period. Last period of the day, and the one I had been looking forward to, despite my disinterest in the actual subject of Biology.

CHAPTER 5

BIOLOGY

No desks? That was the first thought in my mind as I entered the lab/classroom where Biology would be held. Every one of my previous classes had been filled with desks, but the lab I was now standing in only had eight lab tables, each with four stools. I then noticed Summer waving to me, and I went to join her at her lab table.

"Do you have anyone else you know that's going to be at this table?" I asked her, already planning ahead to see if Surya and Sachin could also be with us.

"No, not really. Why do you ask?"

"Well I met these two guys at lunch, and it turns out they also have Biology with us, so I was thinking…"

"Anyone sitting here?" A short Asian boy was now standing at our table. His jet black hair was in a buzz cut, and his thick black glasses nearly covered his dark eyes. "I can assure you that having me at your table will not be a mistake. You see, both my parents are biologists, so I know that I will be able to ace this class, and with me at your table, I can help you also ace this class." I then noticed Sachin standing behind this kid.

"There's nobody sitting on the floor, you can sit there scrub." Sachin was now sitting at the seat across from me to my left, next to Summer.

"Your loss. You'll regret the day that you didn't let George Wang sit at your table." Surya had now entered the classroom as well and took the seat next to me, filling out our table, as George had moved onto the next table, spouting the same nonsense he had just said to us.

"Well wasn't he a delightful person." Summer was frowning as she interjected.

"So, I'm guessing this is the chess playing friend you were talking about?" Surya asked. Turning towards Summer, he continued, "Do you play in tournaments, then? I wish I could, but my parents don't think spending money to play in tournaments when I have no chance to become a Grandmaster is a good idea. I play a lot online though." I could've sworn I heard Sachin say something about Surya trying to impress her, but neither of them seemed to hear it so I let it pass.

"Yeah actually, I do. So are you going to join the Chess Team here?"

"I am. I even got these two to tag along as well." The bell rang, but our teacher still wasn't in the classroom.

"I'm actually not sure if I'm going to do the Chess Team here, as it might end up distracting me from improving. I have an important tournament coming up in which if I do well, I'll be able to qualify for an important invitational tournament next spring. And then, I would need to focus on that instead of a high school team. I'm definitely going to the first meeting though, to see if it is worth my time." Surya looked like he was about to say something, but the teacher finally entered the classroom. She looked like she was fairly young, maybe 25, with blonde hair that went down to her shoulders and glasses that were so thin that you almost didn't notice them. Her bright blue eyes glowed with excitement as she began to address us.

"Hello class, and welcome to Honors Biology! As you can see here, we do not use desks in this classroom, so I hope that you are comfortable with your lab group, because barring any unfortunate events, these will be your lab groups for the entire year." I briefly glanced over to the lab table behind us, where George Wang was sitting at, and saw a smug look on his face, as well as the other three kids at the table. "Today I'll be taking down your names, so I can get your lab tables set, as well as giving out the syllabus for what we will be doing this year, as well as what is expected from you in this class. After all, this is an honors course, so I expect the best effort from each and every one of you. Oh, and I am Ms. Auguste, and I will be your guide through Biology over the next nine months." She then went to the first table to her right, passed out a syllabus and took down the names of each kid. Since we were the first table on her left, that meant we would be the last table she would get to.

"So how did you meet Summer if you were homeschooled before today?" Surya asked.

"Well we actually had English today, and she kind of stopped me from having a full blown anxiety attack, and we decided to become friends."

"So basically, she helped you not make a fool of yourself so you were in her debt and became her friend." Sachin jumped into our conversation.

"No, he's not in my debt I just decided to help out a fellow homeschooler who was clearly not adjusting well to being around a large group of kids." Suddenly our attention was diverted yet again to George Wang.

"Ms. Auguste? Can you elaborate on what the syllabus means here when it says 'ability to work with a group' as a part of your grade?"

"Well seeing as this is a lab based class, the ability of your lab group to follow instructions as well as work together, will be an important part of getting a good grade in this class."

"Thank you for explaining, I was a little bit confused about how to interpret that." George Wang then began to whisper loud enough for our table to hear, but no one else could, "As I said, any group that has me in it is bound to succeed. I've been told multiple times that I'm a natural born leader, and my brilliance in Biology added onto that will make sure that we will all succeed in this class. I bet the kids who spurned me are already regretting their decision."

"Natural born leader? You're just a conceited little brat, wait till I get you after class you..." Sachin continued with a barrage of words I can't repeat, but he looked angry, which I was confused about. Why was he letting this kid affect him so much? Why should we care about what he does in this class after all? He's not a nice guy, so we should just ignore him.

"Alright, let's have a small bet then. Let's see which one of our tables has a better average grade at the end of the year, and the loser owes the winner anything within reason."

"Don't do it, Sachin. This kid is just trying to get in your head, be the better man and just ignore him. People like him aren't worth our attention, and we definitely shouldn't be interacting with them." I realized that this could get out of hand quickly and tried to stop Sachin from doing something stupid.

"Yeah listen to your friend, he knows not to enter a bet that you have no chance of winning."

"Oh, I have no doubt that we could win this stupid bet of yours, I'm just saying we shouldn't be stooping ourselves so low to get into a petty argument with someone like you."

"If you're so confident that you could beat us, why don't you accept? It's only a harmless bet. Unless you're only all talk, and know that you could never back it up." Sachin got out of his seat and before I could stop him went over to George.

"Fine then. The bet is on." I glanced over at Surya who looked worried, and then over to Summer who also looked pretty mad, but I didn't know if it was because of Sachin taking the bet, or because George was a huge jerk. I turned back to Sachin to see him shake hands with George.

"We shook on it, it's too late to back out now. Unless you want to be known as someone that backs out of their word." Sachin was about to respond when suddenly Ms. Auguste was over at their table.

"Is there a problem here boys?"

"No madam, we were just discussing a possible study group we could have. After all, it is easier to get work done in a group." George was lying through his teeth, a phony smile plastered on his mouth. I didn't realize there was so much drama involved in high school. It's only been one day, and I've almost had an anxiety attack, made three new friends, an enemy, and even almost got beat up by a giant named Luke. All the negatives, however, have been overshadowed by my new friends. I'm not completely sold on high school yet, but the friendships I've made today are certainly making it worth it. And not just because I get to prove my parents wrong. I then was abruptly pulled out of my deep reflection I had just been going through.

"Dev? Are you still on Planet Earth?" Even though Summer had phrased it as a joke, I could see in her eyes that she was worried. Now that's an interesting problem. Is she joking or actually worried? Do you believe the tone of the words or the accompanying facial expression?

Is it a mix of both? Do I respond with a joke since she had asked it as a joke, or do I respond seriously since she's worried? I looked up again to be once again met with the blank stare that had been filling my day. "Dev, you really need to stop doing that; answer first, contemplate life after, not the other way around."

"Yeah, I'm okay. Was just reflecting on all that's happened today. It's a bit overwhelming, if I have to be honest."

"I can understand. This is so much different than how homeschooling was. Are we still on for the library after school today?" She turned to Surya and Sachin, "You two can come as well if you want, we were just going to talk about classes as well as teach Dev here how to actually talk to people without freezing up."

"I can't, my mom picks me up after school and she's probably already here." Surya said, looking pretty disappointed.

"Yeah, I probably could've come if you told me earlier . We can probably go tomorrow if you plan on doing this everyday. Give me your number, I'll text you when I can come."

"That's a good idea!" Summer said, and they began to exchange numbers. Summer then turned to look at me and probably noticed the frown on my face. "What's wrong?" How am I supposed to explain how I'm not sure if my parents would be okay with me sharing my number with people, even if they were my friends? I… right, answer first, then contemplate life.

"I'm not sure if I'm allowed to give you my phone number. My mom gave me a whole lecture yesterday about not having social media, and I'm not entirely sure if this is included."

"Ok, then how about we give you our numbers, and if she allows it, then you can text us later today." Why didn't I think of that? That makes perfect sense.

"That works, I think." Before anything could happen though, Ms. Auguste was at our table.

"Sorry, I had to spend some extra time with the table before you, they had a lot of questions about the syllabus. Anyway, can I have your names down so I can put it into my roster?" We gave her our names and then she passed out a packet to the four of us. "This packet contains the syllabus, classroom guidelines, grading scale, etc. You guys are my last table, so take your time while you read through it and feel free to ask any questions that you may have. On the last page, there's a place for parent signatures, which I want you to turn in by Friday, after your parents have looked through this as well."

"I think we will be fine, we shouldn't have any questions, Ms. Auguste." Sachin said.

"We'll come up to you in case we do, you don't need to stand here with us." Surya added. Ms. Auguste nodded and walked away.

"Why did you do that?" I was confused as to why they would chase a teacher away, she only wanted to help us out.

"We need to talk about Georgie, thats why" Sachin replied tersely.

"His name is George."

"Let's compromise then. Jorge. I refuse to call him by his name. He's too annoying and stuck up for that."

"I'm still calling him George. I don't see why we need to talk about him. You got angered by him, he goaded you into a bet, it's a done deal. We just have to make sure we score as highly as possible on everything."

"No! Did you not see what he's doing? He's sucking up to Ms. Auguste in order to try and become her favorite! If he succeeds, she will be more partial when grading him, which is unacceptable! We need to do something about that!"

"Sachin, don't you think you're going a bit overboard?" Surya replied before I could. I'm not sure what Sachin's obsession with George is all about. Sure, he's not exactly a pleasant person, but that's not enough reason to have a personal vendetta against a person. Did he maybe…

"Do you know George? Like, from before today?" I asked,

"Oh no, thank god I didn't know him earlier." Hmm. So if that wasn't it, was it something he said? I began to replay the conversation in my head, tuning out Surya and Sachin who were having heated whispers about what to do with George. I was interrupted from my thoughts by a loud ring. Looks like the period was over. Going into Biology, I was pretty excited about having a class with all of my new friends, but after a long 50 minutes, I'm not too sure anymore. It was fun being in a table with Surya, Sachin and Summer, but all this drama with George and the stupid bet was making me a bit queasy. I just knew nothing good could come out of that.

"Dev? You're zoning out again…" it was Summer.

"What? Oh right, the period is over."

"And I believe we have an important meeting in the library now, that we shouldn't be missing." Right. I packed my stuff and walked towards the library, with Summer on my left, in complete silence. I had a lot of things on my mind right now that needed to be sorted out. Summer must have realized that as well as she let me be silent as we continued walking towards the library. I replayed the events from today, trying to figure out how much of it was like what I had read about on the internet, and how much was unexpected, as well as determining whether or not high school was worth it. I'm still not sure, I think I will need to be able to look back at this day again in the future to be able to fully determine how badly, or how well this day had gone. For now though, I was certain of one thing. Biology would definitely be the class with the most drama this year and I could thank Sachin and his impulsive nature for that. Barring another anxiety attack in English, of course. Or if I managed to get beat up.

CHAPTER 6

CONTEMPLATION

"Hey little brother!" I heard my sister scream from the other end of the hallway. "Did you manage to not get beat up again after the incident with Luke today morning?"

"I'm guessing that's your sister? And what incident is she talking about?"

"My little brother has a new friend? I'm shocked. And he didn't tell you about how he almost got beat up today morning because of that awful suit he is wearing?"

"So he almost got beat up because of a stupid prank you pulled on him?" Uhh, this isn't going to end well is it? Summer wasn't supposed to find out that it was actually my idea.

"Wait, he called it a prank? No, my brother here spent four hours last night googling what to do on your first day of high school. Did he think to ask his older sister who had finished three years of high school about what to expect? No! And what was his grand conclusion? That he needed to wear fancy clothes to make a good impression on people. Hence the suit. And now I hear that he had the audacity to tell everyone that it was a prank by me?"

"Is this true?" Summer was now glaring at me. Note to self: do not make Summer mad, it is a scary sight.

"Well uhh, you see, I was desperate for a friend, and when you were making fun of the suit, I thought the only way I'd be able to not look like a weirdo was to blame it on my sister. Now that I think about it though, that was definitely not cool. Sorry?" I don't think I've ever been so embarrassed in my life. Summer's glare lessened though, so mission partly accomplished?

"So what I'm hearing is that the first thing my idiot of a brother told to someone was a lie, and it was because he cared about his reputation? That is absolute gold. One day of high school and he's almost unrecognizable!" Was it really that bad? I didn't think I was that different than I was before the day started.

"Anyway, what are you doing here? Don't you normally go home after school?"

"Amma told me that you were staying back in the library with a new friend today, so I had to check it out. I've been waiting too long to meet your first friend." Ugh she's embarrassing me. Making me look like some sort of loser, which I've read is a one way trip to no-friendsville.

"Rakshini, can you stop?" Pathetic, I know, but I needed to stop this immediately.

"What's wrong? Afraid I'm going to embarrass you in front of your new friend? Who just so happens to also be a girl?" I could feel my cheeks getting warm. I did not need this right now.

"I'll have you know, I made two other friends as well. Clearly I'm not as hopeless socially as you all want to think!"

"Which is why you're having me teach you how to act normally in front of people and get over your people anxiety?" Summer was siding with my sister? I thought she was my friend!

"I think you and I are going to get along just fine... what's your name?"

"Summer. Summer Williams. Pleased to meet you." She then shook Rakshini's hand. The ultimate betrayal. I can't believe this is happening. Google didn't mention that it was so hard to keep your friends. I thought making them would be the most difficult part of the process.

"Okay Summer, looks like my little brother here is turning a bit pale, would you happen to know why?"

"Dev? Are you alright? Are you mad at me for telling your sister about why we are meeting in the library? Is that why you're freaking out?" How is it possible for someone I met this morning to already be able to tell what I'm thinking? Google didn't prepare me for this either.

"Okay Dev, calm down, take some deep breaths, like this morning in the hallway." Ok, hold it together. I don't need a second anxiety attack in a day. In, one… two… three… and out, one… two… three… and repeat. That's better. I think I'm back to breathing normally again.

"I'm fine. Let's just go to the library now. Away from the devil."

"I heard that Dev!" My sister turned around and walked away.

"You really need to stop over analyzing every single thing that happens Dev. For one, it's not healthy, and two it's better to just ask the person what's happening instead of jumping to your own conclusions." I definitely do not overanalyze stuff. "Dev, answer first, contemplate life after, remember?" Right. I need to work on that.

"I do not overanalyze stuff." Smooth.

"So when you started freaking out about me 'betraying' you for your sister two minutes ago, what was that?" Speaking of that, I need to figure out how she could read my mind.

"Can you read minds?" Smooth again.

"What?!"

"That's the only possible explanation as to how you figured out what I was freaking out over."

"No, you just have a very expressive face. Your eyes were filled with shock, when I told her why we were going to be in the library, and then it slowly turned to fear, and some disgust as well. So I connected the dots, and realized you thought I was betraying you. We can work on that as well, so you can do it with other people." Now where were these lessons when I was a kid? Being able to read minds, or I guess inference thoughts based on facial expressions, is a pretty useful trick. That is, if you're around people a lot. Maybe Amma just didn't think I would need that skill. Who knows. I'll have to ask her about that when I get home. Summer is giving me yet another blank stare. Answer first, then contemplate life. I need to make that my mantra so I don't keep messing it up.

"Ok, I guess that makes some sense." We found some seats in the library and started talking about her classes, and what I could possibly help her in.

"So 2nd period I'm taking this Intro to Computer Science class, would you be able to help me in that as well if I need it?"

"Actually, before I went into physics, I was dabbling in some CS, as my dad is a Computer Engineer, and I decided to look around in that field. Has been a few years, but I should be able to help you out there." This went on for a bit more, as we went through her schedule.

"Okay, I think we are done with my problems now. Now it's time we start with your 'lessons' on how to interact with other people. I think we already have diagnosed your biggest problems of not trying to contemplate the meaning of life instead of replying to people, and your tendency to overanalyze the actions of people around you."

"I still disagree with you on the overanalyzing part." This went on for an hour or so, until soon enough, it was almost time to get onto the late bus.

"Well, I guess this is goodbye, then."

"It's not really a goodbye, we will be seeing each other first thing tomorrow morning." I was taking Sachin's advice from earlier today and improving on my goodbyes.

"Oh yeah! I almost forgot. We got distracted in Bio, so I couldn't give you my number." She wrote it down on a sheet of paper and handed it over to me. On the bus ride back home, I contemplated the last two hours in the library. Some of the advice she had given me made sense, like attempting to be interested in what the other person is saying, and not looking at the floor whenever someone was talking to me. I still don't get why you would need to keep eye contact though. Feels pretty weird if you ask me. My thoughts then began replaying the days events again. I still wasn't sure how I felt about this whole high school business. There was so much drama, yet at the same time I felt like I had indeed made three good friends. Now whether or not that would be able to balance the stress from the drama that comes as a part of high school, I guess only time would tell. As long as everyday wasn't this eventful, I think I would be able to manage. The bus finally reached my house, and as I got off I realized that I had left my backpack at school. I knew where it was though, so I should be okay. I walked up my driveway and into my garage, preparing for a relaxing evening that would be able to shake off the turmoil of the eventful first day of school I had had.

CHAPTER 7

ENLIGHTENMENT

"**S**o how was your first day of school?" It was now dinner. After I had gotten home from school, I had decided to take a nap for about 90 minutes, and then decided to learn how the chess pieces moved. After all, with both Summer and Surya being avid fans of the game, I should probably know the basics to be able to have some common ground with them. While my sisters answered Amma's question in detail, I just sat in my chair feigning interest in what they were saying, while actually trying to figure out exactly how I would answer the question, once their attention turned to me.

"Dev here almost got beat up, and apparently made three new friends. I even got to meet one, a girl named Summer, when he was going to the library with her after school." Leave it to Rakshini to abruptly put all the attention on me. I was now greeted with intrigued stares from Lakshmi and Amma, Appa was just looking at his phone, not paying attention to the conversation at all.

"What am I supposed to say? Rakshini already gave you a summary of my day." I wasn't about to explain everything that had happened that day before I had figured out what I was going to say and what I was going to keep to myself for now.

"Please? I want to know more about this Summer girl! And you're other friends, what are their names?" Lakshmi was almost jumping out of her seat in excitement.

"I'm trying to eat, if you remain quiet I may be willing to share some details once I am done."

"So when can we meet your friends? Are you going to bring them over one day? I really want to see the poor kids that took pity on you by becoming your friends!" Lakshmi was nearly screeching by the end of her sentence. The joys of having to deal with a hyperactive ten year old - was I ever like that? I don't think I was. I decided that the best course of action was to feign interest in the bowl of rice in front of me, to look like I was busy eating.

"Well, I'm not sure about the other two kids he claims to have become friends with, but the Summer girl seems to actually be a good kid. She's even apparently going to be helping Dev here in getting over his people anxiety. She also apparently needed to calm him down this morning in a hallway when he was freaking out, from what I could infer."

"Why exactly were you freaking out this morning in a hallway?" Amma decided to enter the conversation now. Even Appa's interest had been piqued, seeing as he was now glancing up at me over the top of his reading glasses. Why was it that every conversation I was in was going in the worst possible result today. The giant tried beating me up, Summer found out that my suit was not a prank, and now I'm in a tight corner about the anxiety attack I had nearly suffered during first period - something I wasn't planning on telling anyone about.

"Well..."

"Spit it out already!" Why was Lakshmi so eager to hear about my life anyway? Didn't she have better things to be excited by?

"Well I basically had an anxiety attack in first period English, and Summer dragged me out into the hallway to help me calm down. Not really much of a story."

"Why did you have an anxiety attack Dev?" Now Appa had entered the conversation? That almost never happened! It was too late though, the hole had been dug, and I had fallen in.

"I'm not sure why, to be honest, it was probably just because of the large group of people in the classroom. It didn't happen again after that." That should be enough of an explanation to get them off my case. Appa seemed to accept that as well as he went back to his phone, however, Amma still didn't seem convinced. She didn't ask any more questions about that though.

31

"So tell me about your other friends you said you made!" There was Lakshmi again, too nosy for her own good. At least I didn't have anything to be worried about in this line of questioning.

"I met Surya and Sachin at lunch, as they needed a table to sit, and I was at a table by myself. I also ended up having World History with Surya, and Biology with both Sachin and Surya. Summer is also in our Biology class actually, so the four of us are a lab group."

"Ooh, what are they like? Are they as socially awkward as you are? Is that how you guys banded together?" I don't get how she can always be so energetic. Doesn't it get tiring at some point? Instead of answering her, I just started eating quickly so I could finish and leave the table. Then I remembered the whole phone number problem I needed to resolve.

"Amma?"

"What Dev?"

"So my friends wanted to exchange phone numbers with me, but I wasn't sure if you would be okay with that, so I decided to ask you first."

"Why would you think that Amma would be against that? She literally only sent you to this school to make friends, and it's pretty hard to keep your friends if you can only contact them in school." Rakshini questioned me before Amma could reply.

"She told me I'm not allowed to have social media, so I thought…"

"Yes, you can exchange your phone number with your new friends." Amma responded before I could finish.

"Ok! I'm done eating now." I had actually finished about two minutes prior, but now that I had gotten everything I needed, I had no reason to stay at the dinner table. I got up and went back to my room. I pulled out my phone, and entered Summer's number into my contacts. I then sent her what I had learned was a normal way to greet people, "Hi, it's Dev!". I still liked my James Bond intro, but apparently that just made me look weird. I put my phone down and was getting ready to pull out my notebook to continue the calculations I had started at lunch and in my study hall with Mr. Turner. That's when I remembered my notebook was in my backpack. Which was in the library. At school. Now what was I supposed to do? Then I remembered Surya during Bio mentioning that he played chess online. So I opened up my laptop and opened Google and typed 'How to play chess online'. Now that I had learned how the pieces moved, it was time to test my new skills against other people. Before I could decide whether chess.com or lichess.org was a better website to create an account on, my phone buzzed.

Summer: "Hi Dev! I'm guessing your parents let you text then?"

Dev: "Yeah, apparently I was worried for nothing. After all they want me to make friends, and as Rakshini pointed out, it's hard to keep your friends if you only talk to them at school"

Summer: "That's great! Here are Sachin and Surya's numbers. I'll also add you to a group chat we have created :)" She gave me their numbers, and while I inputted them into my contacts, I noticed a new notification from a group. Looks like I had been added there as well. Then I remembered the dilemma I was in before she had texted me.

Dev: "So would you recommend chess.com or lichess.org?" It would make sense to ask a chess player about where to play online right. It was better than what I was going to do, which was surfing Reddit for an answer.

Summer: "Well, I have an account on both, so it doesn't really matter. Why are you asking?"

Dev: "Well, since both you and Surya play chess, I thought it would be a good idea if I learned how to play as well. I don't have to though, if you think it's a bad idea."

Summer: "No, I think it's great. I was just wondering why, nothing else." Why hadn't I used text before? It was so much easier to talk to people through text than it was in person! Talking through text was so much less stress and less worrisome than in person, where I could barely keep my heartbeat normal and would dissect every action of the person I was talking to. Maybe Summer was right about that. Not that I would ever tell her, of course. The best thing about text? I wouldn't even get a blank stare when I forgot to reply to someone! I then quickly created an account on chess.com.

Dev: "Okay, I created an account on chess.com for now… want to play? I want to see how bad I am compared to you."

Summer: "Sure!" I quickly realized, that despite knowing how the pieces moved, I had no idea how to make them work together. At least I lasted 15 moves. I'll take that as an accomplishment. Surya and Sachin were now texting us as well, so this continued for a couple of hours before they had to leave.

Dev: "You don't need to sleep?" It was 9:30 PM, and it was getting close to when I had to sleep as well.

Summer: "No, I sleep pretty late actually. Around 11:30-12 ish xD"

Dev: "When do you wake up then?"

Summer: "6:45 ish, I'm guessing you sleep early since you seem surprised by this"

Dev: "Well normally I sleep at 10:00, and wake up at 5:30, but now that I have to go to school I have to wake up at 5:00, so I'm ready by 7:00 to leave the house."

Summer: "Why do you need to wake up that early to get ready?"

Dev: "I run for 90 minutes in the morning, that's why"

Summer: "Oh ok, that makes sense." We continued talking for a bit more until it was finally time for me to sleep. As I exited my room to say goodnight to Amma and Appa, I heard them talking in hushed voices. Trying to not disturb them, I walked quietly onto the stairs, careful not to make any noise, and listened,

"... right decision?" I heard Amma say.

"Did you see him today? I don't think I've seen Dev this... emotional? before. Sure, he's definitely hiding things from us, but that's what any normal kid would do. And I definitely never thought I would see the day where Dev would spend three hours texting friends instead of focusing on his research, I think as long as he manages to balance his studies and new social life he should be fine."

"I could barely recognize him though. If one day of high school could do this to him, then what's going to happen after two years? Will he even be the same child he was before all this?"

"I don't think we have ever seen the real Dev until today. He's finally gotten a chance to be himself around kids his age and he's embraced it, and allowed his personality to finally take over instead of just robotically focusing on string theory..." I started to walk away here, I had heard enough. As I walked back to my room I thought about what my parents had said. Was I really so different than I had been before today? A sudden gust of anger then filled me. How could my parents have thought that keeping me away from the world was a good idea?

The reason I couldn't be going to MIT right now was that I lacked the social awareness to be able to survive on my own. But whose fault was that? It was my parents for keeping me isolated out of fear that I would be bullied or whatnot for my intelligence. As I fell asleep that night, I contemplated the decisions my parents had made about my life until today, and pondered the consequences.

CHAPTER 8

DOWNHILL

T he next few weeks went by fairly quickly, as I got used to the new school routine I had created. Despite there being a lot less drama over these weeks, every day still had some sort of encounter with George Wang, who had only become even more outspoken and cocky with the first Biology test of the year coming up. It didn't help either that he quickly became one of the most popular kids of our grade, to my friend's chagrin. Sachin, Surya, Summer and I were now in the library as I helped them study for the Biology test tomorrow on biochemistry and the scientific method. While they were looking through the textbook and asking me questions whenever they had any, I was mostly focusing on playing chess games on the internet, in a format known as blitz (which is basically when both sides only get about five minutes for the entire game). Out of the corner of my eye, I noticed George Wang enter the library, with some of his mindless followers he called friends. He then caught my eye and walked over.

"Well if it isn't the four kids who foolishly thought they could outscore George Wang and his lab table on a Biology test," I don't get why he loved to flaunt his apparent intelligence. In my experience, it only chased people away, but for some reason, it's given George a sense of supremacy over everyone, and made him the 'cool kid' that everyone wants to be friends with. "I don't know why you even bother studying, it's pointless to hope that you can ever hope to beat us."

"Shut up and leave, nobody wants you here." Sachin looked like he was ready to punch George. It was a common expression for his face whenever George was around. Despite my repeated attempts to tell him to control himself around George, he just couldn't. Thankfully, we were saved from the situation escalating by the librarian, Mrs. Morris, a lady with gray hair, in her mid 60s.

"Is there a problem here boys?" She said that with a smile, but had a serious undertone to her voice.

"Nothing wrong, Madam, I was just saying hello to some of my friends from Biology." George once again turned on his false smile, something I had grown accustomed to seeing whenever he was around an adult. Was it as obvious to adults, as it was to kids, how fake that smile was? Or do people just grow more oblivious as they become older.

"Well then, move along, and keep your voices down, this is a library after all." Mrs. Morris continues smiling as she moved on to the next table, while George sent us a large smirk before turning around and leaving the library. We went back to studying until it was time to catch the activity busses, content that we had done enough to be ready for the test tomorrow.

One of the things I miss about being homeschooled is how slow the days went by. The hours after school, for some reason, just go by quicker when you go to a real school than it did when I was homeschooled. It could be partly because I now had things to do after school, such as leaf through chess games Summer had told me were instructive to learn, text my friends, and of course continue my research, which normally I wouldn't be doing after a day of homeschooling. I was also getting decent at chess, with my rating around 1400 online, which Summer had told me meant I was an average player, and decent progress for a beginner. Dinner had also become a pretty quiet affair, as I ate as fast as I could and left, still trying to figure out how I felt about my parent's decisions for the first 13 years of my life. After dinner, I quickly skimmed through the Biology textbook, just to make sure I knew everything. I needed a perfect score, just to make sure George couldn't say anything, even if he was perfect as well.

The next day started off well, with the first project of the year being announced in English. Mr. Bakerman, with his usual bout of enthusiasm, caught all of our attention,

"Welcome back everyone, for a very important milestone in your freshman year English class!" Milestone? It's been 13 days of school!

"An important part of this course is learning how to write a proper essay that can analyze the literary elements of books, so in this project you will be in groups of four, working together to write an essay on the next book we will be reading, *Fahrenheit 451* by Ray Bradbury. You may have noticed when you entered the room, that your normal desks have been shifted slightly to put you into groups of four, which is because the group you are in now will be who you will be writing this essay with." Okay, this isn't so bad, I'm in a group with Summer and two boys I'm on reasonably good terms with, Elijah and Liam.

"So have any of you read this book before?" Summer asked us once Mr. Bakerman had told us to get 'acquainted' with our new group. I knew the question was directed at me though, since she knew I had already taken high school classes.

"Yeah, my mom made me read it last year" I had read it three or four years ago, but didn't want to answer any hard questions Liam and Elijah could ask about that.

"Cool, I read it over the summer." Summer replied. Neither Liam nor Elijah had read the book, but that was to be expected, as they were products of the public school system. For the rest of the period, the four of us got a rough outline of what each of us would do for the essay, to have a clear plan going forward, once we started reading the book in class.

The rest of the day went by in a hurry, as my mind was only thinking about the Biology test that day. It wasn't how I'd do that worried me, I was sure I could get a perfect score, but I was having second thoughts about if I had done enough to prepare my friends. However, by the time we were walking out of the Biology classroom, I was confident that we had all done as good as we possibly could have done. While we were in the library discussing answers, we got interrupted yet again by our least favorite freshman.

"You know that going over your answers now isn't going to save you from the inevitable defeat you will be given at the hand of my lab group." He chuckled, which led to the five kids who had been following him in joining him. Thankfully, this time Sachin had gotten the message, which had been given to him through Surya kicking him under the table. George just sneered, and walked away, which lead Summer to let out a sigh of relief.

"I don't see why he has to keep coming over to us." She wondered aloud.

"Probably because he knows that he can get a reaction out of Sachin here. That's all people like him live for." Surya was right, of course, and I think Sachin was beginning to learn that as well. Once we were confident that none of us had gotten more than three questions wrong, we decided to relax a bit. We spent the next hour just talking about normal life things, such as our favorite pastimes and things like that. It was a nice way to wind down after what had been a pretty stressful day for me, and I'm sure for my friends as well. All we had to do now was wait for a day for the test results to come out.

"29/30?!? Impossible! I am George Wang! There is no way I did not get a perfect score on this test, there has to be a mistake! I knew this topic before I could talk!" Clearly George was not pleased with his test results. I briefly wondered how well his lab group had done, but pushed that thought out of my head as quickly as I could. I was not going to lower myself to petty little things such as a rash bet made on the first day of school.

"How did you do Dev?" Summer asked quietly, probably not wanting George to overhear. Not that he could anyway, as he continued to rant about the injustice that had been done to him. I was actually surprised that he hadn't even looked to see which question he had gotten wrong, as he hadn't even opened his test packet yet.

"30/30. How did you guys do?" I replied in a whisper.

"I got a 28, Sachin and Summer both got a 29" Surya whispered back.

"Nice job all of you! And you both got the same score as our friend behind us as well, basing on his little outburst."

"What did you get for question 27? Both Sachin and I missed that." Summer asked. Before I could answer her, we had been interrupted again.

"There is no way that this answer is wrong! Ms. Auguste? I think question 27 had the wrong answer, as it is clearly C instead of A." It looks like he had also missed that question. I guess I could understand, it was a bit tricky, but it had also been in the challenge section of the textbook.

"Actually George, if you had looked through the challenge question at the end of the chapter in the textbook, on page 27, question 41 is actually the same question that you got wrong. It also gives a detailed solution, on page 38, as to why C is a commonly put wrong answer, and why A is correct." I decided to show off a bit, he was getting on my nerves by now, and it was time to take him down a peg.

"You're joking! Who even looks through the challenge questions? Ms. Auguste even told us it wouldn't be necessary to go through them if we wanted to do well." George's face was beet red now.

"You did do well though, so her statement was accurate. However, I felt that I wasn't ready enough, so I looked through the challenge questions as well, to make sure I was confident on all topics. I'm glad I did now, seeing as a question was actually taken from there."

"So what did you get, if you're so smart??" George yelled, even though I was standing right in front of him.

"Dev was actually the only kid in any of my Honors Biology classes to get a perfect score on this test, and it's clear why he did now, with all the effort he put into studying, even going through problems that I had said were unnecessary. You all should be more like Dev in your studiousness." Ms. Auguste decided to step in now, probably realizing that the situation was getting a bit out of hand. George was absolutely fuming, but he meekly nodded his head and sat back down. I returned to my seat as well.

"So much for not letting Georgie get to you." Sachin said teasingly.

"This was more of taking him a notch down, letting him be humbled a bit"

"I don't think you should have done that. He's furious now, and he's definitely going to be blaming you now, especially as you humbled him in front of the whole class." Summer was right of course. George would be out for revenge now. Hopefully it wouldn't be too bad though.

CHAPTER 9

ALONE

H ave you ever had the feeling in a large crowd, that even though you are surrounded by maybe a hundred people, that you still feel entirely and hopelessly alone? Not loneliness, but an extreme degree of loneliness that just makes you wonder why you even exist? That's what school had become now for me. Constantly feeling this was depressing and downright painful at times. The only times I wouldn't feel this was when I was with either Sachin, Surya or Summer these days. Even at home, I was beginning to feel like a stranger in my family, while I was distancing myself from them, to figure out what I meant to them. This painful and depressing feeling I was quickly becoming acquainted with, was all due to George Wang.

The day after we had gotten the Biology test scores, I got my first hint that something was off during first period English. While my group was discussing the first chapter of *Fahrenheit 451* I noticed that Liam and Elijah were being pretty distant and were barely responding to anything I said. I didn't think much of it at the time though, as I just figured that they hadn't read the chapter. The cold stares I was receiving while walking in the hall with Summer after English, however, signalled me that something was definitely wrong.

"Do you know why everyone is staring at us with cold glares?" I turned to Summer and asked.

"I'm surprised you actually picked up on that, I was hoping you'd be oblivious to it."

"Normally, but it's really obvious. Feels like I'm being watched as if I had just murdered someone or something."

"Hahaha, but to answer your question, no, I'm not sure why everyone is staring at us like that."

"I guess we will find out at some point. Not that I care anyway, I don't know most of these kids." I noticed the cold looks from freshmen in the halls after my study hall classes as well, but it wasn't until lunch that I was able to finally get an answer to why I was suddenly hated by most of my year group.

"Did you hear about what George Wang did?" Sachin hadn't even sat down yet and he was already angry. Surya was also fuming, which is what really surprised me. He was usually calm and was good at keeping his emotions in check, so it must have been really bad.

"No I don't. But I feel like this would be answering why I'm suddenly being looked at by the other freshmen as if I had murdered their dog or something."

"It's horrible." Surya was speaking now. "He created a public Instagram account, that can't be linked to him,"

"Well, anyone with half a brain knows it's him..." Sachin interjected.

"and basically found pictures of various awards you've received, research you've published, and things like that, which he used as evidence to make you seem like a fraud, as since you are 'only a high schooler' it is impossible for you to have achieved those accolades, and he basically also accuses the school of faking your grades to make your image of a genius seem realistic."

"So he's convinced the freshmen class that I'm basically some phony that has faked scientific research, and tricked numerous foundations into giving me awards, grants, scholarships, etc. and that I have now bribed the school to give me good grades in order to keep that image up? How dumb do you have to be to believe that?" I could see why they were mad now. I was raging inside, but knew I would have to keep calm, as it would be the best way to keep under the radar.

"What are we doing then, I already have some ideas." Sachin seemed eager to enact his revenge.

"Nothing. We shouldn't stoop to his level."

"Dude, it's your reputation on the line, you should be doing something." This was Surya.

"I could care less about what my reputation is with a bunch of mindless 14 year olds, the people who actually matter already know who I am and that I am not a fraud, despite what George thinks."

"Are you sure? This could end your high school experience before it has really even started." Surya again.

"I have you two and Summer as friends, I don't care about the rest of the kids in our grade. If they want to listen to George, it honestly does not bother me." The first part was true. My friends had turned high school into a pretty great experience, at least for these first few weeks. However, I did care what others thought. I know it's petty, and I know that the opinions of the public shouldn't be affecting how I act, but I could see the stares of when people looked at me. I could hear the whispers about me behind my back. I knew exactly what everyone was saying about me, and it hurt, despite the fact that I knew it shouldn't. I put on a brave face for my friends though and shrugged off their continued questions about how we could get back at George. I knew that as long as I acted as if this didn't affect me, they would follow suit, and it would allow me to be strong in public.

"Dev? You alright?" It was Summer, during English two weeks later. If anything the situation had actually gotten worse since the first day. It had actually gotten so bad that Liam and Elijah had convinced Mr. Bakerman to put them into another group, on the basis that Summer and I had already read the book, of course. It had been happening in other classes as well. In my World History with Surya, people had begged our teacher to not have to work with me, because I apparently was intimidating for them, or in gym class I would be picked last for the games of soccer we would be playing, and then be told to not come anywhere near the field, and would tell the gym teacher that I had a sprained ankle. Incidents like this made me wonder how gullible teachers were, could they not see that I was being ostracized by all but three kids of the freshman class? And older years as well. I had heard Rakshini tell Amma about how I was being 'bullied', and that even some seniors were believing the nonsense that George had been spreading. I, of course, vehemently denied everything when Amma asked me about it, no point in bringing them into high school drama, of course. "Reply first, contemplate life after, Dev. Remember?" I had been getting better at that, but I just had a lot on my mind right now. I tend to get lost in my thoughts a lot when I'm stressed out, something I had learned over the past few weeks, as I felt stress for the first time in my life. "Dev!" I then felt a sharp pain in my head. Summer had smacked the top of my head with her copy of *Fahrenheit 451*. Right, I needed to respond.

"Sorry, I'm just getting lost in thoughts about the last few weeks." Summer's gaze softened a bit, which I had learned meant that she was being sympathetic. "Don't take pity, it was my fault, after all, I had to decide to humble George in Biology after that stupid test."

"It's just not fair. I don't get why people are just mindlessly believing what they see on social media. Or why people like George. Are you sure you're alright though? You look really bad. Like you haven't slept in a week, that kind of bad." I hadn't been sleeping well, she was right about that. It was hard to sleep when all of my dreams consisted of the horrible things people were saying about me, the cold glares, shoving in the halls that had started recently, the notes in my locker that told me that the world was a better place without frauds like me. "Okay, you are definitely not good. Mr. Bakerman! I think Dev is about to faint again!"

"You know what I said on the first day, you don't need to ask just get him to the nurse." Summer dragged me out of English, giving me flashbacks to the first day of school. Before the whole George Wang catastrophe.

"Dev, you need to tell me everything that's going on in your head right now, or I'm actually going to bring you to the nurse, or worse, I'll tell your sister." Ugh. Blackmail.

"I'm really fine." Maybe I could lie to her though. I needed to stay strong for my friends after all.

"Cut it. You're definitely not fine, if the signs of sleep deprivation on your face are any indication." This is bad. Now my friends will see exactly how weak of a person I am, and will probably abandon me as well. Then I will actually be truly alone in the world, with no one to turn to. But if I don't say anything then I will probably be taken to the nurse who will have to call my parents. Or Summer will tell Rakshini, who will tell our parents. I'd rather lose Summer as a friend than have my parents figure out about all the stupid drama and how it has been affecting me.

"Okay, I'm not alright."

"And what's wrong? It's the George Wang stuff right? The notes in your locker? People shoving you? What was the breaking point." I really hate how it feels like Summer knows me as well as I do, sometimes.

"I'm not even going to ask how you know about the notes," I started.

"Everyone knows about them. I've heard people bragging about the latest message they've written to you during lunch. It's not really a secret."

"Well anyway," Here goes nothing. "This stuff has actually been bothering me since the first day."

"I knew it! Sorry, I don't want to come off as excited about the fact you're being hurt, just that I knew that it was this. Sachin and Surya are convinced that the notes were the breaking point." Wait, hold on here. Do Sachin and Surya also know that I'm not as strong as I would like them to believe? Why haven't they just abandoned me then?

"Well, then I guess you know everything right? I don't see why you need to ask." I turned around and started to walk away. "I don't need to hear you saying how you'll stop being my friend, it'll hurt more if I have to hear it from you directly." I started to run down the hall, not even sure where I was headed. I could hear Summer following me, and that only led me to increase the pace I was running at, as I tried to lose her. I couldn't keep it up though. I could feel my body collapse under me, as I fell to the ground, the tears pouring out of my eyes. For the first time in my life, I was utterly alone. Distanced from a family that I wasn't sure how to act around anymore, and friendless in a world that was dead set against me. Those were my last thoughts before the world turned black.

CHAPTER 10

PROGRESS

I woke up in a white room, and the brightness of the room made my first thoughts as I woke up go something along the lines of, "Is this heaven?"

"No you idiot, this is the emergency room." Looks like I must have been thinking out loud. Wait, was that Sachin's voice? I blinked my eyes a couple of times and looked around the room. Surya was next to him, and I looked behind them to see my family as well, with who I was guessing were Sachin and Surya's parents as well.

"So are you going to explain yourself now?" Surya's sharp tone startled me a bit. Was that a bit of annoyance I could hear as well?

"I'm a bit lost, what do I need to explain?" I was genuinely confused, I could barely remember why I was waking up in a hospital, let alone remember why I needed to explain myself.

"About your overall stupidity." That really clarified things for me. I closed my eyes, trying to remember what had happened before I woke up in this room. Suddenly, everything that had happened that morning, assuming I was waking up on the same day, came back to me. I was still confused as to why I needed to explain myself about stupidity. That wasn't usually a word used to describe me. I must have had a confused look on my face as Rakshini walked over.

"About Summer you dimwit. Do you have any good reason as to why you would just accuse her of abandoning you after she was trying to help? And that you ran away only to faint and made her think that you were in critical condition? Do you have anything to say about how you treat a so-called friend who was trying to help you in a bad situation?" Was I really that bad?

"Rakshini, you can question him later, right now I think the Doctor might want to check up on him, he was passed out for a day after all. Might give him some time to think about what you just told him as well." Amma stepped in now. Did everyone think I had done something bad? I needed to figure out what had happened. As people began to leave the room, I noticed Amma staying a bit back, as if she wanted to say something to me."

"Wait, Amma," She turned back to look at me. "Do you think it would be possible for..." Wait this might be a bad idea. How would I explain to her that I wanted to ask Summer about her perspective on what had happened, when I don't even know if Summer wanted to see me. By the looks of it, she was pretty mad about how I had acted, even though I couldn't exactly figure out why.

"She's outside the room, I'll tell the doctor to give you two a couple of minutes, your condition wasn't that bad, it was just some extreme stress which had led to fatigue, he just wanted to talk to you about managing stress and sleep, nothing that needs to be done immediately." How did Amma know what I wanted? And why was Summer outside my room, instead of with everyone else? I sat in my thoughts for a few minutes before I saw the door to my room open, and Summer entered the room. She looked horrible, her hair all frazzled, and her face was red as if she had just been crying. It didn't look as if she had slept at all either, which made me wonder if she had lost sleep because of how bad I had apparently hurt her. I awkwardly made eye contact with her for a couple of seconds.

"So what did you want?" She seemed like she would rather be anywhere else than here right now. Which I guess makes sense since I had apparently made her feel horrible, and acted bad, which of course is what I needed to find out.

"Well, I first wanted to apologize if I hurt you?" I'm pretty sure I shouldn't have phrased that as a question. "I really didn't mean to do anything to make you feel bad, I guess the stress was too much, and made me say some things I should not have said. I know this sounds like a generic apology, but I really don't know what I said to hurt you.

Rakshini said something about accusing you of abandonment, I think, but I actually thought that you were going to do that, it was why I was hiding stuff from the three of you, I thought that if you realized how weak I was, you would abandon me for George Wang, and then I'd actually be alone, and then I thought that since you had realized that I was not okay that I would actually be alone and didn't want to be there when you officially ended our friendship, so I tried running away hoping that… that it would all just disappear or that maybe it was a dream, and…"

"Dev?" What? Oh no, I must have been rambling. "I already knew that. It just hurts that you even thought that I would stop being your friend over such a stupid thing. Seriously? I didn't become your friend because I thought you were this superman kind of kid that never was hurt by anything. I don't know why you thought that you needed to act strong around me - or even Sachin and Surya. We all knew how stupid George and the other kids had been, we just didn't know why you weren't telling us." Wow, I really was stupid. Not something I'll probably say about myself again.

"Oh."

"Really? That's all you've got to say?" She said that with a smile, which I think meant that she was joking.

"Well, I think I need a way to make sure I'm not acting stupid like that again."

"How about you don't think pessimistically all the time? That's probably a start. And maybe you can try considering how the people you are talking to are thinking, before you say something."

"I thought I wasn't supposed to analyze the people I am in a conversation with!" We both burst out in laughter.

"Nice to see you two laughing." A tall man, probably in his mid-40s was now at the door. I guess he would be the doctor. "I was afraid I would be walking into a war zone, with you two yelling at each other, from what I heard had happened from your friends outside, but thankfully that was not the case." He then went on to give me a lecture about how I should not be closing myself away from the world, and some nonsense about how if I am not careful I could end up being hurt by my reactions to stress, and a lot of other stuff I had already learned from the light reading I had done into psychology a couple of years back.

The next few weeks went by without much trouble, as I pushed my insecurities back and was able to ignore the stupid antics of my fellow freshman, and just have an overall good time with Sachin, Surya, and Summer. As we were now a month into school, that meant clubs were starting up, as well as possibly the most mind-boggling thing about high school I had seen yet. I don't think I will ever be able to wrap my head around stuff like 'spirit days', 'pep assemblies' and worst of all, school-sanctioned dances. I'm not sure why the school would be condoning an event that will only lead to some people getting hurt by decisions their classmates may make. Thankfully I wasn't going to go to homecoming, or any other school dances for that matter, and the four of us had made plans to spend homecoming weekend at Sachin's house for an extended sleepover. Before that though, I needed to prepare myself for what could be a very bad experience; the first chess club meeting.

CHAPTER 11

CHESS

I know it is stupid for me to think that meeting a new group of people for the first time is a life-altering moment, but that's just how I am. I knew that a large number of people in the school disliked me, and was scared that I would have to confront some of them during the first chess club meeting. It was also why I had refrained from joining any other school clubs. At least at the chess club, I would have Sachin, Summer, and Surya to help me. We considered Scholastic Bowl as well, which intrigued me because my memory allowed me to be very good at remembering useless trivia, but since Sachin and Surya weren't interested, and Summer was only going to do it because she thought I would need company, we decided against it.

The week before the first chess club meeting, I spent maybe four hours a day just memorizing chess games. Summer had given up on giving me individual games as I was apparently learning them too fast, so she just gave me a website with a bunch of games, and I was in the process of memorizing as many of them as I could. It was pretty useful for my own games as well, as I just tried repeating openings I had seen in the games I had memorized, and I was generally just copying middlegame plans from games I had seen. Surya was a bit put out with my progress though, as apparently I was nearly as good as he was (I was around 1500 online and he was 1600). Sachin, of course, claimed that Surya was upset for a different reason, but Surya had stopped him from saying anything else. Finally, the Tuesday of the meeting had arrived, and after Bio, the four of us walked to the room where the chess club was meeting.

The first thing I noticed when I entered the room was that I didn't recognize a single face. That meant that there were no freshman joining as of right now.

"You kids here for chess?" A tall Indian kid with glasses was now in front of us.

"Uhh yeah. Is this the right place?" I'm not sure why I said that, it was obviously the right place. The kid just laughed though, and then said,

"Yes, it is! Come right in, Mr. Wu will be here shortly to explain the club to freshmen like you. I'm Raj, by the way, one of two captains for the team this year, and I was the first board last year." I'm not sure why some people are just instantly likable, but this kid was. As we walked into the room, Raj motioned for some kids to come over. "I found some freshmen who are interested in chess this year! Oh shoot, I didn't get your names." We told him our names, and he continued, "These are the returning members from our state team last year, Nicholas here is the other captain, and the second board from last year." He was pointing to a short Caucasian kid, with dirty blond hair and dark brown eyes. The kid seemed excited, and began to speak.

"I was worried we were going to get no freshmen again this year. You see, all of us are seniors or juniors, but as you can see we don't have many other kids interested in chess." Other than the seven kids that had gathered around us, there were about five other kids as well, none who were paying attention to the conversation right now. "We tried doing some recruiting this year, but not many people seemed interested. We were worried that the team may be shut down after we graduated if not enough people had joined." Suddenly Sachin turned red, causing all of our attention to go to him.

"Well, uh, I kind of told some other kids we were doing chess since they asked me to come to other clubs, and I guess George got wind of that and told others to stay away. Sorry, I didn't realize it would hurt the team." Realization went over on Raj's face.

"You're Rakshini's brother, aren't you." He said directed towards me. "She told me that you and your friends were interested in chess, which is why I was outside the room, to begin with. It's terrible what the other freshmen are doing to you, by the way, none of the seniors actually believe it, of course, all Rakshini ever talked about freshman year was her genius little brother." It was my turn to turn a bright red now.

"Yeah, so what are your ratings? Do any of you play in tournaments?" Summer clearly wanted to steer the conversation away from George Wang's personal vendetta against me.

"I'm the only one here who plays tournaments, I'm rated around 2100." Raj spoke, I think he understood what Summer was trying to do and agreed with it. "Nicholas, a senior, is pretty good as well, he's around 1900 I would say. Our board three is Wei, a junior, over there, he's maybe around 1700." He was pointing to the tallest kid of the group, maybe around six and a half feet tall, with glasses. "We have two twins, Max and Rachel, also juniors, who are maybe like 1500, they are our boards four and five." Max and Rachel were both brown-haired, Max with a buzz cut, and Rachel with hair that went down to her waist. "And then we have Sai, Arjun, and Havish, who are seniors, and all are around 1200, as our bottom three boards." He motioned to three Indian kids, Sai was short with curly black hair, Arjun was tall with his black hair in a Mohawk, and Havish was about the same height as me, with the exact same glasses I had, and also with a dark brown hair. In fact, we almost looked like twins, despite the fact that he was three years older than me.

"Are you sure that he is Rakshini's brother? He and Havish could be twins!" Arjun exclaimed.

"Or maybe, Havish and Rakshini are secretly siblings," Max responded. The entire group laughed, and I knew right then that I had found a place that I belonged to.

"Settle down everybody and welcome to chess club!" A voice boomed from the front of the class. It belonged to a balding Asian man, who was probably in his 50s, but still had jet black hair. "I am Mr. Wu, for those of you who do not know me, I teach Calculus classes and am the head coach of the Northshore Chess Team. I see a couple of new faces this year, which is always great, we always welcome new members, whether or not you are here for casual relaxation, or want to be competitive and on the team. We meet on Tuesdays and Thursdays every week starting next week... " He went on to talk about how the team works, our weekly matches that start in October, the state tournament in February, and all other logistical stuff that you would expect to be covered in an introduction meeting. After he was done, he made a beeline for us, probably since we were the only new kids and he wanted to get to know us better. "Hello! Do you kids have any questions about anything I just said?"

"Yeah actually, what kind of training do you guys do in practices? I'm Summer, by the way."

"Well during practices we usually start out by doing some warmup tactical puzzles, and then the players play each other so I have a general sense of how good a certain player is when I have to make the roster."

"Okay. If people need materials to study when they are at home, I have a lot." Raj walked over to us now.

"What kind of materials?"

"Well, I have a huge library of chess books that my dad had collected from when he was a kid."

"You wouldn't mind sharing that with us? How good are you by the way? I guess you play in tournaments since you asked me about that." Summer actually turned red here. Was she embarrassed to admit how good she was?

"I'm actually around 2350 FIDE and 2400 USCF. It's mostly because my dad has been training me since I was, like, three years old. He said he would be willing to help train you guys as well, if it would work during practices. Maybe like two times a month?" Mr. Wu seemed interested in this. He then asked,

"Who is your dad? Is he any good of a trainer? He must be if he has trained you to become a 2400 player." If it was possible, Summer's face turned even redder.

"Uh, he is actually a Grandmaster. Henry Williams, maybe you've heard of him? He hasn't played in many tournaments recently though, as he has been focusing on helping me reach the IM (International Master) title. I'm currently a WGM (Woman's Grandmaster), and have one IM norm." Wait, Summer's dad was a GM? I didn't know that. No wonder she was so amazing at chess. She must be one of the top kids of her age in the country as well. I noted that in my head, as I knew I would have to be doing some research on these ratings later.

"Can you give me his contact info? I would love to speak to him about a schedule we could come up with." The room seemed to be buzzing with excitement, as news about how good Summer was, spread to the other members of the team. As they all crowded around her, asking her rapid-fire questions, I turned to Surya.

"Want to play some games while Summer is distracted?"

"Sure, I need to beat you while I still can. I still have no idea how you've gotten this good, it's taken me four years of playing games online to get to the rating I'm at, and you're probably going to be better than me in a few weeks."

"You should try what I'm doing, and just memorize a bunch of grandmaster games."

"Not all of us can just look at a game for two minutes and know everything about it, Dev." Sachin interjected. "Must be nice having an eidetic memory."

"Sorry, I don't want to sound like I was bragging. It's not fair that I was gifted with some talents that others don't have. If it helps, I could try and show you some memory tricks I've learned to help you guys out." I actually felt pretty bad. They shrugged it off though, and for the next hour or so of practice, I just played games versus Surya. Then Max came over and played us in a few games. I actually was able to split my games versus him 1-1, while Surya lost 1.5-0.5. Mr. Wu then caught all of our attention again.

"Hey guys, it's around four o'clock, so we have about an hour till the activity busses. Since it's the first practice, how about you guys set up a bughouse ladder and relax, before we get to work next Tuesday." A loud cheer went up as it seemed that this bughouse thing was a pretty popular thing. Summer quickly explained the rules to me, as I learned that it was a partner game, one player for each color, and whenever you take a piece, you can give it to your partner who can then place it anywhere on the board. As in normal chess, the goal was to checkmate, but this was a more casual and social game with players on each partnership trash-talking the others and stuff. I was a bit overwhelmed, but Summer was able to carry me - well, she just told me where to move- as we somehow managed to finish fourth out of the seven partnerships that had participated. For the first time in high school, I really felt that I belonged, outside of just being with Summer, Sachin, and Surya. While we walked to the busses, I asked Summer,

"So are there recorded bughouse games that I can memorize? So you don't always have to tell me where to go?" She laughed before responding,

"Of course not. If it helps, I can show you some opening moves you can play, and some basic motifs, but the only way you'll get better is by just working on tactics, because bughouse is all about teamwork and tactics. The strategic play that normally happens in chess games doesn't really happen in the craziness that is bughouse." Today was a good day though. It was like the cliche of the light at the end of a dark tunnel, but finally being with a group of kids, even if they were all seniors and juniors, who didn't just automatically believe George's jealous lies and hated me without even getting to know me, was refreshing, and for the first time since the first biology test, I was finally looking forward to going to school again.

CHAPTER 12

FESTIVITIES

What is so special about homecoming? The closer we got to homecoming week the more it seemed that people were making it out to be some life-changing event and a day you would cherish for the rest of your life. I didn't really get that though. After all, it is just a high school dance, right? What's so special about it? It seems like a waste of time. Even if I was sure my parents would be okay with me going to this event, I wouldn't go. Mostly because of the fact that George Wang and his buddies were going and I would rather not have a confrontation with them. Surya, Sachin, and Summer and I had plans for the weekend, anyway. We would be going to Sachin's house on Friday after school and sleepover until Sunday evening. It was now the Monday before homecoming and the beginning of a 'spirit week' which basically meant that every day had a different theme for the way kids could dress. A stupid concept for an institution of learning, and one I would not be taking part in.

Monday was Pajama day. I guess it wasn't that bad, but for a kid that showed up in a tuxedo the first day of school, seeing kids casually walking around school in pajamas was just strange. Just when I thought I could manage with the other kids in pajamas however, I walked into English and saw Mr. Bakerman also in his pajamas. I ran over to my seat next to Summer and said,

"Why do people even want to wear pajamas to school?"

"Well for one, it's more comfortable. It also allows kids to get into school spirit, homecoming spirit and stuff like that."

"Yeah, that's the part I don't get. Why would the school care more about spirit and dances than the education of the kids here?"

"Well, I guess it's so that kids aren't completely stressed out from, like, schoolwork and have a way to relax. It also probably gives them some money as well, as you have to pay for tickets and stuff like that."

"Whatever. As long as I don't have to get roped into this I should be fine."

"You know your sister was nominated by a teacher for homecoming court, right? That means if enough kids vote for her she could be a finalist for the homecoming king and queen."

"Hmm. So what you are saying is that, if I could manipulate the system I could get my sister onto the most embarrassing moment of her high school career?"

"Well, she would have to make it into the top five girls out of the 30+ that were nominated by teachers, and then she would have to beat the other five girls. And seeing how the school hierarchy works, it's probably going to end up going to some random athletes that were nominated."

"Or... I could hack the system. I want to be able to see the look on her face when she is nominated, and how mad my parents would get. Especially as they don't approve of these kinds of events either." Maybe homecoming would be pretty fun after all. Embarrassing Rakshini, as well as making her an integral part of the idiotic assembly we were going to have on Friday, would make this entire week of shenanigans worth it.

"You could do that? I thought you said you only dabbled in coding when I asked you if you could help me with my computer science homework."

"I may have been understating my skills a bit. I would be a bit rusty though, I haven't actively done anything like this since I was 11 and decided that I was more into physics." During my study halls that morning, I refreshed myself on some coding languages, making sure I would know how to get into the school's system and alter votes. During lunch, I also told Sachin and Surya about my plans.

"That would be hilarious." Sachin was bouncing with excitement. "Did you know that George Wang's sister, Allison, was also nominated? I overheard him talking about how she would be winning in a landslide, as she is also apparently extremely popular."

"Wait, George has a sister?" This was the first time I had heard about this.

"Yeah, Allison Wang, Science Bowl star because of her extreme knowledge of Biology and Chemistry, and also one of the most recruited girls' basketball players in the state. Why do you think George got so popular, so fast? It was definitely not for his charming personality or for his apparent intelligence. Everyone knew he was Allison's brother and wanted to be on his good side." Surya always had an uncanny knack to know information on just about everyone in our grade, as well as other grades as well.

"Doesn't help that she also has a lot of guys after her." Sachin added.

"Why do you guys know these things? And why do you care? Anyway, this gives us even more of a reason to get my sister to win, it would anger her as well as George!" And the plan was on. Sachin and Surya even had promised to get me the name of a guy I could vote onto the court after they did a bit of research.

After World History, I walked into my study hall with Mr. Turner. I was hoping that I would be able to work on my new side project during this period, instead of my normal research.

"Mr. Turner? I have a side project in programming that I have been working on. Would it be possible for me to work on it during this period, instead of what we normally do?"

"Do you need my help? I don't really know much about programming, but I could ask one of the CS teachers that are on break right now if they could help you."

"No, you don't need to do that. I should be fine." Well, that went without much of a problem. Which I kind of expected as he seemed like a more laid back guy that still cared about his students and work, but wanted the kids to be more responsible.

If I didn't believe that Allison Wang was George's sister at lunch, I definitely believed it during Bio. We had a work period today, as we were supposed to be working on the review for the test that Ms. Auguste had posted for our unit on Cells. Of course, as you would expect from high school kids, that meant the period was basically just a social hour for kids with their lab tables.

"You know I heard the funniest thing a couple of periods back." It was George, of course. He clearly wanted us to hear what he was saying as he had increased the volume of his voice from what it had been earlier, that we had not been caring about at all. "As you know, my sister has been nominated for homecoming court, but I've also heard that our fraud over here also has a relative that was nominated. An older sister named Rakshini. What kind of name is that anyway? You would think immigrant parents would make sure that they give their kids names that would allow them to blend in." Sigh. I don't know why he tries so hard to trigger me. "According to my sister, she must have bribed a teacher to give her a recommendation so that she could attempt to look popular. It's silly of course, she will probably end up with the least amount of votes, if she's anything like her fraudulent brother. Too bad they won't show the places after the top five."

"You know, Rakshi is actually a very sweet person. And unlike some kids I know, she never tries to put other kids down." Since when was Summer on nickname terms with my sister? Surya and Sachin also looked shocked, probably because this was the first time Summer had responded to one of George's taunts.

"What are you doing?! Just ignore him! I whispered sharply.

"It's your sister he's bad-mouthing, why aren't you defending her?"

"Because I know that Rakshini- also why do you call her Rakshi?- wouldn't care what a kid like George thinks and says about her."

"Aww, is this a lover's spat I'm sensing?" George was actually infuriating at times. And what was that he said?

"No, I was just being reminded that it's not worth my time to respond to you." Summer then got up and left the room, telling Ms. Auguste that she needed to use the restroom. I'm positive she was beet red though, but she had turned away from me too fast for me to get a good look.

"Are you not going to chase after your girlfriend? She looks like she might need some comforting." Also, when had these stupid thoughts of George started? Summer and I were just friends, and that's all we would ever be. I have no time for anything like that; as I said I didn't come to high school to learn about female anatomy.

"Shut up George, you don't know the first thing about any of us." It was Sachin.

"Oh come on. Even a blind person can see that they are inseparable. It makes perfect sense for two outcasts to seek comfort in each other as well." Oh god, if he was spreading this, it could be really bad.

"You'd be the last person I would want to ask about friendships, seeing as you have no real friends, just people who are too scared to stand up to your bullying." Sachin was mad now. This could easily turn bad fast.

"Guys, how about we both go back to our work, and fight each other at a later time." The moment I said that, I realized how bad I had worded that. George realized it as well, from the gleam in his eyes.

"Fine then. Friday, after school at the park across from the Walmart. If you aren't there, I'll make sure that everyone knows how much of a coward you are." Well, this could be bad.

"Make it on Thursday, and we have a deal." Why was Sachin so rash at times? First the stupid bet on the first day of school and now this schoolyard fight? I was not going to be a part of this.

"Have fun beating each other up, I won't be there to watch this stupid thing." I went back to the test review, and ignored Sachin for the rest of the period.

"Hey, Dev?" It was Sachin, I had left quickly after Bio, but he must have caught up.

"What."

"Sorry, I was being stupid again. I don't know why I let him get to me so much."

"It's fine, make sure you win, okay?" He laughed.

"I also have the names of the guys who Allison would be okay with being the homecoming king, so you can make sure they aren't in the final voting. Also, we have the name of the guy that you should vote in. Apparently, he's pretty popular but he also hates Allison, they have a history. His name is Ethan James." Okay. Now that I had the names, all I had to do was get into the school's system at home today and rig the votes.

When I got home I went straight to my room and started on my new project. Once I had decoded the administrator password, I had a look at how the voting system worked. It seemed that every student was assigned an integer variable which was their 6 digit ID number, and the value was initialized at 0, and when a person voted, the student was detected when they typed in their ID and the specific variable value was assigned from 1-15 depending on who they voted for. I simply had to create a program that looked for variables set to 0, and then set them equal to 2, which was Rakshini. I also decided to change any votes that were 7 - Allison Wang - to 2 as well. I made sure there was some distribution among the other 13 candidates so that there would be no suspicion.

"So Rakshini, do you have any news to tell us?" It was dinner, and for the first time since the first day of school, I decided to say something.

"Like what?"

"I don't know... maybe the fact that you're on the voting for homecoming court?"

"Let's be real. I'm not popular enough to win any votes, and I'm not planning on going to homecoming anyway. The vote will go to someone like Allison Wang, you might be familiar with her younger brother actually, George."

"So if you make the final voting, would you go?"

"There is zero chance I will, so sure, I will go, but only if I make it."

"Rakshini, you know how we feel about school dances?" Amma was speaking up now.

"Yeah I know, I'm only agreeing to this because it is not happening."

"I would vote for you!" It was Lakshmi. "I think it would be great! You'd have to dance with a guy though, and cooties are disgusting." She made a face, which made us laugh. I'd forgotten how fun dinner could be at times. Too bad I wasn't sure if they really needed me for anything other than my academic brilliance though.

The rest of the week went by fairly quickly. On Wednesday the finalists for prom court were announced, with Rakshini, of course, being one, to her complete shock. On the downside, the large rant George went on in Biology would have made you think he lost a Presidential campaign, and not that his sister losing homecoming court. On Thursday, I rigged the final votes for Rakshini during my study halls, and heard about Sachin's resounding beat up of George at the park through text. We also got some surprising news though, that put a damper into our weekend plans.

Summer: "Sorry guys, I can't go to the sleepover. My grandmother in Detroit died today, and her funeral is on Sunday. I won't be in school tomorrow either, as we are driving over to Detroit."

Surya: "RIP Summer's Grandma"

Dev: "What's RIP?" I had never seen this before, so I had to ask.

Sachin: "Rest in peace, and how do you not know that." During the pep assembly the next day, we got the unsurprising news that Rakshini had won the final votes and was now homecoming queen, and Ethan James was homecoming king, just like I had rigged. The glare I had received from Rakshini though made me glad that I was going to Sachin's house right after school. It looks like she had realized what I had done. I did the only logical thing a kid would do in my situation, and shot her a large, innocent, grin.

CHAPTER 13

SLEEPOVER

fter the assembly, Sachin, Surya and I quickly left the gym to avoid Rakshini, and quickly found Sachin's dad who was taking us to Sachin's house. During the car ride, we being the immature kids we are, made fun of Rakshini's reaction to winning the vote, and of course, planned how I would be able to hide from her wrath as she finally realized what I had done. Sachin's house was a normal two-story house, with a large finished basement, that would be our living quarters for the next two days.

"So what's the plan?" I asked. We were all sitting on the couch in the basement, having just put our bags away.

"We can play on the Xbox if you want."

"I don't really like playing video games, but I would be okay with watching you and Surya. It definitely would be more fun making fun of how bad you are than actually playing the game." I wasn't going to let on that I had never actually used an Xbox before so they would also have to teach me the controls.

"That works. Do you still have 2k Sachin?"

"Yeah, let's play that." Clearly they have played this game before, but probably not for a while based on the fact that Surya had to ask if Sachin still had the game. Sachin turned on the TV that was in front of the couch we were on, and it didn't take me long to realize that this 2k game was about basketball. I was honestly expecting it to be some first person shooter game because basing off stuff I had heard in the halls, those games are extremely popular.

While they argued for a bit about which players for the 3v3 game they were going to play were better, I zoned out as I took in the fact that I was actually at another kids house for a sleepover. A few months back that would have been unthinkable. If this is what normal kids did, then would it really make sense to leave high school after only two years? Before I could come to an answer I was interrupted from my thoughts by a loud scream of joy.

"I won again!" Again? Have they already played two games?"

"Why is Surya so bad at this?" I decided to act as if I had paid attention to their game the entire time.

"Well, the main reason is probably that Sachin gets to practice a lot with an Xbox while I only play on an Xbox whenever I'm here."

"Are you only filled with excuses?" The banter between the two continued for a while, as they continued to play 2k, and I joined in at times, usually to make fun of Surya's lack of video game skill. We soon started just to talk about life in general though, while the game still went on.

"So how are you liking high school, Dev?" It was Surya who asked the first question to me directly.

"It's certainly different from homeschooling, but…"

"Really? I thought they would be the same." Typical Sachin and his sarcastic responses.

"I think it's a good kind of different. Despite all the stupid stuff like pep assemblies…"

"I will never understand your undying hatred of pep assemblies." Sachin again.

"Yeah, of all the things to hate on in high school, how is it that you've latched onto pep assemblies as your most hated aspect?"

"… and you know the whole George fiasco stuff, I've actually been enjoying it."

"Really? I thought that you would be disenchanted by now." Surya couldn't hide the shock from his voice.

"Yeah, tell us what makes you come back to high school when you know you can just leave us for greener pastures… like MIT."

"My parents would definitely have shipped me off to MIT in your situation."

"Well… on the premise that I know this sounds extremely cringe, it's actually the fact that I got to make friends with you two and Summer."

"How did we become friends anyway? Were we really that desperate that we decided to become friends with a kid who got all of his social skills from James Bond movies?" I knew Sachin was teasing when he said that, otherwise I might have actually been insulted.

"Speaking of Summer, you never did tell us the full story about how you two became friends."

"Yeah, you only told us that she helped you through an anxiety attack."

"That's actually it."

"Why her though? You could have picked anyone in your English class to be friends with." Why was Sachin so interested in this?

"Well she was sitting next to me when I began to freak out, and we had already exchanged pleasantries before class had started that day…"

"Pleasantries, as in you acted as if you were James Bond." Oh come on, are people never going to let that go? I expected better from Surya.

"Well yeah. I didn't know any better back then."

"So why did you sit next to her? There were probably other open seats right?"

"She sat next to me! Why are you guys so interested in this? Are you wishing that I was friends with someone else?" Did they secretly not like Summer? What if they didn't? What would I do then? Would I pick them or Summer? I was filled with dread while I waited for a response.

"So you don't like Summer?" It was Surya, who seemed a little hopeful actually. That confused me.

"Of course I like her! She's my friend!"

"So not as anything more? Are you sure?" What was Surya implying here? And why was Sachin silent here? Usually, he's the one that can't stop talking.

"Sachin? What does he mean?" Sachin paused the game and turned to look at me. Surya did as well.

"Do you not find Summer attractive at all?" That's what they were worried about? Here I am freaking out about the future of my friendships and they just want to know if there is any truth to something that George believes?

"I've never thought about that. I have more important things to worry about in life than stuff like that."

"Seriously? You're a 14-year-old guy and you're telling us that you've never thought about that?" Sachin looked incredulous. I don't get what's so hard to believe about that.

"13. And no, I have research I need to work on, tests to study for, and I'm trying to get better at chess."

"You do realize that even though she's friends with you, at least five guys asked her out to homecoming right? Three of them are even a part of George's posse." Surya also looked surprised. And I was looking at my friends in a new light. Is this what teenagers talked about? I would need to look this up later. For now, I decided to see exactly what they meant by this.

"So? Why should I care that other guys wanted to go to homecoming with her? It's only natural, right? You usually would want a girl to go to a dance with you."

"The stupid rumors that George is spreading about you two are because of the fact she said no to every single one, which made people think you two are together or something like that." Now Surya was being silent while I was talking with Sachin.

"Oh. Well, there's no truth at all to the rumors. I'm disappointed that you two would even doubt that."

"So, if for example, Surya wanted to ask her out, you wouldn't care at all? No jealousy or anything?" Was this as hypothetical as Sachin was making it out to seem? Or was there some truth to this.

"No. I could honestly care less about dating, it's a waste of time. I came to high school to learn how to be around people, not learn about the female anatomy. I would tell you that it's not a wise decision as you should be focusing on studies, but no I would not be jealous."

"I still don't get how you don't find her attractive at all? Like even if you don't care about dating, does your mind just not automatically think that?" Surya finally spoke up again.

"Can we change the subject? This is getting stupid." I would definitely have to be doing research on this later though, so I can make sure that my mind never gets sullied by these kinds of thoughts.

"Fine." Sachin probably realized I was uncomfortable. The conversation moved onto other stuff until Surya again had a question for me.

"You said you were 13? When is your birthday then?"

"March 14th, 2003. I don't care about birthdays at all so please do not use this information as hope that you can 'surprise' me or something."

"Not even a gift?"

"What would Dev even want for a gift?"

"Nothing. I don't care much about random material items."

"Nothing at all?" Surya sounded confused, while Sachin was facepalming himself.

"No. What are your birthdays, since you asked?"

"November 9th, 2001" I didn't realize Sachin was on the older side of kids in our grade.

"July 7th, 2002" So Surya had just turned 14 in the summer.

"Why do people care about birthdays so much anyway? Sure it is the anniversary of when you were born, but I don't really see the point."

"What do you mean?! Your birthday is the most important day of the year! It's the one day in the year that's all about you."

"Sachin's a bit fanatical about birthdays, in case you couldn't tell."

"Okay. You say it's all about you right. Let's take our Biology class for example. We have eight lab tables of four kids each. That means there are 32 kids in our class. Do you want to know the odds of someone having the same birthday as you?" I paused for dramatic effect and to quickly do the calculations in my head. "74.35%"

"No way. There are 31 kids other than me! And 364 other possible birthdays. There is no way the percentage is that high!" I went on to explain the whole math behind the percentages, which basically went along the lines of, 364/365 is the probability that one person does not have the same birthday as him, but since there are 496 possible pairs in a room of 32, the actual probability that they don't have the same birthday is $(364/365)^{496}$, which comes out to 25.65%, meaning that the probability that two kids in our Biology class have the same birthday is 74.35%. Of course, that doesn't mean that it necessarily has to be Sachin that shares the birthday, it's just the odds that two kids in our Biology class have the same birthday.

"Well, thanks for ruining birthdays."

"Thank you for saving me from his nonstop blabbering about birthdays" Soon, we were called up to dinner, which was a fairly quiet affair. After dinner, we went back to the basement, and decided to look for something else to do. Which led us to go onto every man for himself nerf gun war. I was obliterated of course, since despite the fact that I have pretty good speed and stamina, I cannot aim to save my life. I don't think any of my shots were even close to the intended target. It was fun though, and I really was beginning to think that growing up was overrated. Who knew that people could have so much fun that didn't involve research? Another reason to be resenting the decisions my parents had made for me for the first 13 years of my life, I guess.

We probably didn't sleep until about 3:00 AM. We watched a movie, and then played an intense game of Monopoly. Sachin and Surya both ended up teaming up to try and stop my dominance, but it didn't really work out for them. It also didn't help that even once all of us were in our sleeping bags, we kept on chatting about the most random things in life you could imagine. Like, who knew that Surya was afraid of spiders? Or that Sachin plans to climb up Mt. Everest one day. It also made me feel a bit bad though. I didn't have the dreams they did, my whole life up till now was about getting into MIT, graduating with a good degree, and making a lot of money, and hopefully win a Nobel Prize. But high school was opening my life to the stuff I had never considered important before. Like friendships, and crazy dreams like climbing Everest.

I moved my 90-minute run to when I woke up, which was at 9:00 AM, instead of the normal 5:00 AM. Saturday and Sunday were more of the same, as we just did a bunch of random activities, and talked a lot, and slept extremely late. The highlight of these two days was probably when we went outside to Sachin's large backyard and played a three person version of ultimate frisbee. It was also funny watching Sachin and Surya attempt to join me on my run Sunday morning. They lasted around 45 minutes, which was impressive in a way, but they were also panting for the last 25 minutes of their run, and looked like they might have passed out on the spot. Finally, and it was a bit disappointing as well, it was time for me to return home. I expected it to be a quiet evening where I could finally rest after three days of non-stop fun, but I was wrong. The moment I entered my house I was greeted by a loud scream.

"WHAT WERE YOU THINKING?" I wonder why Rakshini was so mad? What did I do to her? I was gone for three days … oh. I'd actually forgotten about the whole rigging of the votes thing.

"Uh, I thought it would be funny? And it would shut George up about how great his sister is?" Smooth reply. There is nothing she could possibly find wrong in that statement. Meaning she will be sympathetic to my cause and stop yelling at me.

"Let me get this straight. You thought humiliating me in front of the entire school was a good way to get back at a petty bully? And you thought it would be funny?" Hold on here, she just put my words in an extremely negative light! This is what I meant earlier when I said that she was always so negative. She could have been sympathetic here, but instead, she's making herself seem like some sort of victim!

"It was pretty funny though! And I got to get pictures of you in a pretty dress, so I think it was a great idea." Lakshmi coming to my rescue, I'm not sure if I should be happy about that or disappointed that I needed a ten-year-old to save me from this argument. Disagreement? Argument might be a bit too strong of a word.

"Also, can I ask how it was humiliating? I would think that it was an honor to have been voted in by your classmates?"

"Because everyone knew that I was not actually going to homecoming! And then I was forced to go! All because you thought it would be funny."

"You see, I'm sensing a bit of hostility here, so I'm going to be the better man here and walk away." I ran past Rakshini, which caused Lakshmi to laugh, and closed the door to my room.

"This means payback, you know that, right?" I heard her scream from my behind my door.

"Would you have rather Allison Wang won?" I actually didn't know what her answer would be, but I was betting on the fact that they weren't on friendly terms.

"You're impossible!"

"Nope, only improbable." She punched my door, I'm not sure what the reasoning behind that was, and left. Finally, I can relax. I didn't realize how tired I actually was until my head hit the pillow, and even though it was only 6:17 PM, I was out cold till the next morning, sleeping right through dinner.

CHAPTER 14

OCTOBER

October has always been my favorite month of the year. There's no real rhyme or reason to it, other than the fact that just like with certain people who you are just drawn to, my fascination with October just happens. That was before though. Now I had an actual reason to like the month of October, and that was because it was the month where we began having our weekly chess meets against other schools in the area. We were now on the bus after school, driving towards a high school in our district, Lakeshore High. Mr. Wu was telling us about what we should expect, and what he would be doing for the board order.

"Okay everyone, settle down. Lakeshore is a middle of the pack school in our conference, meaning we should be scoring a lot against them. These are the kind of schools that if we play at the state tournament, we want to score 60 points or more." The scoring system for these matches was a weighted score, with a win on board one being worth 12 points, board two being 11, and down to board eight which was worth five. A draw on any board would split the points between the two schools. That means if you won on every board, you can get a total of 68 points. A team would be the same color on boards one, three, six, and eight, and since we were the visiting team that meant we would be black on those boards, and white on the other four. "However, since we have new members on the team, I want to give them all a chance to play." Even though Sachin wasn't really interested in playing competitively, it was a well-known fact that Mr. Wu was going to do all he could to change his mind. "So we will be playing, in board order:

Summer, Raj, Nicholas, Dev, Wei, Surya, Max, Sachin" What?! Wei is definitely better than me! Why am I playing a board higher than him?

"Mr. Wu? Why am I ahead of Wei? He is clearly better than me right now."

"Since I want these matches to be of educational value for our newer members, like you and Surya, I put you both a board higher, so that you can get experience versus better players. Wei and Max have a lot of experience already, and know how good players on high boards are, but you and Surya are going to be playing your first real matches, so we thought it was best to test you both." Okay, that makes some sense then. I was now even more nervous though, I had been expecting to play behind Max and Rachel, on board six, but now I was playing on board three ahead of Wei?

"Dev? Calm down." It was Summer, who was on my right, in the aisle seat, while I was next to the window. "It's just a game, but if you go in thinking you will lose, you aren't doing yourself any favors. Just remember, this school isn't that good, so you are most likely better than your opponent, despite the fact that you're on a higher board than you expected." That did help a little, but I was still pretty nervous.

"Yeah, they went 4-6 in the conference last year, and we have one of the weaker conferences in the state." It was Surya who was now trying to get rid of the jitters.

"And whoever they play, definitely does not have as many games memorized as you do, so you should be fine." I applauded Sachin's efforts, but sadly a chess game isn't determined by who has memorized more games, but instead of by the person who just has a better plan and more tactical awareness than his opponent. We arrived at the school, but this only seemed to increase my nervousness. I mean, I had never played a long chess game over the board outside of practice, what if I messed up completely? Raj must have noticed this as he walked over to me.

"Nervous? I can imagine. I was like that before my first match freshman year, and I had been playing in tournaments for four years before that." That was surprising. Why would he have been nervous?

"Why?"

"I didn't want to let everyone down. Back then I was just a freshman who people knew was talented, but I hadn't proved myself in match play yet. So I was worried that I would accidentally blunder and then everyone would think I'm not that good. You just have to have faith in your own skill though. You are better than this kid, you definitely have better training than this kid, the only thing he might have over you is experience, but that would be against kids in this conference, which in all honesty, is a joke." That did help. If even Raj was nervous before his match, and he's so good now, then being nervous isn't a bad thing. Maybe I could use the nervous energy to motivate me to do even better!

I was playing a kid named John McPhee. He told me that he was a freshman, and this was also his first ever match. That made me feel a lot better. Not to brag, but I was apparently improving faster than most people do once they start playing, so I was now confident that I was a better player than my opponent. The game had been delayed a bit as the opposing school had to look for some people who could fill in for their last two boards, but once they found two random kids, they were ready and the match had begun.

My opponent started with his king pawn up two squares, which is known as e4 in the chess world. It's probably the most common first move possible, and it is played at all levels. I thought for a bit, as I had so many options to play. I could be like Aronian, and play a double king pawn position, I could be like Maxime Vachier-Lagrave and play a Najdorf, I could be like Karpov and play the Caro-Kann, so many different options. As I kept deliberating, I could feel time just pause, making me feel as if I had unlimited time for a decision. Then I noticed my opponent was giving me a curious look, and I realized I had already spent seven minutes, of the total 55, for just my first move! I thought back to the most recent game I had seen, Jan Timman versus Anatoly Karpov from 1988. Since Karpov had won that game, I decided to copy him and play the Caro Kann - it must be a good opening as well, Karpov was a former World Champion! My opponent gave me a strange look, as if he had never seen this before - which I figured he might actually have not. He then moved his queen out to h5. Was he seriously trying a four-move checkmate? I pushed my pawn up to d5, as is normal for the second move in a Caro Kann, and my opponent started thinking again. I realized that my move had come with an added bonus that it stopped his Bishop from going out to c4, which would have been the next move for him if he was able to continue with the four move checkmate. I started moving faster as well, as I had more confidence knowing that my opponent was truly an absolute beginner. Eventually, I was able to take his wayward queen, that he had moved way too early on move two, and as it only cost me a knight, my opponent tipped his king over - a signal that meant resignation. I recorded the result then went outside the room we were playing in, to where Mr. Wu and any other members who had finished were waiting.

"Why did you spend so much time on your first move?" It was the first thing Mr. Wu asked me after my game.

"Well, I realized that there were so many different things I could play! I couldn't make a choice either because I've seen so many games that black has won with all of those opening choices. I ended up going with the Caro Kann because it was the most recent game I had seen."

"Hmm. You're going to need to figure out what you like. I can't have you wasting so much time on what should be a trivial decision. You should talk to Summer, she probably can help you figure out what you can play."

"It's fine. I already know I will be sticking with this opening versus e4. I'll make sure to ask Summer if she has any materials on the opening though, so I will be more thorough than relying on a database of games inside my head."

"If that's okay with you, then that is fine." I went over to the rest of the kids. Summer, Max, and Wei had already won as well, and they were with Rachel, Sai, Arjun and Havish who had been here in case the other school had extra players.

"Perfect, now we can have two games of bughouse going!" Havish was currently standing with Summer and Wei, watching the other four playing bughouse.

"Let's put Havish and Dev together, they look like twins, so they should be bughouse partners!" Wei said jokingly.

"Wait no! You and Summer are both better than Dev and I, that would be unfair!" I ended up teaming up with Wei against Havish and Summer, and as more games finished, more people joined in what had become a bughouse ladder. After the last games had finished, we had won on every board, we finally had to return to school. By the time I reached home, it was around 7:00 PM, but all I wanted was for the next meet to happen.

The rest of October, went by, with three more meets, all of which we won, as well as the fall weather going in full swing, something I had always loved about October. We had finished two more units in Biology as well, and our grades were still all higher than George's group, which was only making him angrier. Summer and I had done the best out of everyone on the *Fahrenheit 451* essays as well, which probably didn't appeal to Liam and Elijah, not that I cared about them. If they wanted to listen to George's lies, they can pay the price for it. Nothing else seemed to happen though, and the rest of the month flew by. It was now time for Halloween, however, a holiday that had never really appealed to me. Sadly, I had been roped into dressing up, as apparently our school was holding some sort of costume party on the Monday of Halloween, and Sachin and Surya seemed extremely excited about a chance of winning a group prize. To my chagrin, of all the group costumes they could have come up with, they had all wanted to dress up as the Avengers. It was now the Friday before Halloween, and lunch was possibly my last chance to change their mind.

"Seriously? Not only are superheroes such a childish thing, but you also want to dress up as superheroes from a movie based on a comic book series?"

"Oh come on, it would be perfect! Summer could be Black Widow, Surya can be Captain America, I can be Thor, and you could be Iron Man!"

"It even matches! Summer-Black Widow, that should be obvious. You're a genius, so was Tony Stark. Sachin beat up George, so he's probably the most powerful, just like Thor, and then I'm just Captain America, because who would want to be Hawkeye?"

"Okay, when you said group costume, I was expecting something more like, not childish?"

"Like what? It's Halloween, you're supposed to be childish!" I'm not sure if it would be possible to dissuade Sachin at this point.

"I don't know, we could have dressed up as Physicists! Einstein, Tesla, Madame Curie, and Schroedinger, or something like that. Anything but superheroes based off a comic book!"

"We are trying to win a prize, not show case ourselves off as nerds."

"Earth to Sachin? We are nerds. We all take honors classes, all study for two hours in the library after school, and play chess. So you and Surya, as well as me and Summer are almost the stereotypical definition of a nerd."

"One, I am not a nerd. And two, George is going as Gregor Mendel, because you know he wants to show off his Biology affinity. We do not need to look like we copied him." I was outnumbered here. I decided that I might as well cave in to their request, it's not like this would do anything to antagonize us even more from the rest of the freshman class.

Who knew costume shopping was such a big deal? I thought all you needed to do was find something that fits and then buy it, but apparently not. Summer was making sure we checked every single clothing shop at the mall for the most accurate and cheapest costumes, in order to figure out which one was the best. Even though Sachin and Surya had originally agreed with this idea, I think even they were getting a little tired now. We had been shopping for four hours now! Finally, we ended up buying our costumes though, and it was time to get out of the mall, which I had become far too acquainted with over the last four hours.

"Seriously? You guys dressed up as the Avengers? How old are you? Seven?" Of course, George would make fun of us, he clearly has nothing better to do.

"Really George? Last summer you made us go on a Marvel marathon! And you've got to admit, their costumes do look pretty cool." Well, that was surprising. A member of George's posse talking out against George? The kid was from the lab table behind George, which made it even more surprising that he was, for once, standing up against George.

"Adrian! Are you really sticking up for those losers?" George's voice had gone up a couple of pitches and I was certain that Ms. Auguste would have heard that. Except she wasn't even in the room. Figures that the authority figures are nonexistent when you need them.

"You only call them losers because they didn't want you to sit at their lab table at the beginning of the year. Yet Dev outscores you on every test, Summer has scored within one point of you on every test, and their lab group has been beating yours on the stupid bet you made on the first day. You do realize that it's your credibility and reputation at stake? You already ruined theirs, so they have nothing to lose from this bet. I'm tired of your stupid antics, writing those stupid notes to put in Dev's locker, making fun of every movement they do, while they silently just outshine you in just about everything." I wasn't the only one in shock. Most of the kids on our side of the classroom were staring at Adrian as if he had three heads. He then turned and looked me directly in the eye. "You deserve so much more than what George has caused for you in these last two months of school. I foolishly went along with this bullying, but I'm stopping now, and I hope you can accept an apology for any action I might have taken against you, as well as for not putting that kid down in the first place."

"I cannot believe you are betraying me to try and become friends with a fraud."

"I don't know if you actually believe that, because anyone with a brain who looks Dev up can see he is the last thing from a fraud. Do you realize he was the most sought after undergraduate physics major last year? My uncle personally recruited him to CalTech, which he eventually did not accept to go to. There is no way that if he was a fraud that he would have been able to dupe so many admissions counselors at elite colleges." I could see many kids thinking now.

"Oh come on. If he was really going to be a college student next year why is he here?"

"I'm sure if you had asked Dev nicely, he would have told you." Before the conversation could escalate though, we were interrupted by an announcement on the PA.

"Hello, students! This is your principal speaking! All day we staff members have been taking notes on your Halloween costumes, in order to pick the winners. Now that we have five minutes left in the day it is time to announce them. If your name is mentioned, come down to my office to receive a bag of Halloween candy!" He went on to list some names, none of whom I recognized until, "And finally, for the best academic costume, George Wang, who was dressed up as Gregor Mendel!" Seriously. Why do I feel like they made that up just for him. He was literally the only person dressed up as a scientist.

"May the best man win, I guess." George smirked at us as he left the classroom.

"So what's the deal with Adrian?" I turned to the rest of my table, now that all the commotion had died down.

"You don't know?" Sachin had a teasing tone to his voice. "He has a thing for Summer, this was all probably just him trying to get on her good side." Summer turned red.

"He only asked me to homecoming, nothing else. Not that I would have said yes anyway, he's too narcissistic. And he never actually tried to get to know me. Also, I didn't tell you guys that, so how do you know?"

"You can never hide anything that happens in this school from Surya."

They continued to argue about who knows what. I tuned them out though, I was not in the mood. I felt something deflate inside of me. Just when I had thought that maybe people were realizing that George was wrong, and would start treating us normally again, it had all turned out to be a hormone induced ploy. I hate high schoolers. Or, most of them I guess. The Chess Team and these three kids were pretty cool.

CHAPTER 15

BIRTHDAYS

T he beginning of November brought a lot of excitement. The upcoming World Chess Championship match between defending champion Magnus Carlsen and challenger Sergey Karjakin being the main reason for my excitement. I probably should have been more excited for Sachin's birthday party, but since I am not really a fan of birthdays, it didn't excite me as much as it should have. To top it all off, Mr. Turner and I nearly had a breakthrough, enough for me to publish another paper, with Mr. Turner as a co-author of course. It was also a time of excitement around the school as the Thanksgiving Holidays were coming up in three weeks. Which also meant teachers would be cramming in as much material as they can in those three weeks, so that they can test the day before break.

"Dev? I think we did it." I was in my study hall with Mr. Turner and we had just put the finishing touches on our paper.

"I'm not sure. I'll have to go back through it and make sure our math is sound."

"What do you mean? We have checked it at least seven times already."

"When you're working in 11-Dimensions, nothing is as it seems, meaning it is entirely possible we have either missed something, missed an easier way to reach our conclusion, or of course, missed an extremely easy refutation to our thesis."

"Are you this methodical with every paper you have published? It sounds like a lot of extra work."

"I do not like being wrong, and I do not like making a fool of myself. Both of those combined mean I have to make sure my calculations and theories are always sound, and that there is no way to refute them." Which was true. Even if the theory was not right, I'd rather it not be blatantly wrong. Or worse, have an arithmetic error. I've been told by many people that this much revision is not needed on something as meaningless as a minor paper, and should only be done on major breakthroughs, but I disagree. You never know when what you think is minor could be the foundation for a major breakthrough. Or maybe it is a major breakthrough and you haven't even realized it. All of these factors make me revise everything as if I am having a major breakthrough worthy of a Nobel Prize.

"I guess that makes sense. If I'm being honest with you, I want to just put this out to the world already. Maybe since this is the first real paper I've done."

"No problem, Mr. Turner. I'm sure this will be ready to publish before Thanksgiving Break." Or maybe after the World Championship match, which theoretically could last till November 30th if every game is needed. Not that it will be, since Magnus is just that much better than Karjakin.

Before the match started on the 10th though, there was Sachin's birthday party to go to. Since November 9th was a Wednesday, he was actually holding his birthday on the Sunday before his birthday, November 6th. He was holding it at this bowling alley/arcade place, with time split between the arcade, bowling, laser tag, and of course presents and cake. The party was going to last for four hours, with 90 minutes for bowling, an hour each for arcade and food, and 30 minutes of laser tag, in that order. It was the four of us, and then a couple of Sachin's friends from middle school, and some cousins, all in all, there were 15 kids. We had split into three lanes of five kids each. Summer, Surya, Sachin, and I were with one of his friends from Middle School, Aryan. There was a lot of good-natured trash talk going around across the three lanes, and it seemed like everything was going well.

"What is this? A group of losers going bowling?" I knew that voice and didn't have to turn around to know who said it. "I wonder what the special occasion is? Maybe they realized that it is futile to win a bet

THE HIGH SCHOOL EXPERIMENT

against the great George Wang, and are celebrating their early lead?" Seriously? We had a good 3% average on him, 97% to 94%. Also is it really necessary for him to come and bug us over the weekend? Wait. Why is he even here? He wouldn't have stooped so low to try and stalk us would he? I turned around and saw George surrounded by a bunch of his lackeys.

"Can a kid not celebrate his birthday in peace?" Sachin muttered on my right. It looks like he had turned around as well and saw exactly the same sight.

"Your birthday? Too bad November 6th is not as cool as a birthday as November 9th." Hold on. I actually feel bad for Sachin now. Victim of the birthday paradox. With possibly the worst person to share a birthday with.

"You have got to be kidding me!" Sachin looked like he might cry. Okay, I get it, it's bad news, but seriously, it is just a birthday.

"George, how about you just go to your lanes, I think it would be better for both parties." Summer was trying to keep stuff under control, without escalating anything further.

"Who is this jerk anyway?" Aryan looked a bit lost, which was to be expected as he didn't go to Northshore. "And what are the odds he and Sachin have the same birthday?"

"There was a 74.35% chance that two kids in our Biology class have the same birthday. And you're an eyewitness to those percentages." I should not have said that. I could feel all the eyes shift on me. "What? You can do the math yourself if you want." Why am I not able to shut my mouth here? "Now if you are asking if one would believe George and Sachin were the same age, the answer is no because George acts like a spoiled five-year-old, while Sachin actually acts like a 15-year-old- or I guess 14 as he hasn't turned 15 yet." Oh, I'm really asking to get beat up now.

"What was that? You dare insult the great George Wang?!" Also, when did he start inserting a 'the great' before his name when talking in the third person.

"Has anyone told you how stupid you would sound if you always talked about yourself in the third person? Let alone the fact that you're so narcissistic that you also call yourself great? What have you ever accomplished in life? You're a soon to be a 15-year-old kid and your biggest claim to fame is that you are popular in high school. And that's not even an accomplishment because you are just riding on the coattails of your sister's popularity. You're nothing more than a whiny kid that seems to think he is entitled to all the world's privileges and thinks that everyone should just kneel before him. You're nothing better than a wannabe Adolf Hitler." I really, really hope that I don't get beat up. I could see the shock in everyone's eyes, which concerned me a bit. Was no one else tired of this kid? Clearly ignoring him wasn't working. The only way we would get him to stop is if we stand up for ourselves and call him out on what he really is. The incident with Adrian in Biology had opened my eyes to this. Still doesn't mean I want to get beat up though, so maybe this wasn't the best course of action.

"Whatever, I didn't come here to argue with you losers anyway." And to my shock, George and his friends just walked away. Everyone continued to just stare at me, and to be completely honest I was not expecting this either. Both me actually saying something, as well as George just straight up walking away.

"Okay Sachin, when you told me you made new friends, I did not expect them to be cool like Dev is. I was expecting more of like a social outcast, like you and Surya." Aryan was teasing, of course, he didn't actually want to insult Surya and Sachin.

"You don't understand Aryan, Dev here is the most hated kid in the freshman class! Definition of not cool right there."

"He literally went around introducing himself like he was James Bond on the first day of school!" Surya added. What was this? Was it everyone make fun of Dev day? I had just saved them all from George Wang. I couldn't help but join in on the laughter though.

"Don't forget the tuxedo!" Summer was now joining in as well, and the laughter just increased.

"The name is Shanmugan. Devadas Shanmugan." Sachin mimicked me from the first day. The rest of the party wasn't so bad, as George didn't do anything else, and actually seemed like he was just avoiding us. I personally wasn't a fan of the arcade, I found the games a little stupid, so I found my fun in watching Summer fail at every arcade game she played. Which of course led to her targeting me for all of the laser tag game. I think the number of times I got hit alone, would have been enough for her team to win. Sachin and Surya weren't too happy with that, as they had both been on my team.

"You know that you're supposed to help the birthday boy win at laser tag right? Not make yourself a wide-open shot and give the other team a free win." Surya teased after the game.

"Or maybe you shouldn't antagonize someone for an hour in the arcade, continue to make fun of their lack of skills while we eat, then have to be on the opposite side during laser tag." Sachin pretended to pout, as if he actually cared that he lost a game of laser tag.

"I'm sure Dev here has learned his lesson though, he will think twice before he tries to make fun of me again."

"Only if a game of laser tag is upcoming. You aren't scary otherwise." Summer then landed a soft punch to my shoulder.

"I can make that hurt a lot harder if necessary." A shiny glint in her green eyes made me wonder if she was actually serious about punching me if I acted out of line in the future. The banter between us continued for a while, until it was finally time for us to leave. Minus the whole George fiasco, it wasn't a bad experience for my first birthday party. And once again I could feel a pang of regret that I had missed out on so many things like this as a child. I knew my parents hadn't meant to hurt me, but the more of a childhood I got to experience, the more I wondered if it was worth it. Sure I was already renowned in the scientific community, and could have been an MIT student at 13, but was all that really worth living a half-life? If I had gone to MIT like I had wanted, I never would have been able to make friends, like my parents had said, and I would have never been able to enjoy life, because before high school it was all binary: either I was successful or not. No middle ground, and things like friendships were all but an enhancement to life, not an integral part of it. I quickly pushed those thoughts aside, there is no point in dwelling in the has beens of the past, when I could be enjoying the gifts of the present.

Of course, George hadn't decided to ignore us, despite my hopes. If anything, he had become a lot more vindictive to us now, and we had only been through three school days since the birthday party! Well two and a half, we still had to actually go through Biology with him on

Wednesday - November 9th. The moment he walked into the room with that large smirk on his face, I knew something was up.

"Happy Birthday to you! Happy Birthday to you! ..." At least seven kids started singing, and many more joined in, as is the custom for when it is someone's birthday. Is this really what he had planned? I honestly expected more from George.

"It must be nice to be recognized on your birthday. After all, it is the one day of the year that is all about you." George walked by Sachin and muttered that. So his entire plan revolved around guilt? So original. I then got an idea. I walked over to Ms. Auguste, and whispered,

"You know, today is Sachin's birthday. I'm sure you can find a way that makes him be recognized, like George was." I then walked back to my seat. Now, I had no proof, but I was pretty sure Ms. Auguste knew exactly what kind of person George was, as well as his antics in this class. After all, even though she seemed to give us a lot of 'work' time in this class, she must still be paying attention somewhat to make sure kids are behaving. Now, of course, the only issue with this theory was that she hadn't exactly done anything to reprimand George. I saw Ms. Auguste nod at me though, and she left the room. I wonder what she had come up with. When she came back, she addressed the class.

"Well class, today I was going to teach a lesson, but then I realized that today is actually a pretty special event for our class. Of course, this means that we will be going faster than normal over the next couple days to make sure we are still ready for the test before break, even with one day wasted." There was silence in the room and people looked at each other with confused glances.

"Dev? What did you do?" Surya whispered next to me.

"I don't know, I just told her that it was also Sachin's birthday. I am just as clueless as you are."

"As you all know from the events of two minutes ago, it is George's birthday today. But what you may not know, is that we actually celebrate two birthdays today. Since it is a rare event..." Sachin started coughing.

"74.35%" is what his cough suspiciously sounded like.

"I thought it would be nice to relax and eat some cake. I was able to call a friend who works over at the nearest Stop-And-Shop, and got the order for 20 minutes from now. However, since we already sang 'Happy

Birthday' to George I thought we should also do something for Sachin."
She then motioned for him to come up. She then took out some wax
and put it on the table. "I will write the words 'Happy Birthday, Sachin'
using this wax on the table and light it, then after everyone sings to you,
you can blow it out" Take that George. I turned back to see his reaction,
and saw his face scrunched up in what I believe was supposed to be
anger. It was so distorted, though, that it just looked hilarious. Everyone
else seemed to not care, probably because they were getting free cake.

"You are so going to pay for this." George whispered as he walked
by me at the end of class, after we had all gotten some cake.

"And soon you will learn not to mess with one of my friends." I
really need to stop reacting to him. I couldn't help it though, I finally
understood how Sachin felt at the beginning of the year whenever
George pestered him.

"Why should I be scared of you? You're a fraud who hides behind
authority figures who you have bribed to hide all of your activities, and
now you have your merry band of friends to hide behind." I don't know
what came over me next. I was suddenly filled with blind rage, and I
punched him right in the mouth. I could hear gasps from behind me, as
my friends had seen what I had done. It was too late now. George and
I were now on the floor attacking each other. I was definitely losing,
what could you expect after all, and right before he could put in one
last finishing touch, he was grabbed from behind by one of the school's
on-duty police officers. I only realized how bad the situation was when
I felt my arms being pulled behind my back. The walk to the discipline
office was a long one, as George and I, in our bloodied state, got many
stares from kids in the halls. I had never been so ashamed of myself in
my life. We finally entered the office, as we waited for our counselors
and the principal to enter the room.

"Do you realize how much trouble you boys are in?" Mr. Davidson
and his disappointing tone was the last thing I heard before a familiar
feeling of the world turning black consumed me.

CHAPTER 16

FALLOUT

I woke up in the Nurse's office to a swarm of disappointed faces. As I regained consciousness the memories of my fight with George resurfaced. I knew that no matter what punishment the school enacted on me, my parents' reactions would be worse. A lot worse. I wouldn't have to wait long though, they were already here. A quick chat with the principal about a one-week suspension, and it was time for an awkward drive home with my parents. Do you know that feeling when you know someone is going to reprimand you but they just remain silent, as if they want you to start talking? The silence was uncomfortable, but I stood firm. I knew that anything I said would only make matters worse. When we got home I was greeted by Lakshmi, and her never-ending bout of enthusiasm.

"Did you really beat a kid up? What did he do? Is there a video? I want to see this!" Well, at least one person doesn't seem to be mad at me for this.

"Lakshmi? Go to your room. You too Rakshini. We need to have a talk with Dev. Alone." Well, I guess there was no more postponing. This is possibly the first time I have seen disappointment on Amma's face, and I don't really know what to expect. Just that it is going to be bad.

"So are you going to explain why you punched that kid in the face? I thought we raised you better than this." I can't tell if Appa is mad or disappointed. Probably both, if I am being honest, because at some level I am too.

"Sorry. I don't really know what came over me. I've been able to tolerate his bullying for the entire year, but for some reason, I just snapped today. I shouldn't have done it."

"You know you could be facing a rescinding from MIT." I haven't even thought about that. My record is spotless, though, and I'm too highly sought after for them to let me just go somewhere else.

"Well, if we are being honest, it is me. They wouldn't turn me down just because I got into a small fight at school."

"Dev! How dare you talk to your father like that."

"Where is this ego coming from? This high school has been a bad influence on you. Creating an ego, getting into fights, next thing we know you'll be going around chasing after girls." Okay, now I can read his face. He's mad. Like, really mad. This is possibly the angriest I have ever seen him. Not possibly. It is.

"For all we know he is already being distracted by that Summer girl. Maybe that's what's causing this behavior! He wants to show off his masculinity to impress her, I think that's what these American kids do." Hold on, I'm fine if they are mad at me, I deserve it, but my friends? No way.

"How can you talk about her like that?! You've met her! You even said she's a nice girl! And there is no funny business going on, I am not interested in getting practical experience on the female anatomy. And I'll tell you what's causing this 'bad behavior'. The fact that you guys locked me out from the rest of the world for 13 years. You raised me to have no emotion whatsoever. You told me that the only thing that matters is how successful you are, then you prevented me from going to MIT. You told me that I needed to learn how to be around kids my age, and then lash out at my friends the moment one small thing happens. I heard what you said that night. It also made me realize how much you guys have failed me as parents. I don't know what I am going to do when I grow up, but all I know is I will make sure I am nothing like you guys. I wouldn't want my kids to be ashamed that I am their father." Months of agitation. Months of deliberation. Months of silent anger. They all came gushing out now. My parents wanted to know what happened to me? I'm finally telling them about my life. About how I feel about them.

I left them in the living room, jaws open, and went to my room, door slamming shut behind me.

"Dev? Are you okay?" I could hear Rakshini from behind my door.

"What do you want."

"Am I not allowed to check on my little brother? You seem like you need someone to talk to." She was right I guess.

"Fine, you can come in." She slowly entered my room, closing the door behind her.

"Are you really that upset about being homeschooled for 13 years? I heard everything you said."

"Not about being homeschooled per se. Just about the fact that I wasn't allowed to have contact with the outside world. And then they go and pull this stunt on me, and suddenly everything I was led to believe in my whole life turns out to be a lie. Why couldn't I have been treated like a normal kid? Like you or Lakshmi. You both are also smart. Just because I am a bit above average…"

"I wouldn't call an IQ of 170 a bit above average."

"Okay fine, just because I'm a wunderkind doesn't mean I should be treated any differently. All Amma and Appa have proven by this are that they are no better than the kids in my grade, who single me out because I'm smart."

"Now, maybe I shouldn't be speaking for them, but I was four when you were born. I was in kindergarten, learning how to read and write, when you had already memorized the capitals of every country in the world. I was there throughout your entire childhood, and I know that Amma and Appa only did what they thought was best for you. They saw how you intimidated the neighbor kids on the playground. They saw how you would have no idea how to react to those kids who were just trying to make a friend, when you just wanted to have a study partner. That's why they homeschooled you. They wanted to keep you away from the cruel world out there, from kids who would bully you, and others who would attempt to use you. It's clear now that the decision was not correct, but can you at least try to see it from their point of view? You have every right to be upset, but at least understand where they came from, and forgive them." I don't care. They should have known better.

They should have sought advice. They should have taught me how to deal with it, instead of just hiding me.

"No."

"What?"

"No, I'm not going to forgive them. They ruined my childhood and failed as parents. Maybe one day I will learn to tolerate them again, but never will I forgive them."

"Dev... do you realize what you are saying? You need to realize that humans make mistakes. Amma and Appa are only human, they are bound to make mistakes."

"Am I not human then? I can't remember when I've made a mistake." Oh wow. I really need to learn how to think before I speak. I did not mean that... I really didn't.

"Oh really now? I can think of multiple mistakes you've made just since high school started. And I can see you making a pretty big mistake right now. I'm one of the only people in the world who will always wish the best for you, so maybe you should stop thinking the world revolves around you for one second, and open your eyes. I'll let you sleep on it." She stormed out of the room. What have I done? Rakshini was always there for me when things were rough. Whether it was because I was at a dead-end in my research, or because a giant named Luke was trying to beat me up, she was always there looking out for me, and I had just upset her deeply. She was definitely wrong about forgiving my parents though. They had messed things up too much to get any type of forgiveness from me. I would have been fine if they were only mad at me, but no way was I going to let them insult one of my friends, and try to put the blame on them. I pulled out my phone and sent a text to Summer.

Dev: "Are you still awake? Things are bad here. My parents tried blaming the whole fight on me trying to show off my masculinity, or some nonsense like that. Then when Rakshini tried comforting me, I just made her mad. My parents are a lost cause, but can you help me try and fix things with Rakshini? Also, I don't think you are welcome at my house right now. Apparently you are 'distracting me, and making me be diverted from the right choices."

Summer: "What? Slow down Dev, one topic at a time."

Dev: "1. Parents blame you for my 'violent behavior' 2. I made Rakshini mad, and need to fix things with her... I guess that's it."

Summer: "I'm sure you misunderstood your parents. Or they misspoke; that happens sometimes when people are angry."

Dev: "No my parents messed up. I am not forgiving them. They ruined my childhood, and now they are trying to ruin what might possibly be the best thing that has ever happened to me, in high school and the friendships I made there."

Summer: "Calm down Dev. Anyway, what did Davidson do? How long is the suspension."

Dev: "One week."

Summer: "I guess school is going to be a lot more boring without you. And George of course, he seems to bring entertainment wherever he goes."

Dev: "Are you trying to change the topic?"

Summer: "Yes. I want you to sleep on what you said before. Think about it during your run tomorrow morning with a fresh, and anger-less, head. Goodnight."

Dev: "Goodnight."

CHAPTER 17

AFTERMATH

I don't really get suspensions. Sure it's supposed to be a black mark on your record, but you also get to stay at home, which wasn't too bad. I mainly worked on fixing up my paper that I was working on with Mr. Turner, as well as school work that my friends were giving me copies of so I wouldn't be behind. Things at home weren't that great though, as I was actively avoiding my parents, and was actually spending far more time with Lakshmi than I would have liked. Of course, this meant I was watching way too many *My Little Pony* episodes, and I'm positive I could feel my IQ drop every time I had to watch one.

"So when are you going to tell me the story of how you beat another kid up?" I was with Lakshmi in her room, and she was now grilling me about my suspension.

"What's there to say? A kid was being annoying - had been since the first day of school - and he finally got me to react. Not my proudest moment, I shouldn't have lost my cool."

"Was it exhilarating? It must have been nice to finally give him what he deserved, right?"

"No, not like that. It would have been better if I had gotten him to stop without having to resort to violence."

"You know instead of feeling bad that you had to punch him, maybe you should be happy about the fact that you stood up to him, even if you would have rather not done it that way." I guess she did have a point. At the same time, she is also ten so she doesn't really understand how the world works.

"I could, but that's not the right way to look at it. Whether or not he deserved it doesn't matter, I should not be stooping to his level. I need to have the moral high ground."

"Everyone makes mistakes! You should just laugh this off and move on. Maybe even in a couple of years you will think back at this moment fondly, like a story old people tell their grandkids." I guess I could try to think of this that way. Not really sure how this will help me though.

"Okay, I'll try that. I need to go now, have things to do."

"Come back soon! We can watch the next episode of *My Little Pony!*" I will not be taking her up on that invitation. I went back to my room and started to think about the events of the last week. I decided that even though I didn't understand the point of a suspension, I definitely did not want to go through one again. It had been pretty boring, even though it was basically what my schedule was back when I was homeschooled. Maybe it was because the only person in my family who I didn't ignore was Lakshmi - and let's face it, she's a bit immature for me to constantly hang out with her. My parents had also taken my phone away for the first five days of the suspension, since they apparently wanted to distance me away from 'bad influences'. I'm not sure why I got my phone back, but I wasn't going to complain about that. Then I remembered that I had missed a week of school, and might have missed something other than schoolwork.

Dev: "So is there anything I should know that happened at school over the last week?"

Sachin: "Oh yeah, George only had a two-day suspension, so he's been back since Monday"

Dev: "Okay that makes sense, I did instigate the fight after all"

Sachin: "There are also rumors that his family is pushing for the school to examine your mental health, since they believe you may be prone to violent behavior"

Dev: "WHAT?!"

Surya: "It's only a rumor, Sachin shouldn't have said that over text, we were going to tell you in lunch tomorrow."

Dev: "When did this rumor start?"

Surya: "When George came back to school. He has also been playing an innocent victim, and keeps a bandage on his nose"

Dev: "Wait... I punched his mouth!"

Sachin: "That's what I've been saying!"

Surya: "Well it doesn't matter now. We need to figure out how to deal with this." Looks like Surya didn't want us talking about the fight, which I guess makes sense. I started thinking. Now George had a new way to turn people against me, and this time he actually had a point. I was the one that punched him first after all. That's when I knew I had to fix things with Rakshini. If anyone could help me through this right now, it was her. I walked over to her room, keeping the advice Summer had been giving me over the last week in mind.

"Rakshini? Is it okay if I come in?" I asked after knocking on her door.

"What do you want Dev?" She seemed as if she didn't really want to be talking to me right now. Which I guess is understandable.

"I wanted to talk about what happened last week."

"Okay come in. Make it quick though." Okay. Deep breath. Summer told me the first thing I needed to do was make sure my mind was clear, so that I don't let random emotions come in the way of the apology. Or something like that at least.

"I shouldn't have acted so egotistically when you were trying to comfort me. Or in anyway acted as if I were superior to all people." I think I got the emotions down correctly. Summer had told me what to say and how to say it, and I had been practicing all week, even without my phone. Still wasn't sure how me acting annoyingly egotistical angered her, but Summer said it was what I was supposed to do.

"You've been talking to Summer." What? "There's no way you would have been able to pull that off without talking to someone else, and let's face it Sachin and Surya aren't exactly going to be the best kids to ask for help. I don't care though, it's the thought that counts." Okay good, I thought she was going to stay mad at me because I couldn't do this by myself.

"Uh yeah. I knew I messed up though! I just needed her help to figure out what exactly I did wrong, and then her help on how to fix it."

"Still socially inept I see. You know, I don't agree with Amma and Appa about your friends being bad influences. Anyone can see that they've actually been able to help you become a better person. Not that it's some sort of accomplishment, you were just a robot before."

"Hey! I was not a robot." It was nice being able to joke with her again. "On a more serious note, I'm still not forgiving them. They ruined my life."

"Okay, you can be mad at them, they also should be disappointed in you, but saying they ruined your life is a stretch." I was extremely tempted to lash out at her again, but I knew that it was probably not a good idea. "Just think about what I said last week, that they only try to do the best for you."

"Okay fine, I'll think about it. Anyway, did you know that George Wang and his family are trying to get the school to test my mental health? Apparently I might be too prone to violence."

"Ignore it. Rumors like that aren't worth you getting in trouble. Just ignore anything that boy says to you, he isn't worth your time."

"I'll try. I was able to do it for two months, shouldn't be too hard." I actually believed this. My actions last week must have been due to too much stress or something. Maybe the horror of having to dress up as a superhero during Halloween caused it. I went to bed that night a lot calmer than I had over the last week, knowing that everything should be fine now.

Stares. Glares. Whispers. That's all I noticed when I entered the school. It seemed that everyone wanted to see my 'grand return to school.

"What are you looking at?" Rakshini glared at the people I had noticed, clearly, she wasn't happy about it. People scattered after that, clearly not wanting to be on the wrong side of her anger. I still don't get how she was able to make people scared just by raising her voice, just like she had on the first day of school. I walked to my first period English class, feeling a sense of deja vu from the first day. I took my seat next to Summer, trying my best to ignore the fact that everyone was trying to look at me without being obvious about it.

"So how was your one week vacation?" Summer said, clearly trying to lighten the mood.

"Pretty boring, actually. I ended up watching way too much *My Little Pony* than what I would have liked. I did finish up on my paper though, so assuming Mr. Turner thinks it's ready, we will probably be publishing it."

"Well, that's cool. Are you going to let us read it?"

"Well I guess you could, but I won't guarantee that you will comprehend it."

"I'd still like to see it, it would be rude of me not to see something that you publish, right?" I just shrugged my shoulders, I wasn't sure what the social protocol in this situation was. Before our conversation could continue, however, the bell rang, signaling the beginning of the period.

"Hello, class! Nice to see y'all here again. Today, I wanted to talk about the final exam and what it entails." Groans could be heard from multiple kids.

"Mr. Bakerman, it's not even Thanksgiving Break yet!" One kid, Hazel I believe, exclaimed.

"When you've been teaching as long as I have, you realize that the time between Thanksgiving and finals goes by way too quickly for what I am about to say. As you know, the final will be 20 percent of your grade, however since this is an English class, we have a slightly different format for the final. In addition to a multiple choice test on the day of the final, which will count for 50 percent of your final exam, I am also expecting you to turn in an out of class literary essay on our next book, *Northanger Abbey*." Sigh, I've read this book as well, and it is possibly one of the most boring books out there. Not really a fan of Jane Austen as a whole, but this is possibly one of the books I least liked from her, up there with *Jane Eyre*. "I find that if I tell my kids about this essay after Thanksgiving Break, with all of the rush that happens in all of their other classes and cramming for finals, they will forget about this essay until the night before, and then I'm stuck reading 50 essays filled with spelling mistakes, horrible grammar, and will make me wonder why I even became a teacher." A couple of kids laughed, I guess Mr. Bakerman had said that as a joke, as he had also paused to let the laughter die down. To avoid that horrible experience, I started giving the essays a week before Thanksgiving, as most kids end up writing the essay during the break, which makes grading them a lot more enjoyable." Okay, this wasn't too bad, maybe a couple of hours spent one day during break, and I'll have a passable essay. The rest of the period wasn't too bad, as we were able to get time to read the book or work on our essays.

I had gotten used to the stares. It really wasn't that hard, as I had been stared at since day one with the tuxedo. What I wasn't used to was some voice I didn't recognize yelling at me on my way to lunch.

"Hey kid!" I didn't even register that he was talking to me, because I didn't recognize the voice at first. "Hey! Are you ignoring me?" I turned around, wondering what this kid was yelling for, only to be face to face with Luke - the giant that had nearly beaten me up on my first day.

"Uh, what?"

"I heard you've learned how to fight. Then again after your last experience with me, that would be expected." He chuckled at this, as if he had told a joke. Maybe it was a joke for him, I'm not sure.

"To be fair it was one punch, and I still lost the fight."

"I like your spirit kid. And good thing you ditched that tuxedo." Wait. Is this kid being nice to me? Was he not trying to beat me up on the first day of school? I am confused.

"Why haven't you tried beating me up again?"

"Because no one should be going through the stupid drama that you have had to go through, and I'm definitely not going to be adding onto it." That's weird. A delinquent feeling sympathy for a victim - a former victim of his as well. "If you need any help beating up on bullies, you have my number." He then handed me a slip of paper, patted my back and walked away. That has got to be the strangest interaction I have had with someone my entire life. I knew other people had noticed the interaction as well, as I could feel the glares on me, but they were now of confusion, instead of hatred.

"You know, the strangest thing happened to me right now." I was in lunch with Sachin and Surya now.

"George Wang offered to become your friend?" Surya asked.

"I don't think it was a guessing game... but here's what I'll guess: George Wang was expelled!"

"Not everything in my life revolves around George Wang, you know."

"Of course not, it revolves around you!" Sachin retorted.

"It is your life after all. Just like my life revolves around me and Sachin's revolves around Sachin."

"Anyway, now that you two have been philosophical, let me get to my story before getting any more enlightening proverbs from you two. So you know how I nearly got beat up the first day of school by some giant named Luke?"

"Uh no."

"You didn't mention it actually." Whoops. I guess I hadn't told them that story. I briefly filled them in on that backstory before moving on,

"So anyway, the giant comes up to me today and tells me that if I ever need help protecting myself from bullies, I should give him a call and gave me his number."

"Okay, I have one question. When you say giant, how tall is he actually? 5'6?" Figures Sachin would try to flex his height advantage on me and Surya.

"Hahaha. No, he is like 6'5 and also like really large. Not fat large, more muscly large. Probably a football player or something. Or a sumo wrestler."

"Hmm. I wouldn't trust him." Sachin said.

"Or he could genuinely be a nice guy? You have to at least contact him Dev. Maybe he will be the solution to George!"

"I don't want to seem like a coward, hiding behind him though. At least for any George problems. Maybe if anything else happens, I can contact him."

"Okay, you both claim to be smart, but you're missing the obvious solution here." Sachin was using a know it all tone. "He's a senior right? Don't you have a sister that's a senior?" Right. That was pretty obvious.

"Right. I'll ask her next time I see her." Then I remembered my conversation with Summer that morning. "Hey, my paper is ready to be published, and Summer said she was interested in reading it, so I'm asking you guys as well."

"Nah, I'm good. Maybe in a few years when I'll actually understand the stuff."

"Sachin! Of course, we want to read it, Dev. Probably won't understand it, but it's still a cool accomplishment." Hmm. Social protocol is weird. Why would it dictate you to read something you don't understand just to support a friend?

"Okay, I'll send you guys a copy after I have Mr. Turner give it one last look over." The rest of the period went by as normal, nothing really stood out from it. As usual, the rest of the day went by without much commotion, until of course, the daily confrontation with George Wang.

"I didn't realize that this school let delinquents back in. I thought they usually expel kids who are prone to violent tendencies." It was times like this that I wished I brought earplugs to school. It would definitely help in ignoring this kid. Then he turned to me. "Seriously though. Is that the real reason you were homeschooled? Not because you are some sort of boy wonder, because I think everyone knows you aren't, but because you are too violent to be around other kids? How much did you have to pay your 'friends' to be around you and risk getting beaten up?" See, when he spouts nonsense like this, it's easy to ignore him because I know it isn't true.

"George? Have you been paying attention to anything I've said in the last 30 seconds? Or are you too busy bothering Dev, who was trying to pay attention to my lecture." I guess we could ignore the fact that I hadn't realized that Ms. Auguste was lecturing either, but at least I could pretend I was."

"Sorry Ms. Auguste, Dev was just asking me for clarification on what you had just said." Would she really believe that excuse?

"I'm sure the rest of the class would like to hear it as well. After all, we can't have you and Dev having a better understanding of this topic than everyone else, and I'm sure there are other kids who would love clarification." I could hear other kids snickering at Ms. Auguste's handling of George, especially as I'm sure no one believed George's excuse. I didn't have to turn around either, to know how red George's face was.

"Sorry Ms. Auguste, but I was actually asking Dev what he needed clarification on, when you interrupted us."

"Oh, I see, I was interrupting you? Next time, have your side chats after I am done lecturing, George. I don't want to see you bothering another studious kid again, Dev hadn't said a word to you and was looking at the board the entire time." George was silent after that, but

I assume that he had nodded his head, as Ms. Auguste had turned back to the board and continued her lecture on Mitosis. After class, Ms. Auguste asked me to stay back. "Dev? Do you need me to move either you or George? I'm sure there would be another lab table willing to switch with either of your tables."

"No, it's fine, I can handle him. Last Wednesday was an accident, I didn't mean to lose my control." That and accepting this offer would only make me look cowardly. I didn't need that to happen, I already had a horrible reputation, didn't need to be called a coward as well.

"If you say so. I want you to know that I know everything that happens in this classroom, and if you ever need me to step into a conflict, I can help."

"Thanks, Ms. Auguste, but right now I don't think I need you to do anything."

"If you say so. Keep up the good work in class, and I'll see you tomorrow." I still don't get how a physicist like me has his best grades in a fake science like Biology. Not that it was by much, other classes were never below a 98.5 percent, they just didn't beat the 100 percent I had in Biology. The horror of that.

CHAPTER 18

TOURNAMENT

The weekend before Thanksgiving was the first Saturday tournament for our chess team. This tournament would be the first gauge of how good we were compared to other schools in the state. There would be around 30 schools at this tournament, with 20 of them being the best schools in the state. I decided to forgo my morning run this day, since we had to be at school at 6 AM to get onto the bus that would take us to Country High School, where the tournament was taking place.

"Is it really worth it? Getting up at this ungodly hour?" Sachin asked us. We were sitting on the bus, each of us to a seat, seeing as there was a whole bus for 20 kids.

"You guys will really enjoy this, trust me. These tournaments have been my best memories of chess club during the last three years." Raj answered, overhearing Sachin's question.

"I'm not sure about these school tournaments, but USCF tournaments are always fun. Even when you have to wake up a bit early." Summer joined in.

"I think it's pretty cool. We get to see all the great players from across the state in one place, it will be fun learning from them." I joined in. I was pretty excited about this tournament. It would be the first time I got to put my skills against a quality level of opponents.

"How did I end up becoming friends with a bunch of chess nerds."

"Well, you've been stuck with me since we were in 1st grade, the rest of them just joined us for the ride."

"More like you dragged me to chess club using a bag of chips."

"True."

"Now let me sleep in peace, I have a 90 minute bus ride I can use to make up for the fact that I am sitting on a bus at 6:00 A.M."

"You didn't have to come to this, you know." Summer chimed in.

"How could I not? Otherwise, I would have had to deal with you guys talking about what an amazing time you had here, and I wouldn't want to miss out on it."

"You're sending mixed signals here Sachin. You either want to go and are okay with waking up early or you sleep in and don't go." Raj spoke again. It was too late though, Sachin was out cold.

"I guess he chose both." I joked. Most of the kids on the team actually chose to sleep as well, probably because it was so early and it would make sense to actually get some sleep in so that they didn't get tired during the tournament. Halfway through the bus ride, Mr. Wu passed out a sheet of paper, which turned out to be the board orders for the teams today. The Varsity team would be eight players, and each of the two JV teams would be five players each. There were no real surprises this time, Mr. Wu had told us that he wanted to put out what he believed was our best lineup, so that we could truly see how we stack up against the rest of the teams in the state. The lineup was: Summer, Raj, Nicolas, Wei, Me, Max, Rachel, Surya. The first JV team was Sai, Arjun, Havish, Sachin, and some kid that was just casual about chess. That also applied for the third team, with the players coming here just to have fun on a Saturday, which was completely fine. Nothing much happened the rest of the bus ride, as I spent most of the drive staring out the window.

"I see that your team got some freshmen." A tall Asian kid had walked over to our table in the skittles room and was now talking to Raj.

"Yeah we did, and they are pretty decent as well."

"Wait, is that Summer Williams? I thought she was homeschooled." Wait... Summer is famous? Or at least known in chess circles? I looked at her inquisitively.

"Okay yeah, some people probably will recognize me. I am one of the top junior players in the state, remember?"

"Okay." I turned back to Raj and the Asian kid.

"Still won't help you guys defeat us. We got some freshmen as well, and we won state last year with no seniors. I'd be surprised if we score less than 60 in any match."

"If you say so, Ethan. I'd like to play you guys this tournament, just to show you that we can put up a fight against you."

"Your goals are lofty. Good luck though, and may the best team win." The kid, Ethan, sauntered off, probably to find someone else to annoy.

"Who was he?" I asked.

"Ethan Lee. He actually was my neighbor and went to our school until my sophomore year. Then last year he moved to the city because the chess programs there are better. He's a national master, and the second board for Johns High School - the team that won state last year. They are definitely the favorites to win it all this year as well."

"He seemed like an interesting person."

"Just a world-class jerk. He would be tolerable if he was still with us, but going to Johns just inflated his ego even more. It'll be fun if I have to play him, though."

"Who's their top board, then?" Summer joined in.

"Ramesh Chandra. He's a sophomore, and won every single game he played last year, which was part of the reason Johns demolished the competition at state. I believe he is an International Master as well."

"Oh yeah, I've played him before. I've beaten him two times, drawn once, and lost once. I should prepare for him though, he got really good over the summer, which was when he got his IM title."

"Wait... so he wasn't really good- by your standards- last year?" Raj looked shocked.

"Well, I've always been better than him, ever since we were like six. It was only in April that he gained 150 rating points, and then won the North American Youth tournament in July to get his IM title. He's higher-rated than me now, which I'm kind of mad about, so I should probably go and prepare for him, in case we do play them." Summer then walked over to her laptop and started going through what I was guessing were her opening files.

"So how good is their board five?" I asked Raj.

"I'm not sure what their lineup is this year, but expect it to be around 17 or 1800."

"Oh wow. No wonder they were so good."

"Yeah." I then went over to Summer, to see what she was looking at. I noticed it was a game that she had played against the Ramesh guy from last January. "So how exactly do you 'prepare' for someone?"

"Well, most good people have games you can find online, or maybe games you have played against them, and then you can use those games to figure out what openings they play, and do research into them, maybe find a sideline that is good to surprise them in, or maybe a good novelty in the mainline, or something like that."

"So how do you know what's the mainline and what's a sideline?"

"The program most people use is called ChessBase, which basically has a huge database of master games, and you can see what the most played lines are. And there's this thing called the online database which gets updated every Sunday, so you can use that to see the newest trends that the top players and other GMs are following in certain openings."

"Okay, that makes sense. Do you mind if I just watch you prepare then? Might give me some ideas of what to play as well."

"Yeah go ahead. We have an hour before the round though, if you want to go play blitz or something with Surya."

"I thought blitz was bad before a tournament."

"It can be, but it's also a nice way to relax."

"I think I would rather try and learn something new."

"If you want." The next hour I watched - as well as tried to help- Summer looked through games that Ramesh had played over the last few months, until it was time to go to the tournament hall.

"Ok guys, we are playing Athens High School this round. They aren't that good of a team, they went 3/7 at state last year, so we should do well against them. Treat this as a warmup for the state tournament, meaning every game counts for tiebreaks, so make sure you don't play any stupid moves that may cost you." Mr. Wu was giving us his normal team breakdown speech, something I had gotten accustomed too during our weekly meets.

My game was not that exciting. My opponent gave me a free queen on move five, and I quickly won the game. It was kind of a let down really, I was hoping I would get good games today, and even though I knew I would get better opponents in future rounds, the game was still a little of a downer. On the bright side though, we won on all eight boards for a 68-0 sweep. It was now the lunch break, which for some reason was before round two, instead of after round two. You would think it makes more sense to put the break halfway through the tournament right?

"Hey! Guess what!" It was Sachin, and he looked happy, which was worrying.

"Should I be worried?" Surya took the words out of my mouth.

"I drew! It was a really crazy game though, I never knew that even a rook wasn't enough to win against a bare king, but I guess you learn something new every day." Summer, Surya and I just glanced at each other, trying to figure out which one of us should tell him that a draw is probably not an accomplishment in that situation.

"So... why don't you show us the end position?" Summer asked. Sachin seemed way too excited to show us, was he really this naive? He then showed us the final position, which was a king and rook against a king, with Sachin having the rook.

"And then I played this! It looks like it just wins because the black king has no moves, but it turns out it's a stalemate because the king isn't in check! You know, I wasn't really a fan of playing chess, but seeing this and the complexities and the cool rules that prevent even an extra rook from being enough to win, makes it pretty interesting." Was Sachin okay? He seemed a little bit too excited here.

"You do realize you actually had a checkmate right? If instead of moving your rook to where you did, if you moved it one square in front, it was a check and the king has no squares, meaning checkmate." Surya decided to break the news to Sachin. Sachin starts laughing. A lot. And then he fell off his chair, with how much he's laughing. The three of us just glanced at each other again - what exactly were we supposed to do?

"Are you okay Sachin?" I asked after around 30 seconds.

"You guys... are... so... gullible!" He managed to say between laughs.

"What?" Summer was just as confused as Surya and me.

"Of course I played the checkmate! The look on your faces when I told you I drew! Totally worth it. It makes me wonder if I should have actually stalemated."

"Seriously Sachin?" Surya didn't seem too happy about Sachin's prank.

"You would understand if you got to see your faces. You guys looked hilarious!"

"I don't get why you'd joke about it though, you should be happy that you won!"

"I am! And I got to prank you so it was a win-win!"

"Okay guys, let's just go eat." I stepped in before the banter between Sachin and Surya could continue. After a few slices of pizza, it was time to get ready for round two.

"Okay guys, we are playing North Central High School, they placed second in the state tournament last year, so they will be a tough challenge for us." Mr. Wu was once again debriefing us with how good the other school we would be playing was. "Their only losses last year were to Johns High School, three times throughout the season, so they have a valid argument to be the second-best team here. They also only graduated their seventh and eight boards, so the core of their team is still intact. I don't expect us to win, but that's not an excuse to not try and get blown out against them." We took our seats at the table and began to set up the board.

"Hello!" This tall, freckled, white kid with dusty brown hair was staring at me.

"Hi, are you my opponent?"

"Yeah, I'm the board five for North Central. The name is Dave."

"Same."

"I'm a freshman."

"Same."

"I was homeschooled for a long time."

"Same."

"I have two sisters."

"Same."

"Are you listening to me?"

"Yep. I just happen to be the same for everything you just described."
I then shot him a grin. I think I would be making fast friends with this kid.

"So your name is actually Dave?"

"Well it's actually Devadas, but basically everyone I know calls me Dev."

"Oh ok. So how long have you been playing chess?"

"I actually started this school year."

"Seriously? I've been playing chess since I was 11. What's your rating then? I'm around 1700." He seemed genuinely shocked, which I guess was a normal reaction.

"I haven't played any tournaments, but I would probably approximate myself as 1500."

"That's amazing dude. How have you already improved so much?" Before I could answer, however, the tournament directors had motioned us to be silent and the games were off. My opponent opened with e4, which I had become accustomed too, as most people seemed to be preferring it at my level. As usual, I responded with my Caro Kann, and he went into the advanced variation of it, something I was happy about. I played my moves fast, but my opponent seemed a bit uncomfortable in the line, as he generally paused for one or two minutes for every move. Which was confusing, since we were following a Shirov-Karpov game from Las Palmas 1994. By the time he deviated on move 16, I had used almost no time, while he had burned 30 of his 55 minutes. The game developed slowly, as I took my time, gaining space on the queenside, while my opponent seemed to be without a plan. He would spend a lot of time on every move, and I couldn't really see any real reason for any of his moves. Eventually, I was able to break through on the queenside, which coincided with my opponent being low on time, and after a few mistakes by him, I ended up winning material, and the game.

After I recorded my result, I looked at what other games had finished. Summer had won, Raj had drawn, but Surya and Rachel had lost, but all the other games were still in progress. I quickly added up the scores, realizing we were up 25.5-16.5. We were in good shape to win though, we only needed 9 points out of the remaining 26 that could be taken. I then began to watch Nicholas, noticing that there was a small crowd around his game. Both players had around seven minutes, and nearly all the pieces on the board, which made it extremely complicated. Out of the corner of my eye, I saw Max tip his king over, a sign of resignation. 25.5-23.5, this match was still extremely close, with both the 3rd and 4th boards still playing. Most of the other matches in the room had also finished, so many players from other schools had also crowded around trying to see what was happening. I took a glance at Wei's position and saw he was up a pawn in a rook endgame. It would be hard to win, as rook endgames are notoriously known to be drawn, but he also had a small edge and could play it out for as long as he wanted to. A few minutes passed, and now both Nicholas and his opponent were under two minutes, and making their moves fast now. If you took one glance away from the board, you could miss a series of moves. It looked like Nicholas had an advantage though, his pieces were slowly crowding around his opponent's king, forcing his opponent to be defensive. Soon the attack became unstoppable, and after a flurry of moves made with them having five seconds on their clock, Nicholas emerged victorious. 35.5-23.5 ... wait that means we won! Everyone crowded around Nicholas, patting him on the back, whispering good job, etc. Wei's game was still going on, so we still had to be relatively quiet. Wei managed to actually win his game though, so we had a final score of 44.5-23.5 against the second best team in the state!

"Good job, you played well." Dave had come up to me while we were walking outside of the tournament hall.

"Thanks. Did you know the opening? We were following Shirov-Karpov from 1994 for a large portion of the game, in case you want to check it out later." Dave and I continued to talk about our game, talking about what we considered important moments and suggesting improvements we could have made. Eventually I needed to get back to the rest of the team though.

"Ok, good luck in the rest of your tournament! Also here's my number, in case you want to talk later." I took his number and went back to Surya and Summer, who were waiting at our table in the skittles room. Sachin was already in round three for the JV section. We talked about each other's games for a bit, with Summer basically telling us what she thought we could have done better, from what she had seen. Round three we had been paired down, surprisingly, and won 68-0 against a team that wasn't much better than our round one opponent. That left only one match, against Johns High School, who had also won their first three games of the tournament.

"So you guys managed to beat North Central? That's impressive, I guess, but still will only be enough for 2nd." Ethan Lee had walked over to our area of the skittles room, and was talking to Raj again.

"Shouldn't you be over with your teammates?" Raj was clearly trying to get the kid to leave.

"They can be a bit boring at times, and I don't get much time to hang out with people I spent years with, which is why I am here now." That and he probably likes to brag about how great his team is, while act condescendingly about ours, but no way he would say that out loud.

"Well, I think Mr. Wu wants to talk to us, and would rather not have kids from other schools around."

"Oh okay, see you in about 15 minutes then." As he walked away, I turned to Raj and asked,

"Why does he always have to come over here?"

"He just likes to keep his ego inflated, it's best if you ignore him." A few minutes later it was time to go to the tournament hall, to play our match against Johns. I reached my board to see that it was already set up. Actually, all the boards were set up, as the Johns kids were already at the table waiting for us. I sat down at my board and said hello to my opponent, only to get no response. He was just staring at me. Huh, I guess he's trying to intimidate me or something, whatever. Soon it was time for the game to begin. My opponent opened with the queen's pawn two squares, d4. I started to think since I hadn't expected this. I really needed to win, after all, this was the best opposition I could get, so I might as well go all out for a win, right? I thought of all the great attackers in chess, Kasparov, Tal, and so many others and realized that many of them got attacking chances with the King's Indian Defense. I decided might as well go with it, and started making moves on the board. My opponent was blitzing all his moves out, while I was spending a couple of seconds trying to think of games I had seen in this line. Eventually, I got surprised though, as my opponent played a move I wasn't expecting. I decided to continue with a typical plan, of pawn storming on the king-side, but after a couple of moves I couldn't really make any progress. Meanwhile, he was crashing through on the queenside, and I had a problem - in the fact that I couldn't avoid losing a pawn. The rest of the game went quickly as he put the finishing touches and finished me off. That opening experiment didn't go well. I wasn't the only one who had already lost. Max and Rachel had lost as well, so we were down 21-0. The other matches were only about halfway through, with everyone having around 20 minutes left. I decided to go watch Summer, after all, it wasn't often you got to see an International Master play in person. I looked down at Summer's notation to see what opening it was, only to see that it was actually a repeat of the game I had seen her look at this morning, between her and Ramesh from January. He had deviated though, probably an improvement over his previous play, and they were now in a roughly equal middlegame. Nothing much seemed to be happening, so I decided to go check out some of the other matches, and come back later when we were closer to finishing.

I decided to check out Dave's game, as well as the rest of his team. After all, it would help our tiebreaks if North Central finished 3-1. They were playing Washington High School, who had placed in the top five at state last year, so I had expected the match to be close. By the time I got there though, North Central was already up 29-0. Dave's game was still in progress though, so I decided to see how he was doing. It didn't take long to realize he was completely winning though, he was up a rook and his opponent was just playing out of inertia. I checked out some of the other matches going on, before returning to our match. When I got back, Wei had won and Nicholas had drawn, so we were only down 26-14. I started watching Summer's game, which had drawn a bit of a crowd. The first thing I noticed was that Ramesh only had 30 seconds on his clock, while Summer still had 18 minutes. I looked at the position on the board and saw Summer was now up a piece, but it had probably been as a result of a sacrifice by Ramesh, as she was now under attack with her king wide open. She was calm though, as Ramesh was frantically making his moves, checking her king, while she nonchalantly moved it to the other side of the board, away from the attack. Once her king was safe, Ramesh resigned, since he was down too much material and had no time on his clock. 26-26! We had clawed our way back into the match now. Not even 15 seconds after Ramesh had resigned, Ethan had offered Nicholas a draw. This confused me because he looked much better, my evaluation being validated by Nicholas immediately taking the draw. 31.5-31.5, and it was all down to Surya. The crowd had shifted towards the eighth board, where Surya was playing his opponent. Surya had 3 minutes to his opponents 7. Just like against North Central, a large crowd of kids from other schools had also gathered around, as well as kids from the JV section, to see the final game of the match. I looked at Surya's position, and I was immediately confused. Surya had 2 bishops and a knight extra, but his opponent had a queen. I had never seen anything like that before. I knew mathematically that meant they were equal on material, but didn't know how you would evaluate who was better. I don't think Surya or his opponent did either as Surya looked worried and confused, while his opponent was deep in thought. After a five minute think his opponent made a move and offered a draw. Surya took it immediately. 34-34! We had just drawn to the best team in the state!

"Why would you take a draw?!?!" Ethan walked over to his board eight.

"I didn't know what was happening! The position was too complicated and I thought I would blunder." The board eight responded.

"You could have won a piece! Instead of playing ..." I didn't hear the rest as Mr. Wu was calling our team over.

"Good job kids. I don't think I've ever been more proud of a group of kids before, but we also have to realize that this was not the state tournament, so this doesn't mean anything yet. They were also missing their bottom two boards, who had some other commitments this day, preventing them from playing, meaning the board eight results could have been different. We also need to work on improving our bottom boards. Against both North Central and Johns, we lost on three of our bottom four boards, which is not a recipe for success in important matches at state. We can't be relying always on the top boards to score well. Anyway, now we know what we have to work on before the state tournament, as well as what kind of expectations we can have. I expect you guys to be working even harder over the next three months so that we can do even better at state." That made sense, despite going 3-0-1 and tying for first at this tournament, we clearly had weaknesses on the lower boards, myself included. I definitely need to find a response to d4. Maybe I should even switch to playing that, seeing how hard it is to play against based on my experience. The rest of the day went by quickly, as the awards ceremony, and the bus ride home just went like a blur while I was deep in thought about how I could improve.

CHAPTER 19

AWKWARDNESS

I t was now the dreaded Monday and Tuesday before Thanksgiving Break. The days in which it felt like every single teacher in the school was giving us a test, making everyone extremely stressed. Well mostly everyone. I was just mildly annoyed about the number of tests I had on Tuesday, but I didn't really need to study to do well. The perks of being way ahead of everyone, I guess. As usual, we were in the library after school, with me helping Summer, Surya, and Sachin get ready for our Biology test on Cell Division.

"Hey, I thought I would find you four here." It was Ms. Auguste, but she wasn't alone. Behind her was a girl with brown hair, a little bit over five feet tall, with brown eyes.

"Hey, Ms. Auguste!" Summer said cheerfully.

"Kids, this is Emily. She's in my 3rd-hour biology class, and came to me for some help. I figured that since you four are here every day after school, that it would be better for her to study for my class with you guys, if that's fine by you."

"Yeah it's no problem." Sachin replied quickly, which was surprising because he was the most vehement in not associating with any of the other kids in our grade because of how they all believe George's rumors.

"Okay then, I'll see you guys in class tomorrow." She then walked away, with an awkward silence following her.

"So, Emily, what do you need help on?" I decided to cut the silence short, and start doing the job that Ms. Auguste had assigned us.

"Uh yeah, I made a list of stuff I wanted to, uh, ask Ms. Auguste, I guess I could, uh, show it to you?" I'm not sure if I was reading her correctly but she looked... nervous? Scared? Both? Well, I guess she was probably a bit uncomfortable. I decided to smile, I've heard that helps make people more comfortable.

"Yeah, that would help." After a few more minutes, the tension seemed to leave, as she stopped stuttering when she was asking questions. After about an hour of this, she seemed to be distracted by something.

"So why does George Wang hate you guys?" Figures. "I mean he's been saying since the beginning of the year that you guys are egotistical and not even smart - and that you've bribed the school to fake your grades." The last part was directed to me, obviously. "The last hour has made it clear that you guys actually know your stuff though, so then I have to ask, why does he hate you guys?"

"To be honest, I'm not 100 percent sure why..." I started.

"Oh come on. Dev here basically decided to knock him down a few pegs after the first biology test, in front of the whole class." Sachin interjected.

"That and we kind of didn't let him sit at our lab table on the first day of school, which probably insulted him in some way." Summer added.

"Doesn't help that Dev tried beating him up at school, and he lost a fight to Sachin outside of school." Surya added.

"Oh wow. I mean I'd heard most of these stories, but hearing your side makes him sound kind of petty. At the same time, it's believable because that's exactly the type of kid he is. That's what he did in middle school as well." Emily said what was her longest string of words without stuttering since she first came here.

"You went to middle school with him?" I asked.

"Yeah." The conversation went on for a bit. Eventually, it was time to go. "Anyway, I shouldn't have been so antagonistic of you guys like the rest of the freshmen are. I mean, I knew what kind of kid he is, yet still believed whatever he said about you guys."

"It's fine. At least you're okay with us now." I said.

"So is it fine if I come back tomorrow after school?" For some reason, she turned red when asking this. I guess it was kind of embarrassing, since only a few hours ago she believed all the negative stuff said about us. I tried putting myself in her situation, trying to talk to people who

I originally didn't have a high opinion of. Like if I suddenly wanted to become friends with George, or something like that.

"Ignore Dev, no matter how much we've tried, he still just spaces out sometimes. Yeah, you are welcome to stay after school with us whenever you can. Normally we would be at chess on Tuesdays and Thursdays, but since tomorrow is the last day before the break, we don't have practice." Summer decided to reply since I was lost in thought.

"Sorry about that, I'm really trying to work on it." She laughed at that. Was that a joke? People are weird.

"Okay, I'll see you then." She then left, leaving the four of us at the table.

"That was... strange?" Surya started.

"How so?" I asked.

"Well, she seemed pretty easy to convince about George. Would it be this easy for everyone if only we tried talking with people?"

"Well most people are extremely nimble-minded, so theoretically yes, but the problem would be more along the lines of; would they let us talk to them." Sachin said.

"Well yeah. I still don't see how that's strange though." I mean isn't that normal for people? Once they realize the truth they just go with it?

"I guess it was more... unexpected?" Summer was strangely quiet though.

"What's on your mind?" I asked her.

"Nothing!" She answered a bit too quickly, making it clear that there was something. She also turned red though, which confused me even more. What could be so embarrassing that she wouldn't want to talk about? Sachin then suddenly had a mischievous glint in his eye.

"You know, we have another issue that has come up with the introduction of Emily into our study group." I didn't like the tone he had. Or the fact that he was grinning at me specifically. At least I wasn't the only confused one though. Summer and Surya also glanced at him curiously.

"And what is the issue exactly?" I decided to see what Sachin was thinking about.

"Really? None of you noticed?" We all shook our heads, clueless to what he was talking about. "Our new acquaintance has a major crush on Dev. How did you guys not notice this?"

"Because we were here to study for the Bio test tomorrow, not make speculations about a girl we just met." Summer stated briskly. She seemed a bit defensive as well, but I was probably hearing things.

"This is just speculation by Sachin. Nothing important to think about, and definitely not an issue. " I decided to try to end this topic.

"Okay fine, just watch her tomorrow. Look how nervous she is around Dev, and how she only acts like he exists and the rest of us are in the background. Or the fact that she laughs at random things Dev says." Sachin seemed kind of annoyed.

"All of those could be explained by the fact that she was nervous being around us because she believed stuff George said, and then wanted to make sure she was in our good graces." I'm not sure why I was even arguing with Sachin. It's not like I cared whether or not if it's true. I had better things to do than wonder how I affected other people.

"Fine." We packed our stuff and went to the busses. When I got home, I did my normal pre-test routine of skimming through the textbook just to make sure I would have it for reference in case I had a blank during the test.

"Dev? Are you here?" The voice surprised me. Why was Amma asking for me? I wasn't aware we were on speaking terms.

"What do you want." I hated how curt I was around them nowadays, but after what they had said about my friends, unless they apologized I wasn't going to change that.

"I wanted to talk to you... you know about the whole suspension argument." Was she finally ready to apologize?

"What do you have to say?"

"Well, Appa and I were thinking..."

"Just get to the point."

"Maybe we should just send you to MIT starting from next semester. You clearly have shown that you can handle yourself around other people, so there really is no point in you going to high school for another three semesters." Classic. I can see what she wants. She wants to remove me from the 'bad influences' that are my friends at this school by sending me across the country to MIT.

"No."

"What?! You've always wanted to go to MIT? You were devastated when we decided to send you here instead."

"Well for one, this is just another ploy by you to try and separate me from the one good thing that resulted from your actions. And two, the only reason I wanted to go to MIT is that you ingrained it into my head nearly since the day I was born. Who knows what I actually would have wanted to do if you guys hadn't been so controlling of me!"

"Dev! You shouldn't be talking to me like that!" Surprise! Amma was angry.

"I'm sure if I actually respected you, I wouldn't talk to you like that." Well, that came out a bit harsh, I guess. It still doesn't mean I didn't believe it. Her eyes went wide, and she quickly left the room. A part of me felt bad for hurting her, I mean she and Appa only wanted what they thought best for me, if Rakshini could be trusted. The problem is they just don't understand what I need right now, and until then they deserve any hurt I may give them, accident or not.

The Biology test the next day wasn't so bad. I know I got a perfect score, it was a lot easier than I had expected it to be. We were in the library going over what we had gotten, and any questions that might have troubled them, when Emily arrived.

"Oh my god, thanks for all the help you gave me yesterday! I actually was able to answer most of the questions on the test confidently, and it was definitely because of the review we had yesterday." Hmm, maybe Sachin was onto something. She definitely did seem to be forgetting the other three kids at the table.

"It was no problem."

"So it's no problem if I continue coming here for help when I need it then right? I know you said it was fine yesterday but in case you changed your mind…?"

"Nope, no mind-changing has happened. I'm always open to helping anyone in distress." Huh. That doesn't really sound like me, does it? Must be some book I read recently or something.

"Thanks again! Is it okay if we go ahead in the next chapter today then?"

"Uhh yeah sure." I glanced at the rest of my friends, only to be greeted with a knowing look from Sachin. He was almost radiating smugness. Summer was confusing though, she looked... disappointed? I'd have to ask her later. Surya just looked like he was about to laugh. I still don't see how me being slightly uncomfortable makes him laugh.

"Also is it okay if I get your number? In case I ever need help on homework at home or something."

"Yeah sure." The next two hours were extremely awkward. Sure she's a nice girl and everything, but once I saw the stuff Sachin had mentioned yesterday I couldn't un-see it, and it just made me feel weird. I almost would rather have to tutor George Wang for two hours, I could deal with his insults, but outright admiration and borderline fawning just was different. It's not like I asked to be smart, I'd rather be admired over the kind of person I am, and not because I happen to be extremely intelligent- if that makes any sense. At the same time though, it's not like I hated it. It was kind of nice. This was confusing, I'd have to ask Google later how to react in a situation like this. The awkwardness was annoying me, and I would need to end it.

CHAPTER 20

THANKSGIVING

Do you know what the worst part about Thanksgiving break is? I don't get to see my friends in person. I have to resort to text. Especially since I don't think my parents would let me go to one of their houses or something. And don't get me started on Emily. If you thought the questioning I got during the sleepover about Summer was bad? This was 100 times worse. Especially as Summer was joining in on the teasing. Google wasn't much help either. Apparently people in my situation don't go asking the internet for help. Then again usually people in that situation are probably popular enough to have a group of friends to ask for help. Meanwhile, my group of friends was more interested in making fun of me. In good nature of course. I definitely would be teasing if I were in their shoes. It didn't help that Emily was texting me multiple times a day, to my horror. It always started out related to Bio, but she would eventually move the conversation. It was subtle, I didn't even notice the first couple of times. Eventually I caught on though, but at the same time, I didn't really mind it. I guess a part of me was just desperate for friends that it would go at any length to have one.

"Have you punched anyone new?" Lakshmi just barged into my room without knocking. Figures she would have no respect for personal privacy.

"Since I punched George? No. And no, I'm not planning on punching anyone soon."

"Do you have any new stories about George? He's funny." She then begins to mimic him. "29/30?! How could I ever do so horribly!!" I laugh. Her impression was hilarious. Especially how she contorted her face. I definitely shouldn't have told her that story though, can't have her deciding to make fun of any kid she doesn't like, after all.

"Lakshmi, that's not nice." I tried to say it with a straight face, but I couldn't.

"If it wasn't nice why are you laughing? And he's not nice so he deserves it." Some part of me wanted to agree with her, but at the same time, I needed to be a good example for her.

"It doesn't matter. Just because someone's mean, doesn't mean you treat them any differently than a kid you like." Lakshmi pouted. I heard a knock at my room, followed by Rakshini walking in.

"So what are you two up too? Nothing good, I imagine basing on the laughter I could hear from downstairs."

"Lakshmi was just mimicking George. I told her it's not nice, you don't need to do it."

"Ah, the infamous George Wang. It seems that he's all Lakshmi will talk about nowadays. I wonder why."

"Hey! She asked for stories, so I told her, I didn't think it would make such an impression on her!"

"Anyway, I came here because Amma and Appa want you guys down for lunch." Sigh. I really hate mealtimes. Well, to be fair it was mostly a silent affair, but the silence was killing. I really hated it.

"Okay, I'm coming." I started to get up to leave my room when I heard my phone buzz.

"I wonder who is texting you, little brother?" Before I could reach for my phone, it was in Rakshini's hands. "Emily? I wasn't aware Summer had changed her name?" Kill me now. She had an evil glint in her eyes, not so different than Sachin whenever he wanted to tease someone. This was a bit more sinister though.

"That's not Summer." I could feel my face heating up. Why was it heating up? I shouldn't be embarrassed because I was kind of friends with someone new right?

"Oh really? Because I wasn't aware you had made a new friend that you hung out with."

"I've never hung out with her before."

"Then why is she asking you if you're free tomorrow to hang out?" Uhhhh. This was embarrassing.

"No idea, really! I don't know why. I only know this girl because Ms. Auguste asked me to help her out in Bio!"

"Sounding a bit defensive, Deva?" I could hear the teasing in her voice. I was more focused on something else though.

"Why are you calling me Deva? You know I only go by Dev right?"

"Because it annoys you... and distracts you."

"Distracts me?" Then I realized. She no longer had my phone. I turned to Lakshmi, who was grinning.

"Have fun at the mall tomorrow at 3:00 PM!"

"I'm sure you two will get a lot of Biology studying done."

"Why are you two so evil?"

"It's simple. We are three days into the break and you haven't left your room except for meals. And the timing was perfect for me to meet my little brother's new friend."

"Yeah, but I barely know this girl, and now I have to hang out with her?"

"Get to know her. See you at lunch." Rakshini left the room, with Lakshmi running after her. Why has my life turned into a horror show now? I have no idea what I am going to do. I picked up my phone from the seat Lakshmi was sitting in. Sigh, more texts.

Emily: "How long can you stay for?" How do I respond to this? Is it too late to cancel?

Dev: "Hold on, I need to eat lunch, I'll talk later."

Emily: "No problem!" Now what do I do? Well, I'm going to lunch... only because I just found something I dread more than meals with my family now. As I walked down the stairs, I heard voices from the dining table.

"He's what?" I could hear Amma's eyes bulge.

"Going to the mall tomorrow for a couple hours. I'll drive him there, as well as chaperone if you guys care." Rakshini replied.

"Okay, he can do whatever he wants." Amma didn't seem too thrilled. I took a seat at the table, not making eye contact with anyone. To my shock, no one actually said anything. Then again, it wasn't really a shock, that's how every meal has been recently. I quickly ate my food, and then went back to my room and fell face-first onto my bed. High school is horrible. Wait no, I take that back. The drama resulting from high school is horrible. What was I going to do now? Thanks to my sister, I would have to spend a few hours at a mall with a girl I barely knew tomorrow. Not to mention that said girl may have an ulterior motive to setting this all up. I did what I knew best, and texted my friends.

Dev: "I hate Rakshini"

Sachin: "What did your sister do now?"

Summer: "I'm sure it wasn't that bad, you're probably overreacting"

Dev: "She set up me and Emily to hang out at the mall for a few hours tomorrow"

Summer: "Nevermind. That's bad."

Sachin: "What do you mean bad?"

Surya: "Yeah, it's a disaster!"

Sachin: "No, I'm serious, this is a golden opportunity to get back at your parents!"

Dev: "I am so confused"

Summer: "Should Dev really be antagonizing his parents further?"

Sachin: "Think about it."

Surya: "*thinking*"

Sachin: "Look, your parents don't like Summer because she's distracting you, or whatever right?"

Dev: "I guess yeah?"

Sachin: "You can take the blame off Summer, and put it on Emily!"

Summer: "No no no no no no no"

Surya: "Sachin are you insane?"

Dev: "I'm still lost"

Summer: "He wants you to either pretend to be going out with her, or actually go out with her, to annoy your parents."

Dev: "NO WAY I AM NOT DOING THAT!"

Sachin: "Hey! Maybe they'll get so mad they'll stop you from contacting her!"

Dev: "I don't need them more mad than they are."

Sachin: "Think about it"

Dev: "I can't believe I thought you would be able to help" I was really mad. How dare he try to suggest I do something like that!? 'Would it really be so bad though?' a small part of me asked. I pushed that away. I can't let myself be distracted from my work, even if I am only pretending.

I hate how sometimes time feels to fly faster than it should be. Before I knew it, it was already 2:30 PM on the next day, and Rakshini was pestering me to get ready to leave.

"I don't want to do this."

"Too late. Now get in the car. Your friend will be waiting, you're picking her up in five minutes remember?" The drive was awful. I was wishing I was anywhere but in the car. Well most of me was. There was an annoying small part of me that was actually excited. Probably because I had been kept away from my school friends the entire break.

"Hey, Dev! Is that your sister?" We were now picking her up.

"Yeah, that's my sister, Rakshini."

"Nice to meet you, Emily. I haven't heard about you at all though, so you're going to have to fill me in on how you two met."

"Oh, it's nothing interesting, he was just assigned to help me through Biology by our teacher."

"See I told you." Might as well rub in any small victories I do get on this day.

"Okay fine, I just wanted to double-check my brother's story. So anyway, tell me about yourself, we still have about 20 minutes till we get there." Emily and Rakshini kept talking for the rest of the car ride, while I was entranced by the road outside my window.

"Dev, we are here!" I must have zoned out as I hadn't realized we had reached.

"Okay, I'll pick you two up at this entrance at 6:00. Have fun!" Ugh. I guess it was time to get this over with.

"See you later Rakshini!" Emily waved back at the car. As she drove away, she turned to me. "Do you not get along with your sister?"

"Normally I do, I'm just kind of annoyed at her right now."

"Oh ok. That's normal for siblings I guess. I wouldn't know though, I'm an only child." We started walking into the mall, and I couldn't help but notice that she was standing a bit too close to me.

"So what do people usually do at a mall?"

"What?! Have you never been here before?"

"No actually. I was homeschooled and didn't have any friends that were interested in this kind of stuff." Probably best not to mention that I had no friends.

"You've been missing out then!" She grabbed my hand and started dragging me to different places around the mall. Who knew there were so many different food vendors? Or stores that sold jeans. Or an arcade. I didn't even know people still went to arcades now! Despite my reluctance, I have to admit I actually had fun. I'm not sure why, she was a bit much at times, and way too hyper, almost like a 14 year old Lakshmi, but for some reason she was still fun to be around.

"This was fun." I said while we walked towards the exit.

"So you wouldn't mind doing this again?" Uh oh, I could see what would be the result if I wasn't careful in my answer.

"Yeah, but it would have to be a while. Maybe during Winter Break or Spring Break. Normal school year won't really work." Maybe this will make her less interested, if I don't seem available.

"That's fine! I had fun too." She shot me a large smile. I wasn't sure how to read that smile. Or if I should be worried about it. I was saved by Rakshini though, who had honked her horn to catch our attention. As we got into the car, she gave us a knowing look, not that I was sure what she knew.

"Did you two had fun?"

"Yeah." We both said at the same time.

"Okay, so that means I'll probably have to be your driver for future dates?" I blushed, and could see Emily turn red as well.

"This wasn't a date, Rakshini. Dev and I are just friends."

"Oh, I see. Well if that ever changes, you know who to contact." I absolutely hate my sister. It's like all she wants to do is embarrass me! I think Emily was pretty embarrassed too though, since she didn't say anything the rest of the car ride.

While I had wished my Thanksgiving Break was a bit more exciting, I guess I shouldn't have really expected much. I mean, we don't celebrate Thanksgiving, and with my parents and I not on speaking terms, I really shouldn't have hoped for much. Maybe that's why I enjoyed my afternoon with Emily, I was so desperate for something interesting that I had even enjoyed three hours in the mall! A place where people go shopping! Yeah, that's why I enjoyed it. It still doesn't explain why I can't get the large grin she shot me at the exit out of my head though.

CHAPTER 21

FINALS

If I thought that the stress people had before Thanksgiving was a lot, I was wrong. Finals hysteria is a lot worse. While November felt like it went by super slowly, December was going by at a rapid pace, and it felt that all we did in any class was talk about finals. I wasn't too concerned about finals, other than the *Northanger Abbey* essay, which I had finished over Thanksgiving, but for some reason I still wasn't too confident in it despite revising it nearly every day. What was worrying though, was George Wang's relative quietness. I was hoping it was just that he was focusing on getting ready for finals, and not that he was planning something new against us in any way. Well, I guess there was that one time after school when he noticed Emily at our table and made a face. By George Wang standards that's nothing, and I was getting concerned about that. We were now in the second week of December, with finals next week, and we were now in Biology. The first surprise was when I walked into Biology and noticed that it wasn't Ms. Auguste at the teacher's desk, and instead some old lady, who I'm guessing was a substitute teacher. I walked over to the lab table, where Summer, as usual, was already there.

"Is Ms. Auguste not here today?" I asked her.

"Looks like it. So we probably will just be doing a quiet review or something." Surya and Sachin now joined us.

"Free day!!" Was the first thing out of Sachin's mouth when he sat down.

"I'm sure Ms. Auguste had something planned for us to do today, so probably not a free day." He and Surya continued arguing about whether or not we would actually be doing anything that day for a few more minutes, until the bell rang, signalling the start of class.

"Okay, settle down!" The sub's efforts hadn't worked as kids from across the classroom continued to talk. "QUIET!" That worked. It was also a sign that this sub clearly did not have a lot of patience. "Okay, as you can see I am clearly not Ms. Auguste, but we will make do. Looks like we have a review game, based on your lab groups." She then turned on the projector, which allowed us to see a giant Jeopardy board. "As you can see, this will be a biology themed Jeopardy. All six units you have had are a different theme, and unlike normal jeopardy, there are seven questions per unit, each question worth a different value from $100 to $700. The lab group that wins this game gets five points of extra credit, which I am assuming is to make you all try." This, as expected, got everyone's attention. Apparently George Wang didn't like this idea though.

"This game isn't fair! Dev claims to have an eidetic memory, so he would know the answers to all the questions instantly!" Wait hold on. When did I ever claim that in front of him?

"I'm not sure when I claimed that in front of you George."

"Well it's all over the internet in a bunch of random articles about you." Right, he had done research on me when he bagan his campaign discredit me. "That and you have perfect recall of every page in the Biology textbook, which you've shown off multiple times."

"Ok whatever."

"So how about we change the rules a bit, Dev against the entire class!" Figures George would try something like this.

"Well... I guess if Dev would be fine with this, it wouldn't hurt. And in the case if he loses, the top four scores each get five points."

"Wait... If I agree to do this, then it wouldn't be fair if I only got five points, right?" Might as well try and get something out of this. If I didn't agree, George would make it seem like I didn't want to expose myself or something, so I kind of have to do this. "Since the offer was 20 points split among four kids, I think I should deserve at least 15. Also I'd like you to make sure that Ms. Auguste knows this was not my idea."

"I think that's fair. I'll tell Ms. Auguste, and she can determine how much you get. I guess it's time to start then. She passed a whiteboard out to everyone, and made everyone go to the right side of the room, while I stayed on the left. I guess it was time to show off exactly what I could do.

I got to pick the question first, as I was the one against the odds. That's an interesting dilemma, should I start with the smaller values, and then go onto the harder questions, or just start straight away with the hard questions for maximum value. I decided that if I wanted to win, I should be taking the large values out of the way.

"Cell Division for $700." To my surprise I was actually taking every question. I had expected that I would have a good chance to win even against every other kid, but halfway through the board I was the only person to have answered a question. I had mathematically already won as I had answered all the 700s, all the 600s, and 500s. I decided that there was no point in going on. "Organisms for $400". As she read the question, I sat back down at the lab table, signalling that I was finished.

"What? Do you finally not know an answer?" Figures that George would try to say something.

"No, I know the answer, but as I've mathematically already won the game, there's no point in me even finishing the game. Might as well let you guys actually review instead of just watching me get every question right." Before George could reply, the substitute stepped in.

"He's right, it defeats the whole purpose of the game if he just answers every question. I'll tell Ms. Auguste to give the three kids with the highest scores from now, will also get extra credit. George's face was extremely contorted. I'm not sure why exactly he wanted me to answer everything, but clearly he has some sort of ulterior motive for this. As the game progressed, I tuned out, not really caring what would happen with the rest of the kids.

"Not so confident, are you?" George snarked after the bell rang. I had no idea what he was talking about, so I just kept walking. "Were you really so scared that someone would get a question right, that you dropped out of the competition?" No point in responding to this, this is just classic George Wang taunting. He probably doesn't even believe the words coming out of his mouth, but he just wants a reaction.

"You're talking a lot for someone that didn't answer a single question." Summer stepped in between George and I, clearly trying to make sure I wouldn't repeat my earlier act of violence against George.

"Typical Devadas. Needing a girl to protect him when he's too scared to do anything." I resisted the urge to respond to that. Not because I saw it as some sort of insult to me, but because it was extremely derogatory towards Summer, making her seem weaker, or something, just because she's a girl. I turned to see Summer with her face red in anger. I clearly needed to do something if I wanted this to not end badly. I grabbed her hand and started to pull her away from George.

"Come on, don't let this kid distract you from the fact that the chess team winter break party is happening right now." Summer sent one more glare at the smirking George before following me to the chess team room.

"That kid really has no life." Summer sighed, as we walked towards the room.

"Just ignore him."

"Like you did in November?"

"Hey! I've learned from my mistakes."

"I guess there's been some improvement, but seriously what do we need to do to get that kid to stop bothering us."

"Eventually he will do something stupid and people will stop following him around. Until then, we should just barely acknowledge his presence and make fun of him when it's just us."

"Or we could follow in the footsteps of a kid I knew back in November..."

"Hey!" We both started laughing here, which is how Surya and Sachin found us as we entered the chess team room.

"What happened with you two?" Surya asked.

"George Wang." We said at the same time.

"Should have guessed that it would have been the king of idiots himself, Jorge Wang." Sachin responded. Raj then walked over to us.

"Are you guys excited for today?"

"Well seeing as I am predicting two hours of bughouse, yeah I guess I am excited."

"Well your prediction is correct." And with that a bughouse ladder was formed, and as expected Summer and I (but mainly Summer) were able to defeat everyone we played, and ended the day as the unofficial winners of the bughouse tournament. Thoughts of George Wang had been subsided, the joy of bughouse overtaking that in my mind.

Sachin: "Did you guys see this?" It was around 8 PM, I had just finished dinner, and was treated to that message on my phone.

Dev: "What?"

Sachin: "George's latest post"

Summer: "Seeing as neither Dev nor I have social media, the answer should be obvious"

Sachin: "Right"

Dev: "So what exactly did he do?"

Sachin: "Well basically he made a lengthy post about Bio today, except skewed it in a way to make you look bad. You know, saying that it was all a set up, and you were given the answers before hand, which is how you answered all the questions, and even claimed that you dropping out was a sign that you couldn't remember enough answers, which is why you had to stop"

Surya: "Did you really expect anything else? This is the same kid that tried to get Dev expelled for his supposedly violent tendencies"

Dev: "Ignore it, it's complete poppycock and anyone with a brain would know that"

Sachin: "Seriously? Poppycock? Who even uses that word anymore?"

Summer: "Why don't you ask Auguste for help? She did tell you to go to her if you wanted to put a stop to this"

Surya: "^^^"

Dev: "It would be a sign of weakness. We can handle this by ourselves"

Sachin: "Yeah, and it would still leave us have a horrible reputation. And it would kind of back George's whole propaganda thing about how the teachers are in Dev's pocket"

Dev: "Exactly. And anyway, eventually George will go too far in what he says, which would end this whole thing since people would stop listening to him"

Summer: "I guess... I don't like it though... " I put my phone down and collapsed onto my bed. I thought back to my thoughts from the first day of school. Nothing had really changed since then - I was still shocked at the amount of drama it was causing in my life, but with four months under my belt, I think it is safe to say that I have been able to manage any stress from the drama… outside of when I punched George, of course. I was pulled out of my contemplation by my phone buzzing again.

Emily: "Did you see what George did?!"

Dev: "Yeah, Sachin told me"

Emily: "It's awful! What are you going to do?"

Dev: "Ignore it. Eventually people will realize that George is just filled with nonsense… like you did."

Emily: "You would think that I wouldn't have been the only one to realize it by now though?"

Dev: "No, you were the only one that was willing to be our friend, even if it needed some pushing from Ms. Auguste"

Emily: "I don't get how you're so calm about this. I would be devastated if my name was put under a smear campaign, like George is doing to you"

Dev: "Except I could care less about what High Schoolers say about me. The people who really matter already know everything that matters. You should take that advice too, what people think of you in high school should be the least of your problems"

Emily: "I guess… anyway I gtg now, cya tomorrow."

Dev: "Wait, what do gtg and cya mean?"

Emily: "How do you not know those abbreviations? Got to go and see you!"

Dev: "Okay… I get gtg, but how does see you become cya?"

Emily: "You're a genius right? Figure it out :p"

Dev: ";p ??"

Emily: "Bye!" High Schoolers are weird. Why does everything need to be shortened over text? And what is the point of emojis? I get like ' :)' and ':(', but stuff like ':p' ? Confusing stuff.

"Mr. Bakerman? Are we ever going to switch seats in this class?" It was Liam. The kid to my right.

"No, I wasn't planning on it… but if anyone wants to switch, I guess I'll let some change happen. I remember how it used to be when I was a kid, and I hated being in the same spot for an entire year." I couldn't tell if he was actually that clueless, or if he was just going with it. It was pretty clear why Liam had asked that question, and I'm sure every other kid in our class knew why as well. There was a mad rush as kids got up from their seats and scrambled to find new desks. What happened next shocked me though.

"Is anyone sitting here?" It was Harry, a kid I hadn't really talked to - or noticed at all actually - this year. He was in my Biology class as well, but he always seemed like a silent supporter of George to me.

"Uh no. You can take that seat if you want."

"George is a jerk." He said as he sat down. "I know, I'm way too late in saying that, but at this point someone's got to, right? I was there, I know you didn't want to do the Jeopardy thing, and was coerced into it by George. I don't get why no one else is calling him out on it though. Oh, I'm rambling aren't I. Sorry, I'll stay quiet if you want."

"What? No, it was fine." Summer spoke up. "I'm just used to waiting out long unending speeches from Dev. And Dev was probably just frozen after the first four words you said."

"It's okay if you don't want anything to do with me though, I get that the way I just went along with everything before now wasn't right."

"No, it's fine really. I was just shocked that someone was actually standing up to George. I'm Dev by the way, but you probably know that." I shot him a grin, something I had learned from Summer, to let him know that he was on friendly terms with me now - or something like that.

"Okay, cool beans." By this time the commotion had settled down. Everyone had found a seat and it was back to normal class time. Nothing much happened for the rest of the period, as we were just reviewing random vocab that we had learned over the course of the year.

Over the next week, George Wang had been relatively quiet, but I was certain I could feel his smirk whenever I wasn't looking at him. It was now the day before the Biology final, and Ms. Auguste was passing out the "Working in a group" grades for each lab table.

"75%??? Ms. Auguste, I'm sure you must have made a mistake."

"I assure you, I do not make mistakes in grading."

"But… this is 15% of our class grade! There's no way I got so low on this!"

"Well, I'm sure if you want to talk about your grades, you can come up to me privately later. I don't think anyone else in this classroom wants to hear details about your grade in this class."

"I protest this! My lab group finished every lab on time and perfectly! We clearly worked together well, as well as showed an ability to follow instructions properly."

"Now, I won't go into details, but the grade is clearly based on how you were able to work as a group to finish every lab. And generally if one person does all the work, that isn't really group work, is it? Especially when that one person actively prevents others in his group from doing anything. *Which you would know if you had turned over to my comments on why you got the grade you earned.*" Ms. Auguste had a pointed tone in her last sentence, showing that she was getting a bit angry at George.

"Let me guess. You're going to give Dev and his group a perfect score, to maintain Dev's spotless GPA. I'm not even sure why I bother with this school, when clearly all the people in charge are in his parent's pockets."

"Get out."

"What?" Ms. Auguste reached into her pockets and took out a pink slip. She scribbled something onto it, and gave it to George.

"Go to your administrator, now. We will be having a talk with her after this period ends." George turned pale at the sight of that. "Also, I am a teacher first, and professionalism is my number one priority. I assure you that every grade you receive is what you have *earned*. Not what I decide to give you." George walked out of the classroom, and for the first time, I couldn't see any confidence in him. He looked defeated. I'm not sure what compelled me to do what I did next though.

"Ms. Auguste, I'm going to the restroom." I said as I followed George out of the classroom. I'm sure she knew that was not what I was doing, but she didn't comment on it. I caught up to George, who hadn't noticed me behind him. "Wait! Hold up!"

"Come to gloat about how you're not in trouble?"

"No actually. I wanted to apologize."

"What?!"

"If I offended you. On the first day of school. I didn't mean to reject you or anything, but I already knew who my lab table was going to be since I had met them in previous periods. And I guess I'm sorry for punching you. And for any other thing I might have done to offend you. I never wished for you to ever actually get in trouble or anything, and if somehow you find me to blame for this, then I apologize for that as well." I turned around and headed back to the classroom before he could respond, the last thing I saw was him staring at me, with his jaw dropped.

The rest of finals week went by without any issue, as I breezed through my finals, fully confident that I had aced them all. I guess all the studying Sachin, Surya, Summer, and even Emily had done with me as well had paid off, as they all did well on their finals. Emily had even managed to get an A- in Bio, which had seemed impossible only a month earlier. It was now time to take a well earned two-week break and forget about school completely.

CHAPTER 22

REALIZATION

My family doesn't celebrate Christmas, so Winter Break is mainly just two weeks of staying at home and not going to school. Of course, that meant for me that I was spending most of my time in my room working on my research. Well, that and having to deal with Lakshmi whenever she was bored - which was often.

"So what happened with that George kid?" Lakshmi was jumping on my bed while she asked that question. Do all ten-year-olds have that kind of energy?

"Nothing much, actually. I did apologize to him though."

"WHAT?! Why would you do that?"

"Not sure... It was in the spur of the moment."

"Do you need to get your brain checked? For damage? Because that's the only explanation I've got for that."

"I think it was smart by Dev to do it." Rakshini called out from the door of my room. I'm not sure how long she had been standing there, but she had clearly heard enough of the conversation.

"Do you have brain damage as well?! How was it smart?"

"He took the high road, and showed that he's the better person."

"No! Now he looks like a loser that is scared of Georgie!."

"Except now George has no standing for any hate speech because any perceived insult that he could have used to justify it is now no longer on the table." They went on like this for a while, as I just sat there and looked at them, content to let them argue about a topic that had nothing to do with them.

"WHY DID YOU DO IT?!" Lakshmi had turned her attention back to me.

"It felt right, so I did it."

"So you didn't think it through at all?" Rakshini chimed in.

"No, it was entirely impulsive."

"You're weird. Next thing I know, you'll be telling me that you are friends with George Wang." Lakshmi jumped off my bed and ran out of my room, probably to go watch *My Little Pony*.

"That was a good thing you did. A lot of people would have used that moment to retaliate against him, maybe call him names or something, but you showed that you're a better person than that." Rakshini then walked out as well, leaving me even more confused than I was a couple of minutes earlier when she and Lakshmi were arguing. I needed answers, and I knew where I would get them.

Dev: "I have a question"

Summer:" What?"

Dev: "You know how I apologized to George, right?"

Summer: "What about it?"

Dev: "What's your opinion about it? Did I make a mistake?"

Summer: "Nonono it was definitely the right thing!"

Dev: "Why do you think that?"

Summer: "It showed what kind of person you are. And in case anyone really needed any convincing, it showed that you would never be the kind of person to bribe teachers to give you perfect grades or whatever George has said about you."

Dev: "Hmm." I then heard Amma call me downstairs for dinner. Which was strange, since it had always been one of my sisters who had done it the last few weeks. "Anyway gtg, ttyl!"

Summer: "Hold on, since when did you start using abbreviations?"

Dev: "I was introduced to them by Emily, then did some research into commonly used ones."

Summer: "Only you would actually google how to speak over text, smh."

Dev: "I'm taking that as a compliment. I actually gtg now tho, dinner time" As I walked downstairs I had some more confidence in what I had done. If Summer had thought it was a good idea, then it must have been. Any worries about why Amma was suddenly speaking to me again had been thrown out of my mind. Until I was nearly done with dinner, that is.

"So what were your grades?" Amma asked me.

"What?" I am confused. I had assumed they had already seen them.

"Are we so irrelevant to you now that you won't even bring your grades up with us anymore?"

"Uhh, I got an A+ in every class except gym class, which was an A-?"

"We know."

"What's your problem, then?"

"That you didn't see it fit to tell us." Now I'm just lost. What is her problem? I kept my grades at her expectations, and she was the one that didn't want to talk to me, right?

"Well, I figured you guys would have already seen them."

"Anyway, now that we all know that Dev is setting expectations that I'll never be able to follow, who wants to know what happened in the most recent episode of *My Little Pony* that I watched!" Figures that Lakshmi would be trying to change the subject. Surprisingly, Amma did just drop the whole grade thing, and I was able to finish eating in silence. As I headed back to my room, I began to wonder if my relationship with my parents would ever be the same. I definitely needed to fix it, it wouldn't be right if it was like this forever, but at the same time, I wasn't sure if they would ever be the ones to initiate any kind of repair. As I plopped onto my bed, I pulled out my phone again, noticing that I had a couple of messages.

Emily: "Did you really apologize to George?"

Sachin: "You have got to see what George just posted!"

Unknown number: "Hey this is Harry, is this Dev?" I opened the group chat first, as I figured that would give me answers.

Dev: "What did he do."

Sachin: "He retracted any statements he might have said about you bribing teachers. However, he is still claiming that you're an extremely arrogant know-it-all and for his newest take? A master manipulator." Well, that was interesting.

Dev: "That's an improvement right? Just ignore anything he says."

Surya: "This is the perfect opportunity to say something though, with people actually doubting George."

Summer: "No we don't. If Dev says something, he comes off as too eager to correct his reputation, or something like that"

Dev: "And here I thought that Winter Break would be an opportunity to forget about High School drama."

Sachin: "Wait! I didn't even get to the part where his family is hosting a huge New Year's party on the 31st, and from the looks of it, nearly half the school will be there."

Dev: "Ignore it."

Sachin: "U sure?"

Dev: "Ya" I then turned to the other unread messages I had. I opened Emily's first, I would save Harry for last, after all, he is an unknown.

Dev: "Ya, I did"

Emily: "That's so kind of you! You didn't need to tho ;)"

Dev: "idk it felt right"

Dev: "kinda felt bad for him"

Emily: "just shows how nice of a person u r"

Emily: "def not the monster he tries to make you look like"

Dev: "Haha"

Emily: "anyway, u going anywhere for the break?"

Dev: "Nah, staying at home, working on research, dealing with Lakshmi's obsession with My Little Pony"

Emily: "oof. Wanna hang out sometime? Maybe watch a movie or something?"

Dev: "idk lemme see how far I get into my research... assuming parents give it the ok"

Emily: "ok, lemme know if you can. The last time we hung out was fun!"

Dev: "ok gtg bye"

Emily: "bye!" That was strange. Well, it was time to see what the Harry kid wanted.

Dev: "Yeah this is Dev."

Harry: "did you really apologize to George?" Here we go again!

Dev: "ya... just felt right idk"

Harry: "so you didn't have any real reason to apologize?"

Dev: "I kinda felt bad for him so…"

Harry: "wow… after everything he did? also, r u going to his new years party?"

Dev: "Nah, I'm pretty sure I wasn't invited."

Harry: "but if u were invited…?"

Dev: "Nah, I'd like to stay at home, avoid high school drama for a few weeks"

Harry: "gotcha. k cya in school then." How did he even get my number? I suddenly realized that I had no idea how he could have gotten my number. Whatever, I'm not complaining. As I lay down in bed I pondered how much my life had changed over the last few months, mainly due to high school. Just a few months ago I lived, breathed, and died for my research, yet now, while my research was still my most important priority, I had a lot more things going on in my life than just that. And I had people to talk to now outside of my family, which was really something I hadn't really expected, even when I was told I had to go to high school to learn social skills, or whatever. Once again, however, I was interrupted from my thinking rather abruptly.

"DEVADAS COME DOWN RIGHT NOW!" Sigh. What did I manage to do now? I also got a text from Summer.

Summer: "Hey, my parents invited your family over for New Year's Eve… thought you should know before your parents do, so you aren't shocked when they ask you about it." Well, that explains the yelling.

Dev: "A bit late on the notice… haha thanks for the heads up anyway"

Summer: "np ;)" Well at least I have some idea what Amma was so worked up about now. I ran down the stairs, not wanting to get in trouble for taking my own sweet time downstairs, you never know what can tick off an angry parent when they're in this kind of mood.

"What is the meaning of this?!" Amma's phone was now pressed into my face, apparently expecting me to be able to see what was on the screen with it right next to my eyes. I took the phone from her hand and read what was on the screen, a text message from a Henry Williams asking if we were free on New Year's Eve. How do I respond to this? Do I tell them I didn't know about this? That would have been true if I hadn't checked my texts before coming downstairs. And what exactly do I tell them to do? The more and more I think about it, the more confused I am about how to actually respond... and what they're expecting as a response... I need to say something right?

"Well, I think it means that they're inviting us over for a New Year Celebration... probably for, like, dinner and to watch the ball drop or something?"

"And why would we agree to this?" I could feel the aggression on each word Amma spoke.

"Maybe it wouldn't be a horrible idea... we could get to know the parents of a good friend of Dev's..." Appa spoke up. I was shocked. I hadn't expected him to actually be open to this. Then I thought back to the original argument and realized he had never actually said anything negative about Summer- his main problem was with how I was acting. Whatever, he still didn't say anything to prevent Amma from bashing her.

"You actually want to meet the parents of the girl that is corrupting our child?"

"If anything, it's the Emily girl that is distracting him more than Summer."

"He didn't know the Emily girl when he punched that poor kid in the face."

"Still... Rakshini said she liked Summer remember...? She can't be that bad. And it's rude to decline an invitation like that."

"I don't like this, we are only making Dev think his choices are correct." Do they even realize I'm in the room? Like, I can hear every word they're saying?

"Summer's dad is a chess grandmaster as well, I could probably learn something from him just by talking about chess with him." I have no idea why I decided to speak up. None at all. Am I becoming too impulsive? I think I am. I'll have to ask Summer about that.

"This chess is almost as bad as video games for you... you're focusing so much on it now. I'll let it slide for now, but one drop in your research progress or your grades, and we definitely will be talking about how much time you're spending on that game." Well... I guess Appa isn't totally happy with me, just not mad at Summer? I just nodded my head as a response and then continued to watch my parents decide whether or not we would be going.

"Okay fine, we'll go. But only so I can see exactly how bad of an influence she is on Dev." Well... looked like Amma finally agreed to let us go? I went back to my room to tell Summer that we would be going, even though I was sure my parents had already told her parents that as well. However, as I plopped down onto my bed, I only had one thought on my mind... "finally I have some time to think to myself undisturbed!"

I thought about all the changes in my life over the past semester of high school, and the many influences on my life that didn't exist half a year ago. Mr. Turner, and how we had developed a nice business relationship, and had brought out a fun side to doing research. Ms. Auguste, and her hidden favoritism towards my friends and me. Mr. Bakerman, and his complete obliviousness to the social world of the students he teaches. Mr. Wu, and his tough love that just forced you to put your best efforts every time. Raj and the other chess team people, who had become somewhat of a second family in their acceptance of me. Emily, and how she always confuses me yet somehow allowed me to just relax. Surya and Sachin, who had allowed me to actually develop a personality and enjoy things that weren't related to my research. Rakshini, who was my biggest supporter through all the drama and horrors I had gone through. Lakshmi, who always amazes me with her positivity and her never-ending source of energy. Summer, who if I hadn't accidentally sat down next to on the first day of English, I would have not even survived one period of high school. Without her, I wouldn't have been able to navigate any of the complex social structures of the world... or maybe it's just high school. That's when I realized, right before I fell asleep, that without Summer I never would have been able to develop socially- that she was the glue that held my entire social understanding together. Realizing that I couldn't imagine how I would survive high school without her constant companionship, giving me the strength to continue through all the nonsense that goes on in high school.

CHAPTER 23

WEIRDNESS

The next few days passed by quickly, as the anticipation of going to Summer's house on New Years. Before I knew it, we were all getting into the car and driving over, but instead of excitement, which I was expecting to feel, I was instead filled with dread. I thought of two reasons as to why I was being filled with dread. The first, and probably the main reason being I wasn't sure how Amma would be acting. She's made it clear she is not a fan of Summer right now, and I'm worried she will take it out on her family and embarrass us all. However, I was also confused about how to act around Summer now, after my epiphany a few days back about exactly how important she was to my life at this moment. Was I supposed to treat her differently now that she was on an elevated status above a normal friend? Or do I just continue acting as if nothing has changed at all? And worst of all, what if she doesn't view me in the same light? Imagine the horror if she just viewed me like a normal friend and I continued thinking this way. It's settled then. I treat her normally since there's a good chance that I'm probably just a normal friend to her. Things like this are complicated. It sometimes makes me wonder why people even believe in the social construct of friendship. Like, imagine one person thought of another person as a friend, only to learn that the other person actually hates him! You would think scenarios like that would scare people away from making friends… it nearly worked with me. I pushed those thoughts aside, New Year's Eve was a time for celebration, not depressing thoughts like that.

"Welcome! I'm Henry, and you must be Mr. and Mrs. Shanmugan." Summer's dad greeted us as he opened the door. "You obviously know my daughter Summer, this is my wife, Jenna, and my four sons, Orion, August, Blaze, and Glen."

"Nice to meet you too. This is my son Devadas, as you probably know, and my two daughters Lakshmi and Rakshini." Appa stepped in and shook Henry's hand. We all went to the living room, where we sat down and watched as the adults all talked about random stuff.

"So how did you convince your parents to come?" Summer whispered as she dropped down next to me on the couch.

"Well actually, my dad was the one that thought we should come here," I replied. Summer's eyes widened at that, as she couldn't help but let out a gasp of shock.

"I thought you said they both thought I was some sort of distraction to you?"

"Yeah, apparently it's just my mom. My dad is actually more concerned about Emily, if you can believe that." Her green eyes shined mischievously.

"Speaking of that... what exactly is going on between you two?"

"What do you mean? Nothing is going on."

"Why are you turning red then? Are we sure her feelings aren't reciprocated?" Sigh. I really didn't want to go into this right now. I honestly don't see what is so funny about my predicament, that my friends are always teasing me about it.

"I don't know... maybe because I'm embarrassed that my friends keep on teasing me about this?" That came out harsh. "Sorry, I didn't mean for that to come out so harsh."

"It's fine, I kind of deserved it."

"Okay. So what are we going to do?"

"Well, dinner will be ready in an hour. Until then I guess we are just going to have to bide time on this couch and make sure our parents get along." I glanced over to our parents. Appa and Henry seemed to be getting along just fine, laughing at a joke. Amma and Jenna, however, didn't seem interested in engaging in conversation.

"Well, I don't think we need to worry about our dads..."

"Clearly." Rakshini then walked over and squeezed in between us on the couch.

"So what are you guys talking about?"

"Nothing!" We both said at the same time. Rakshini raised her eyebrows.

"You sure? It looked like an interesting conversation from where I was."

"Well I was just going to introduce Dev to my brothers, you can join us if you want." Was she? We hadn't talked about that. Not that I minded, this was my first time seeing her family. Summer then got up, and I followed her to the kitchen where her brothers were apparently cooking. "Hey guys, this is my friend Dev, and his older sister Rakshini! Dev, these are my brothers Orion, August, Blaze, and Glen." She pointed to each one as she said their names.

"Hi, I'm Dev."

"Yeah, we know... you're about 95 percent of what Summer talks about nowadays..." The one named Blaze commented, with a smirk on his face.

"Hey! I don't only talk about him all the time." Her face turned red though, so it made it kind of hard to believe.

"Yah that's why he said 95 percent, the other five being normal conversation." Glen joined in.

"You do realize that we didn't even know you had two other friends named Sachin and Surya until October?" Blaze continued.

"If it makes you feel better, Dev basically only talks about you as well!" Rakshini joined in, causing the four brothers to laugh.

"Come on Dev, let's go somewhere else." Summer then walked out, and I followed her.

"Leave your room door open!" Orion yelled as we left the kitchen. As we started up the stairs, Summer turned to me.

"Sorry, for some reason they think it's hilarious that I'm friends with you."

"I could tell. My sister was the same when she first met you."

"I honestly don't understand how they are still immature. Orion and August are already in their 20s, you'd think they'd at least act like adults."

"On an unrelated note, how is it to have four older brothers?"

"Annoying at times... for some reason, everything has to be a competition with them, but at least I can destroy them all at chess, to make up for my extreme unathleticism. Most of the time it's fine though, despite them trying to act super protective of me 24/7."

"Hmm. I guess Rakshini is pretty protective of me, so it must be an older sibling thing. Not that I do anything like that for Lakshmi."

"I think you're a special case… you know, with that brain of yours causing problems for everyone."

"I definitely do not cause problems for anyone, the problems come to me!" We were now in her room. The first thing I noticed about it was the fact that there were three chessboards sprawled across the floor of her room. "How do you even walk in here?! It feel like nearly every inch of the room is covered with a chessboard or a chess piece!"

"It's not that bad… I'm sure you also have stuff just laying down on the floor of your room too."

"Actually no, I can't stand messy rooms… I'll make an exception for you, though."

"It's not that messy!"

"Well let's see… there's no room to walk, your bed isn't made, your desk is just filled with random papers… and is that another chessboard? Either way, it's not organized, and don't get me started on the dumpster fire that is your closet." I was laughing by the time I finished, and so was Summer.

"Okay yeah, maybe I do need to clean it up a bit." She then proceeded to take all her chess boards and pieces and throw them in the closet. "See, now there's room to walk!"

"Your closet is even messier now." I said deadpanned. She closed her closet door.

"And now you can't see it, so doesn't affect you."

"I still can't unsee it."

"Whatever… so what do you want to do?"

"I don't know… anything works." I walked around the room, before noticing something on her desk. "Where did you get this picture?" It was a picture of Summer and I playing bughouse after one of the rounds of the Saturday Chess Tournament.

"Oh, uhh, I think either Sachin or Surya took it."

"It's a nice picture." I didn't really know how to react to this. Maybe I'm just overthinking this but as far as I'm aware, she doesn't exactly have any pictures of Sachin or Surya. I could tell that she wasn't exactly comfortable with this either since she was suddenly fascinated with the floor. I decided to change the topic, since this was clearly uncomfortable for us both. "Oh yeah, I meant to ask you this. Do you think I've become too impulsive?" Smooth change of topic if I may say so myself.

"No, I think you've always been impulsive, you just haven't had situations where it has shown until this year."

"You didn't know me before this year, so how would you know that?"

"Well, I was there as you were transitioning into high school, and I kind of noticed stuff." This intrigued me. Was it possible she had analyzed more about my personality than I knew about myself?

"Like what?"

"Well for one, you were very quick to jump to conclusions about things. Like when you thought I was 'betraying' you for Rakshini on our first day. Or how you concluded that I would think that you are a loser if you told me it was your idea to wear a suit. Things like that showed that you are very impulsive in your thought process, and now you're getting a chance to actually do things and your impulsiveness is now showing in your actions as well." Hmm. She had a point. I've always been a quick thinker, which I had always considered a strength, but I guess now I'm seeing one possible negative side of that, which is impulsivity. I was now having what I guess could be coined an existential crisis. What was the point of the uniqueness of every human if it was possible to be read openly like a book. What was the point of even having my own personality, if there were people out there who knew me better than I knew myself? "Dev? Are you okay?" I could hear her calling out, but it felt distant, as if she was calling from miles away. I turned to see where she was, only to feel everything shaking, as if I was spinning. Then I was actually shaking. Well, that was because Summer was shaking me. "Dev, what's wrong? Calm down." I slowed down my breathing, and slowly things came back into focus. I noticed that I was now kneeling on the floor, and I'm not entirely sure when that had happened.

"Thanks, I'm not sure what came over me."

"No problem, that's what I'm here for."

"Honestly, I don't know what I'd do without you sometimes." Oh god, why did I say that out loud? That was really stupid, wasn't it? Summer had turned red again, something that was becoming commonplace today. Before anything else could be said though, Lakshmi barged into the room.

"DINNER IS READY!" For once I was actually happy that Lakshmi was interrupting something, since the situation was extremely awkward before she came in. "What were you doing on the floor?" She must have noticed us both kneeling on the ground.

"I thought I lost an earring on the floor, so we were looking for it." Summer replied quickly. I have no idea how she even managed to take off the one earring without Lakshmi noticing.

"Here, let me help!" Even more surprising to me was how two minutes later, the earring appeared in Lakshmi's hand. "Found it!" I just gave Summer a questioning look, to which she responded by mouthing 'You're welcome'. As we walked downstairs I decided to engage in some conversation.

"So what have you been doing Lakshmi?"

"I was watching a movie because everyone was ignoring me." Well, that sounded depressing. "It was okay though, I had fun!" Or not. She clearly was fine by herself. As we sat down at the dinner table, I noticed that our moms were still not getting along. On the other side, our dads looked like they had been friends for life at this point. I noticed that Rakshini was getting along fairly well with Summer's brothers as well. Dinner started off quietly, as even though everyone was engrossed in conversation, I was drifting away to my own world. Summer seemed distracted as well, not really looking like she was paying attention to her surroundings either. Until Glen decided to do something about it.

"What happened between you two?" I could feel the entire table stare at Summer and I. And boy was it uncomfortable. Like everyone's judging eyes were on me all at once, and it felt like they were peering open my soul. I could feel myself shrink in my seat.

"What do you mean?" Summer replied.

"You two have been off in a different universe ever since you reached this table. Dev has been too focused on his food, while you haven't even touched your food yet."

"Nothing happened." Summer replied. "I guess we just have a lot on our minds." Why was it that she always seemed to speak up whenever I was incapable of doing anything? As everyone returned to whatever they were doing before, I turned to Summer, once again looking at her questioningly. Then I felt it. Instead of the normal warmth I usually felt whenever I was around her, I felt nothing. As if she was a stranger. And it was weird. She smiled at me but it didn't reach her eyes. That's when I knew I had messed things up. I returned to my food, finishing it quickly. The rest of the night passed quickly. I spent the hours before the ball drop talking with Summer's brothers, getting to know them a bit more. I even helped them clean up the dishes- something I had never done before, even at home. I actively ignored Summer as well, not wanting to embarrass myself again. As the ball drop approached, Henry turned on the T.V. and we all crowded around it. I could feel Summer walk up behind me, as if she wanted to say something, but I ignored it. As the countdown happened, it felt like every number that was counted down only increased the tension between us. As the rest of our families celebrated the New Year, we remained silent, as if the next words to come out of mouths would be life-changing. I didn't say goodbye, but as we left her house I turned back and gave a small wave. I had never understood how a person could have a "sad smile" until I saw her facial expression after I waved. She was smiling, but it was melancholy. The weird feeling from before hadn't left. I fell asleep confused, and could only describe the party, and my interactions with Summer as weird.

CHAPTER 24

SURPRISES

The rest of winter break went by pretty quickly, with nothing really standing out. I'm pretty sure I acted catatonic as well, not really moving out of my room, and not registering anything that was happening around me. That was the main reason why break passed by quickly. Eventually, it was time to go to school... something I was not ready for. Two weeks may not sound like a lot, yet as I entered school for the first day of the new semester, it felt like it had been a decade since I had last passed through these halls. I took my seat between Summer and Harry in English, not knowing exactly what I was going to do. As Mr. Bakerman started to lecture us about what to expect over the next semester, I noticed Summer slip a piece of paper onto my desk.

Is everything okay? Was scrawled on the paper. I didn't know what to do. Was I supposed to respond in person or write a note with my response? That was quickly resolved by another note though. *Just write on this and pass it back.*

Uhh, I guess everything is fine.

No, it's not, something happened at my house that affected you. Was it the food? Well, I wasn't sure what to say. How was it possible that she didn't know. Unless she was just trying to get me to say it.

The food was good. I liked it. There, I can be cagey if I want to. Not that I'm sure why I don't want to say anything. Summer probably wouldn't end our friendship right? But it would definitely be weird.

Did I do something wrong? She sounded worried, but of course, maybe I am just reading too much into the note.

No, you're good.

What is it then? You didn't respond to my texts, you're barely giving me any answers now, I feel like I did something to insult you, except I can't figure out what! Hmm, this is a difficult situation. Either I hurt her feelings or I embarrass myself. Suddenly I remembered how scary Summer can be when angry. Yeah, it's definitely better to embarrass me.

Well, the problem is with me, you don't need to worry. I guess I could start with that.

Is this about what happened in my room before Lakshmi came in? Figures that she knew what I was worried about.

Yeah... I was being weird, sorry about that. Well, I guess I should brace myself for the worst.

Don't worry about it, I don't think I'd enjoy high school either if we weren't friends. Huh. That was not what I expected. I could feel a heavyweight leave me though, as if I was suddenly free from something.

So you're telling me I've been freaking out about that for nearly a week for no reason?

Yep. Some advice? If something is bothering you, maybe talk about it instead of isolating yourself from everyone.

Even if it means embarrassing myself?

If they are actually your friends, you don't need to worry about that. Well, that's something to think about. I then got nudged on my right shoulder.

"Hey, be careful, I think Mr. Bakerman might have noticed the note passing." Harry whispered. I nodded my head, as did Summer, who must have overheard. The rest of the period went by without much commotion, as I zoned out of Mr. Bakerman's descriptions of what he expects from us, and all that. As I walked out of English, I noticed Harry was running after me, as if he had something to tell me. So, I slowed down, and let him fall into place next to me.

"Did you hear what happened at George's Party over break?"

"Uhh no."

"Oh, his mom apparently used the whole thing as a promotional thing to convince people that you were having a bad effect on her son. Something about how you play psychological games with other students, while you try to demonstrate academic superiority over them.

She used the Biology Jeopardy incident as her prime example. What I find surprising about it though, is that George has been largely quiet."

"Okay. Thanks for telling me."

"No problem." As usual, the next few periods went by fast, until I was at lunch. Before Sachin or Surya had even sat down, words were out of their mouth.

"Where were you?"

"What happened?" Sachin and Surya asked at the same time. I had no idea what they were talking about, so could only respond with a blank stare.

"Why didn't you respond to any texts?" Sachin asked, clarifying the earlier questions. Which made a lot more sense as a question.

"Sorry, I was just busy with stuff." No way was I going into detail about the mess I had made.

"Okay, whatever. Anyway, did you hear what happened at the party then?"

"Yeah, the Harry kid told me after English. Anyway, how were your breaks?" As they went into detailed explanations about their breaks, I began thinking of how I would describe mine after their eventual questions about it. However, surprisingly, the questions never came. I guess my explanation of 'busy' from earlier was enough for them.

After lunch, I was surprised yet again, this time in my World History class. Since when was Emily in my class? Surya looked surprised as well.

"Why did your schedule change?" Unlike me, Surya was still able to be coherent. I was still silent from surprise.

"Oh, I decided to take regular English, since I didn't really like my original teacher, and thought the grading was too harsh. I guess it changed my schedule, leaving me in this class now."

"Oh, ok." As we took our seats, I noticed that our teacher was already at the front of the classroom, as if he didn't want to waste any time with his announcement today.

"Okay class, today marks the beginning of a new semester, as well as the beginning of our study into the Renaissance time period. This is usually the highlight of the year in this class, as we have an extremely fun project due at the end of this unit. For this project, I will be splitting you into pairs, in which you will then create an exhibit about anything you want about the Renaissance. Whether it's a painting, a building, a person, a new invention, the possibilities are endless. I will want a topic proposal by next Monday, however." I wasn't really sure how this would be fun, but at the same time, I wasn't really opposed to this. As long as I had a decent enough partner...

"Dev, you will be paired with Emily." And I'm screwed. Not that I have anything against her, but I really didn't need to deal with her fangirlish behavior during a school project. That and I'd much rather be with Surya.

"So what were you thinking we could do this project on?"

"Uhh, how about we do it on Copernicus? You know..."

"Helio-centric universe right? Sure, he sounds interesting." After our teacher gave us the go-ahead we started looking up things we could use in our mini-exhibit. After around 15 minutes, however, we were interrupted by the rubric for the project being passed out. I hadn't even had time to look at it yet when Emily asked, "So what are we going to dress up as?"

"What?!"

"Yeah, look right here! It says that if you dress up in an outfit related to your exhibit you get five points of extra credit!" Hmm. Now, I had already dressed up for Halloween this year, and it was definitely not something I wanted to do again. But it was for extra credit... not that I needed it.

"I don't know... I don't really like wearing costumes..."

"But it's extra credit!"

"Yeah... but I probably don't need it."

"Well, I probably will! And even if I don't, there's definitely no harm to doing it!" Ugh, painful decisions. Look selfish, or ruin my credibility by dressing up in some sort of costume. "Okay fine, think about it, we have a while until this is due." There we go. Now I have time to think of a solid argument that will help me not wear a costume. I looked over to Surya, who seemed to be struggling with his partner - some Asian girl named Katie - as well. Looked like they were having a quiet argument about what they would even be doing their project on. Compared to that, my situation looked amazing, which made me feel bad for Surya.

My study hall with Mr. Turner was nothing out of the ordinary as I just told him about the progress I had made over break, and he double-checked what calculations I had done. Nothing happened during gym as well, since as it was the first day of the semester we received our lockers again, and then sat on the bleachers for 40 minutes, basically what happened on the first day of school. As I walked to Biology, however, I began to think about what I should be expecting. This being the first time seeing George Wang since the apology, I really didn't know how he was going to react. As I walked into the classroom, I could sense something was different. Or maybe it was the many stares I was receiving. I sat down at the table across from Summer, who just smiled at me, causing me to smile back. Was that another way for people to greet each other? It seemed like an effortless and efficient way to greet someone, if that was the case. As Sachin and Surya took their seats at our table, I noticed that George was still not in the room. Which was strange since he generally was in the room after me, but before them. Not that I'm too sure why I'm caring so much about George right now. I started to go through my backpack, getting anything I might need for this period when I was interrupted.

"Dev?" The voice was quiet, and almost sounded… scared? I turned around to face the person in question, only to see it was George Wang. I don't think I covered my shock well.

"Yeah?"

"I just wanted to say, my group forfeits the bet. It's clear you guys are going to beat us by a mile, and there really isn't any point in waiting till the end of the year. So… yeah, nice job. I shouldn't have overreacted to you guys saying the seats were taken, since it's clear that you four had already planned to do that before you knew I existed." If I hadn't been able to contain my shock before, I definitely couldn't now. I think it's possible that my eyes had jumped out of my head. I quickly regained composure though, and replied.

"It's fine, it was a dumb bet anyway. Let's just call it off entirely."

"WHA--?!" Out of the corner of my eye, I noticed that Summer had punched Sachin in the shoulder to stop him from saying anything else.

"You sure? We would be okay if you decide to follow through with the bet."

"No, it was a rash decision by both sides, and a pretty petty reaction to a major misunderstanding. As long as you don't bother us for the rest of the school year, I don't think anything needs to be done."

"I can do that I think." For the first time, George looked up from his shoes, which had been distracting him the entire conversation, and held out his hand. I stared at it, confused by what he wanted.

"He wants you to shake his hand Dev." Summer called out. Ohh, okay. I shook his hand, and then turned back to my lab group, before realizing that the entire class had been watching the interaction. And that it was now 3 minutes into the class period, and that Ms. Auguste was smiling at us, as if we had done something amazing. "That was a really nice thing you did, Dev."

"Wait… hold up, why on earth would you let off that poor excuse for a human?" Sachin exclaimed. Before any of us could reply to that, Ms. Auguste called the attention of our class.

"Okay, now that Dev and George are done, let's get back to Biology, shall we?" As she began to give the normal explanation about what topics we will be covering, and how we should expect harsher grades on labs now that we were experienced, basically a Biology version of our lecture in English, I started writing in my notebook. I wasn't even paying attention to what it was, but by the end of the period, I realized I had an entire page describing all the new people I have met over the last semester, along with what I thought about them. Most shockingly was what I had written about George: A misguided kid, starting to realize that he isn't entitled to everything he wants. Was that true? Or was that me trying to make excuses for a kid that had tortured me for an entire semester. I decided to crumple up that page before anyone else could see. I definitely didn't need anyone to see that. After class, as I was walking out with Sachin, Surya and Summer, Ms. Auguste called me over.

"Go along, I'll meet you guys at the library," I told my friends as they were deciding whether or not to wait for me. "What did you want, Ms. Auguste?"

"I had two things I wanted to tell you. First, I wanted to congratulate you on how you handled George. You took the mature option there."

"I didn't do anything special, it was just the right thing to do."

"Yet I'm sure most kids your age would have acted similarly to how your friend Sachin wanted to." I guess she did have a point, but maybe that could be because I gained some extra maturity through homeschool? Who knows. "Anyway, the second thing I wanted to ask was if you wanted to tutor Biology for half a period during lunch? You've done a great job with Emily, and there are other kids that could probably use some extra help as well." Was today 'National Surprise Dev' day or something? I guess it couldn't hurt if I did this, though. I would still be able to spend half my period with Sachin and Surya. I didn't even think about the horrors of a physicist tutoring in Biology- the less I thought about that, the better.

"Sure, I guess I can do that."

"Okay." She pulled out a form from her desk. "I just need you to get your parents' signature here, to agree to have your lunch reduced to half a period, and I'll need it back by Friday." Well, that could be a bit problematic, but I'm sure my parents would sign this. I nodded and said bye, and went to the library to meet up with everyone else.

CHAPTER 25

EMILY

"So what did Ms. Auguste want?" Summer asked as I sat down at our table.

"Basically just wanted to know if I was free to tutor in Biology for half a lunch."

"Wait… don't tell me you accepted?" Sachin asked

"Why wouldn't I? It's a good opportunity, despite the fact that Biology isn't really a science."

"What about lunch with us?"

"He still gets to spend half the period with us, Sachin." Surya stepped in.

"Still…"

"I think Dev should do it!" Emily said.

"Agreed." Summer didn't seem to happy about it though. As if it was repulsive to her that she had to agree with Emily.

"Anyway, enough about your Biology tutoring, what possessed you to call the bet with George off?!"

"Wait, what happened? What bet?" Emily asked. Sachin then filled her in on what he believed was a massive mistake by me. "I think it was nice by Dev to call the bet off. It shows that he's a better person than George."

"But we could have gotten revenge for everything he did last semester!" Sachin was extremely animated about this.

"It would have made Dev look bad though." Summer, Surya and I were just watching this back and forth between Sachin and Emily.

"He's already hated by most kids in our grade, does it really matter if he might make himself look worse? He should have taken the chance that people might start liking him for humiliating George!"

"No, the mindless group would just hate him more for humiliating George. People are already starting to warm up to Dev, doing something like that would only make them think that he really is what George says he is!" What was really surprising to me was that we hadn't garnered any attention from the other people in the library. Somehow both Emily and Sachin had still kept their voices low, despite their heated argument.

"You wouldn't know what it was like for Dev and us, you were with George until Thanksgiving remember, and by then the worst was over! And let's be real, you only warmed up to us, and saying these things because of your major, uh, admiration for Dev, or at least your fantasy version of Dev!" Some sort of line must have been crossed here right? Like sure they were arguing but I'm pretty sure some things need to be left unsaid. I glanced over at Summer and Surya, who both had gasped at what Sachin had said.

"Uh, guys? I think you both need to calm down." I decided I needed to step in now, but I also realized it was probably already too late.

"Stay out of this Dev. I want to see how she responds."

"Well, you won't get that pleasure then. I can see when I'm not wanted." Emily stood up and stormed out of the library. Now, what was I supposed to do? Sachin had clearly overstepped in what he had said, but was it a good idea to go after Emily and make sure she's okay? Because that could upset Sachin- who is also a good friend.

"That was rude, Sachin, I'm going to go see if she's okay." Summer made the decision for me, got up, and ran after her. That was surprising to me, since from all the tells I had noticed about Summer around Emily, it was that she didn't really like her. I then decided to get up as well.

"You too?"

"She's my friend Sachin, and she's pretty upset right now, I have to check up on her."

"Was Sachin wrong though? We all know that's why she became your friend." Surya spoke up for the first time.

"That might be why she decided to become our friend, but I'm pretty sure that's not why she stuck around. And she was right about how getting 'revenge' on George is a stupid idea."

"So you're putting her friendship with her over us?" Sachin asked.

"I'm not valuing any friendship over any other, I just see one friend who is hurt right now, and needs my support."

"But you're not siding with me here?"

"Why would I? You're an important friend, but what you said was out of line."

"So would you go and console any person I might happen to insult?"

"This isn't a random person, it's another friend of mine, I'm not sure what you aren't understanding here."

"Except she isn't a real friend. She just wants to become more intimate with you, for lack of a better phrase." Surya stepped in to defend Sachin as well.

"So why didn't you question Summer when she left?"

"Because Summer hates Emily, so it just deprived me of words!" Sachin responded.

"Whatever, I'll talk to you guys later." I walked off before they could say anything else. By the time I was out of the library though, I realized I didn't even know where Summer and Emily were. It wasn't hard to find them, however, as I quickly noticed some noises off to the right, near the science hallway, so I went in that direction.

"I'm surprised you're here. Not that I'm not appreciative of it, but I always got the sense that you didn't like me." I know, I shouldn't be eavesdropping, but my curiosity got the better of me, and I decided to stand still and listen to them.

"Well I'll admit I wasn't a fan of you, but what Sachin said was out of line, so I had to check and make sure you're alright."

"He was right though. That was why I decided to try and become friends with you guys. Not now though, I actually liked spending time with you guys. I honestly thought that Dev would have come after me though, but maybe that's just me wishing too much."

"Trust me, Dev definitely would want to be here right now. Before I came out, he looked conflicted, like he wasn't sure how to act without hurting any feelings. And if I didn't know any better, he probably got up right after I left, and isn't here now because Sachin tried to stop him."

"You think so?"

"I know it. In fact, I wouldn't be surprised if he was on his way right now." I guess now was a good time to approach them. Also, how does Summer know me so well, if I didn't know any better I'd say she could read my mind.

"Hey, are you okay?" Time to act like I was not listening to the last minute of conversation.

"Yeah, I'm fine. It just hurt that Sachin was so mean."

"Yeah, he was a bit out of line. I think he's mad at me now as well, since I came here."

"I'll go and fix him. I don't know what his obsession with getting revenge on George is." She then winked at Emily, which confused me. Were they friends now? Emily turned red at that though, so I'm not sure. What does winking mean? So many complex social terms people need to know.

"What's wrong?" Emily broke the awkward silence that had been a result of my confusion.

"Shouldn't I be the one asking you that?"

"Probably... but you're the one who looks like his head is about to explode so..."

"My head is not going to explode!"

"So what's troubling you?"

"What?"

"Whenever you don't understand something, your head looks like it's going to explode." Why does everyone seem to know more about me than I do!?

"I was just trying to figure out what Summer had meant when she winked." To my surprise, Emily turned a deep shade of red. "What?"

"It meant nothing."

"I don't believe that."

"Just drop it, please?" Oh well, I guess I'll just have to ask Summer about it.

"Fine." This led to a long silence, where we both were just leaning against the lockers in the hallway. I'm not sure what she was thinking, but in my case, I was trying to figure out what a person is supposed to say in this situation. "So…"

"Yeah?"

"What are we doing?"

"Standing in a hallway and doing nothing?"

"Well… yeah, I guess." And it was back to silence. I decided to sit down, as there was no reason to be standing. Which led to Emily joining me on the floor. And continued silence. Eventually, she spoke up.

"Have you ever thought about the future?"

"What?!"

"Like where do you see yourself in 10 years? Or 20?"

"Not really."

"What?! How?"

"Well I'm kind of focused on my research, I guess. And in getting better at chess."

"Seriously? Those are the only two things you think about?"

"Well, I also think about the past. And 'what if' scenarios."

"You actually have such a boring life."

"No, I don't! I enjoy life, well I do 95 percent of the time. Sometimes it's bad like when you're making no progress on research, or if George said something that really hurt. But other than that, life is really great!"

"Oh come on, you haven't even lived life. No offense, but you basically lived under a rock until you started high school."

"And you have? What could a 14-year-old girl have done that makes her life fulfilled."

"Well for starters, I've traveled a lot."

"Hey, I've been to a lot of different universities to present research."

"Have you ever had an actual vacation? Like where you just go to a place to sightsee. Or just spend an entire day at the beach?"

"No? But how does that matter? I've accomplished a lot.

"You have a lot of academic success, I'll give you that, but you know nothing about the real world, outside of what you have read in books."

"Hey!" I hate to admit it, but what she was saying kind of rang true for me. Not that I was going to admit it.

"Oh come on, you know it's true."

"Okay, so how would you describe a 'normal' 13-year-old boy?" I used actual air quotes, to emphasize my skepticism of what she was saying.

"Well for starters, he would know how to act around people without the need of google. He probably would be extra interested in proving his masculinity through sports. He would be extra obsessed with how he looks, since he would care about his popularity. He probably would actually know some celebrities, and not be oblivious to pop culture, probably would be obsessed with girls as well…"

"Hey, I know who James Bond is! Also, I run for 90 minutes every day if that counts. And the rest of the stuff is just petty!"

"First of all, James Bond was started in like the 60s, so no that's not modern pop culture. Two, I never said 13-year-olds were mature."

"So basically I'm just an extremely mature kid for my age? Thanks for the compliment. It still doesn't mean I haven't 'lived life' or that I'm not normal."

"Well, I'm not saying that being mature is a bad thing. And come on, your entire life revolving around research and chess? That's definitely not anywhere close to living life. Hmm, oh I've got it. Let's do an experiment, since you're such a science guy. Close your eyes and just spend two minutes imagining where you'll be in 20 years."

"That's not an experiment! That's just an activity!"

"Just do it."

"Whatever, I don't get the point, but I'll entertain you."

"The point will be seen when we analyze the collected data and draw a conclusion."

"Hold on, if you're so bent on following the scientific method, you skipped the first few steps."

"Fine. Question: Is Dev actually living the most out of his life? Research: Collected through being his friend for about one and a half months. Hypothesis: No, he is not. There now we are at the experimental stage."

"Okay, this is really stupid. How are you even going to quantify the 'data' to get your results?"

"Just trust me."

"Fine." So I closed my eyes and began to imagine a 33-year-old Dev. "Well, I have a Nobel Prize in Physics for unifying the gravitational force with the other three fundamental forces, probably through string theory. I guess I would have some sort of chess title, maybe like a National Master or something. I'd be the premier physicist in the world, known by the general public, akin to Stephen Hawking today. I'd probably have to be teaching some classes at whatever university I'm conducting research at. Oh, I guess I'd still be friends with you, Summer, Sachin, and Surya. Hmm, that's probably all you'll need to know about 33-year-old Dev."

"And after collecting and analyzing the data, it has been concluded that Dev indeed has no life."

"How?!"

"Everything you said was related to physics, with chess, and as an afterthought; your friendships."

"So? It just means I have some serious expectations for myself and I'm focusing on that over anything else!"

"You have no considerations at all into your personal life!"

"So? Does that matter if I win a Nobel Prize?" I then was sharply reminded of the sleepover, where Sachin and Surya had random dreams and stuff and I didn't. Is this what Emily was trying to get at? That there's more to life than being successful?

"Would you rather be like Tesla, and die alone, married to a pigeon? Or like Bill Gates, who has a life outside of Microsoft."

"I'm shocked you even know who Tesla is."

"Unimportant."

"Okay fine, since you apparently have a life, where do you see yourself in 20 years?"

"Well, for one I'll probably be married to someone I fall in love with, maybe one child, depending on when we get married. I'll be an elementary school teacher somewhere as well. I'll probably have spent a year traveling Europe, as well as visited the other continents other than Antarctica. I'll probably be driving a kind of fancy car, but not like sports car fancy. I could go on, but I think you get the idea."

"Yeah, I get the idea that you spend way too much time fantasizing about the future."

"Hey! That was a bit mean."

"Sorry, that's just my opinion."

"You seriously have the social skills of a first grader."

"I'll give you that, I guess."

"At least you have the sense to believe that."

"I'm not hopeless you know. I do know that everyone hates Justin Bieber, whoever he is."

"If that's the extent of your cultural knowledge, I feel horrible for you."

"Whatever." We sat in silence again, not really knowing how to continue the conversation. However this time, we were interrupted by Summer, who came back to the hallway we were in.

"Have you guys just been sitting here in silence for the last hour?" Wait, has it already been one hour?

"No!" We both said at the same time.

"Yes, it's been an hour, Dev. Anyway, I talked to Sachin, knocked some sense into him, I think he's a bit embarrassed though, so you might not get an apology from him for a few days." The last part was directed to Emily, I guess. "Anyway did you two have fun?" There went another wink to Emily. What does that even mean?!"

"No, I was just being lectured about how I have no life outside of physics at all."

"Well, she's right!"

"Et Tu, Summer?"

"If quoting Shakespeare is your attempt of proving that you have pop culture knowledge, you just proved my point." Emily chimed in.

"I hate you guys."

"Yet you still are with us."

"Because I'm in a horrible situation. You guys make up 50% of my friends."

"Therefore you love us."

"Love is a strong word, let's just use tolerate."

"Come on you two, if you keep bickering, we're going to be missing the busses." Summer then walked off, with Emily and I chasing after her. I really do have strange friends.

CHAPTER 26

HYPOTHESIS

Inspired by Emily's 'experiment' I created a hypothesis of my own. The question I am trying to answer is whether or not people who grew up homeschooled end up with a different sense of normal than people who grew up in the public school system. My hypothesis is yes, and the way I was testing it was through two unknowing test subjects: Emily and Summer. I thought it was best to use those two as I didn't want to deal with any variables concerning different genders, which would have been the case if I had used Sachin or Surya instead of Emily. The tests were subtle, not enough to alert either of them that I was testing them, and usually posed as me feigning interest in some subjects, such as: who is Justin Bieber?

Over the month of January, I was also tasked with finishing the World History project with Emily, which had ended up in me begrudgingly having to dress up for the extra credit. However, the project wasn't as repulsing as I had originally thought, as it was now doubling as one of the subtle tests on the difference between a homeschool kid and a public school kid. The counter data obviously coming from my work with Summer in biology labs as well as any English activity that had to be done in partners. I think the History exhibit went well though. I was able to find some manuscripts he wrote online, and printed them out as a part of the exhibit. Emily had a model of the solar system, which worked since after all, he was the one that suggested the model. There was some awkwardness in the costumes though, as Emily had to dress up as his wife, since we couldn't think of anything else that really fit (well, we did consider dressing up as the Earth and Sun, but an entire day in those costumes was definitely not ideal). So yeah, dressing up as a married couple from the 1500s was definitely awkward, and led to a lot of teasing from our friends, but for five points of extra credit, I'd say it was worth it (well, that's what Emily said, and I kind of just made that my excuse). And seeing as we got a 55/50 on the exhibit, I'd say it was a success.

I had similar success in pertaining to partner stuff with Summer as well, but she was definitely easier to work with. While Emily would constantly badger me with questions, and try to be social during classes, Summer was usually focused on class, and not as off-topic, which was a relief. Summer fawned over me less, but I'm not blaming Emily directly for that, hormones are a stupid thing, and something most people can't control. I also decided to observe their interactions with other people in the classes that we had together. While Summer generally stayed in a closed group of friends, Emily was extremely outgoing, and seemingly would talk to anyone that wanted to. That definitely helped during our history project though, seeing as she was able to gather people to our exhibit and explain stuff, while I seemingly couldn't talk coherently in front of a group larger than three kids. Summer wasn't as bad as me, but she definitely wasn't going to initiate conversations with anyone that was not her friend.

Outside of the time spent on experimenting, I also focused a lot on chess, as with the state tournament coming up the first weekend of February, it was time for a final push for improvement. Mr. Wu was definitely motivated, as he was generally not playing the top eight during our meets, leaving us to study during the games. Henry had also come in during a couple of practices to give us lectures on what he thought were important lessons for practical chess play. Which was his code for heavy endgame training. As he explained it, what's going to separate us from any other school in the state is how well we play with only a few minutes on the clock, and generally, that would mean you're in an endgame. So of course, if our endgame intuition had been trained well, then we would be performing better than our opponents when low on time if we were in an endgame. The lectures were tough though, as he purposely chose challenging examples to make sure we were all trying hard - that and he probably only had so many positions that Summer hadn't seen.

George Wang had also kept his word, and was basically ignoring us, which was a pleasant turn of events. While it definitely reduced the drama I was having in school, it also left me open to thinking about things other than him, which was a really nice change. It had also changed the workings of the student body in our Biology class. Led by Harry, kids were slowly more open to coming to our lab table whenever they had questions. I guess they had heard about the fact that I was tutoring Biology during lunch. In fact, some of my classmates were kids that were occupying my lunchtime. While I wasn't really friends with any of these kids, it was definitely a nice improvement from the outright hatred I had been receiving for most of the school year. The change in how school was working had definitely increased the speed of my days, as suddenly instead of dreading going to school, I was actually enjoying it. Sadly the 180-degree turn in school life was not the case for my home life, as my parents were still not talking to me- or at least Amma wasn't. Appa was definitely warming up to me again, I'm not sure why though.

Before I knew it, January was almost over, and my experiment was still going on, with me wondering how I would be able to continue the tests. So far I have been able to test their pop culture knowledge (equal), ability to work with me (edge to Summer), socialness (edge to Emily), what they think about in relating to the future (no real difference), taste in music (Summer was more inclined to listen to 80s music, while Emily was more modern in her taste), and to my horror, their taste in a life partner. The last one was an unfortunate consequence of inquiring a bit too much into their dreams of the future, and definitely conversations I wished I never had. However, that had led to me wondering if I would be able to perform a similar test on two guys. Which was why I was now texting Dave, the kid I met at the Saturday chess tournament. I told him it was a survey that I had to do for a statistics class, which I'm sure he didn't buy, but he was definitely okay with answering the questions. After I was done with him, I would subtly get answers to the questions from Sachin and Surya as well. If I ever felt bad at all for using my friends as test subjects, I was able to convince myself that it wasn't that bad since the experiment was not harmful in any way. Well, not harmful for them. I, on the other hand, had been thoroughly scarred by Emily and Summer.

The last week of January, however, brought a change to the complacency that I had grown accustomed too. It started in first period English on the Wednesday of that week. We were now starting our Shakespeare unit, and to my horror, the first play we were reading was Romeo and Juliet. That in itself wasn't bad, what was bad was how I had somehow been voted into playing Romeo. You see, Mr. Bakerman thought that for our first introduction to Shakespeare, we should 'act' the play out. In reality, that just meant we sat in front of the class and read out the lines, but it was the *in front of the class* part that was horrifying for me. Like I mentioned before, I still wasn't used to speaking in front of a large group of kids I didn't know on a personal level, so as a result, I stammered way too much, and when I wasn't stammering I was mumbling. What a great way to start out the school day, am I right?

However, it was like all the bad karma I had accumulated had decided to bite me back all at once on this day. On my way to my second-period independent math class, I was intercepted by someone I wasn't aware I knew.

"Are you Devadas Shanmugan?" I was now face to face with an Asian girl about three inches taller than me, who had extremely long black hair. And she didn't look happy.

"Yeah, that's me. Did I do something wrong?"

"Yeah, I want you to tell me what you did to my brother!"

"I'm sorry, but you must be mistaking me for someone else, I don't think I know your brother, and as far as I'm aware I haven't done anything to make them upset recently."

"So you're telling me that you do not know a George Wang?" Oh. Looks like I was face to face with the infamous Allison Wang.

"Oh, sorry I didn't recognize you. However, whatever he said I did, I didn't do it. We haven't spoken to each other since the first day of the semester, you can ask anyone that knows us both, and they would tell you that as well."

"Well, you did something! He's been a shell of himself in the last month, and it can only be because you got him in trouble at the end of last semester!"

"I'm sorry, you're saying *I* got him in trouble??? Are you that delusional to think George didn't do anything wrong?!" We had attracted a crowd, probably because it was Allison Wang who I was talking to.

"Coming from the guy that punched him in the nose..."

"Mouth!"

"Whatever, you punched him in front of the whole school, so clearly you're the instigator in whatever trouble my brother may get into."

"Clearly you don't do your research. You should be asking your brother for the story before randomly intimidating a freshman you think did something."

"My brother was right about you. You have the balls to lie through your teeth and speak with so much confidence that if I didn't know any better I'd actually believe you."

"Have you talked to him in the last month? I'm sure he wouldn't have told you that."

"You don't know my brother as well as you think you do then. Because that was about the only thing I could get out of him!" I was shocked. Was George not as reformed as I thought he was? Was the mild mannerism an act to make me complacent? Was I wrong to think George had really changed?

"Leave the kid alone Allison. Your family has put this kid through more than enough trouble this year." The giant named Luke was back again.

"Who asked you to step in, Luke?"

"The fact that I know your phoniness, the fact that your brother is even worse than you, and that I know Dev is nothing like how you guys say he is."

"Whatever." She then glared at me. "This isn't over kiddo. Mark my words, anyone that messes with my brother will have to deal with me. And once I'm through with you, you'll wish you never went to this high school." I couldn't help but compare her face at that moment to a harpy from Greek Mythology. Or a female demon. Both really being the same thing anyway.

"I told you to text me if you ever needed my help, yet I find you in the middle of an argument with the most popular girl at this school?"

"To be fair I thought I had handled George by myself. I didn't know his sister was worse."

"Well, now you know. Watch out, she has a lot of influence, and I won't always be around to protect you." He walked away, and with every step I took towards math, I could feel the fear increase in me. I thought I was done with my bad luck for the day, but despite the fact that the rest of the day was relatively quiet, fate decided to throw one more twist at me during my after school meetup in the library.

"So when were you going to tell Emily and me that you've been testing us?" Summer brought up. Oh no, this could be bad. Time to plead ignorance.

"I have no idea what you are talking about."

"Oh come on Dev, Summer and I do talk you know." Emily gave a cloying smile which could only mean trouble.

"And...?"

"You think we wouldn't notice that you were asking us both the same questions?"

"Or that you suddenly warmed up to a partner project with Emily after Mr. Bakerman started giving us partner stuff to work on?"

"Uh... So do you guys have anything related to Biology you want to go over?" My last attempt to avoid this subject would be to change it entirely.

"Nope, the current conversation is a lot more interesting than Biology!" Sachin replied happily. He seemed to be reveling in the scrutiny I was under right now.

"Yeah, answer the question Dev!" Surya chimed in. Welp. I was doomed.

"It's Emily's fault!"

"Excuse me? What did I do?"

"You created your thought experiment. That's what inspired this. Therefore it's your fault."

"Oh, you are so not blaming me for this. Especially as I am a victim here."

"Victim?! The experiment is harmless! I was just seeing if raising a girl through homeschooling is different than regular schooling!"

"Seriously? Did you think to conduct your own experiment? On your friends? Especially as I can probably google that question right now and get a lot of results."

"What Emily said. And I'm not even going to bring up the fact that it hurts that you were my first friend and right now you only see me as an experimental subject." Uh, yeah this is bad. Maybe I did do something wrong.

"No! I didn't mean to hurt you at all. It was harmless! I still think of you guys as friends."

"Mhm. You better think of a nice excuse as to why this was a good idea quickly, otherwise, I'll unleash Summer on you."

"Summer has already spoken though."

"Do you really want to deal with an angry Summer?" Nope, niet, nada. I shook my head vigorously. "Then answer my questions."

"Okay, I'm sorry it was a bad idea. I was being rash and impulsive, and friends are not supposed to be test subjects." Time to go on full-on apology mode. To salvage anything.

"That was a quick change of tune, Dev."

"Definitely. Looks like someone is whipped."

"Spot on, Surya." Whipped? What does that mean?

"What does that mean?"

"Basically that the moment Emily or Summer wants something, you go out of your way to appease them." Surya decided to answer, while Sachin was laughing.

"What do you think we should do, Summer? Should we forgive the idiot?"

"What else can we do? We both know it's because Dev has the social skills of a preschooler."

"Hold on, I thought I was at a first-grade level! That's what Emily told me!"

"That was before you decided to treat Summer and me like guinea pigs."

"Well to be fair, I couldn't really do this experiment on guinea pigs." I should not have said that. Which I realized from the glares I got from the two girls. "Sorry, I didn't say that, I was being dumb."

"I hope so. So we're forgiving him?"

"Looks like it. Otherwise, the idiot will be begging us to forgive him until we do it."

"As usual, you're right, Emily." Well looks like I was safe for now.

"Is that relief I see on your face?"

"You're definitely not off the hook just yet. We're just forgiving this transgression for now. You're still on probation." Well, looks like I'm not that safe.

Experimental Results: Tests abandoned. Human experimentation is not a good idea.

CHAPTER 27

STATE

A fter that horrible day, it was time to turn my attention to the next big thing in my life. I am, of course, talking about the State High School Tournament. We had been seeded 3rd, behind Johns and North Central, even though we had beaten North Central at the Saturday Tournament. At the same time, it made sense, we only had those that tournament available for the seeding committee, since our conference was pretty bad, while the schools ahead of us had a much larger sample of games. The tournament was upstate, so it meant we would have to be staying overnight at a hotel, as well as miss a day of school. I had kept my grades above 98.5 percent, the cutoff my parents required me to meet, so I was allowed to go on the trip. We would be leaving Thursday after school, while the tournament was Friday and Saturday, and with us returning back Saturday night. I was both excited and nervous about this. While I was pretty sure I had improved since November, I still hadn't been able to test out my new black opening against d4, the Grunfeld, in a tournament game. I had also decided to play the English opening, or 1. c4, as white, since I thought it would be a good way to surprise people, the same way I had been surprised by d4 against Johns. Our state team hadn't changed since the beginning of the year, but only the top 12 (eight players and four alternates) players from our school were going. In order, this was: Summer, Raj, Nicholas, Wei, Me, Max, Surya, Rachel, Sai, Arjun, Havish, and Sachin. Yeah, Sachin had somehow managed to improve quite a bit. He probably wasn't actually the 12th strongest player on the team, but he was close enough to whoever that actually was, that Mr. Wu was picking him over anyone else for the last spot, as he is a freshman.

Before I knew it, it was February 2nd, the Thursday we would be leaving for the state tournament. The entire school day went by extremely slow, almost as if time didn't want the school day to end. Eventually though, after a century of waiting, the final bell rang and it was time to leave. Well… it would be in about 30 minutes, since the bus actually needed to get here first. So we were just in the library like we normally would be after school.

"So you guys won't be here tomorrow, right?"

"Yep, two days of only chess!" I responded.

"Why did I sign up for this again?" Sachin asked jokingly.

"Well you are an alternate, so you probably won't get to play." Surya joined in.

"So basically I get to stand around and watch you guys play chess for two days!"

"Honestly that would be better than playing. A lot less stressful."

"Stress? We're playing for fun!" I countered Surya's point.

"And possibly for a state title." Summer said.

"So?"

"That is extremely stressful!" Surya answered.

"Just do your best and then at least you know that you couldn't have done anything else."

"Chess is a cruel game though. As the old saying goes, one bad move can destroy 40 good ones." Summer pointed out.

"Yet it's still fun."

"Well obviously. I'm just saying that unlike a normal tournament, team ones are just more stressful since you have other people you have to focus on. Like for example, there may be some situations where during an individual event you'd take a draw, but the team situation could force you to go all-in for a win and take unnecessary risks."

"Whatever, I'm just excited to play new people."

"Anyway, now that you guys have thoroughly ignored me with your geeky chess talk, I think it's a good time to tell y'all good luck!" Emily piped up, clearly not liking being left out.

"You should join chess next year, it'll be fun!" I told her.

"Nah, I'm not patient enough to sit and move pieces for two hours just for a game. But you guys seem to like it, so have fun!" After that, we had to leave, and it was time for a four hour bus ride.

I hate long drives, so I pass the time by sleeping through it. Makes the drive feel a lot shorter. By the time I had woken up, we were at the Olive Garden we would be eating dinner at. After about an hour spent there, we headed towards the hotel, which was only ten minutes away.

"Are you guys excited about tomorrow?" Raj asked the four of us.

"A bit nervous, but yeah mostly excited." Summer responded.

"I just want it to be over because of how stressed I am." was Surya's answer.

"Yeah, I can't wait to play all the best schools!" I replied. Sachin was asleep, so he didn't answer.

"Yeah, basically a combination of those responses was what went through my head my first year. It'll be fine though, just relax and have fun, and this will be a memorable two days for you guys." To that, I just sent Summer and Surya a smug "I told you so" look. After I got into the room I was sharing with Sachin and Surya, I decided to go to bed again. Nothing wrong with being as well-rested as I could be before an important day.

I wish I could say the first day of the state tournament had lived up to expectations, but three rounds in we hadn't really been challenged yet, with three 68-0 wins. It was expected though, since we weren't playing top-level competition yet. My games had all finished within 20 moves, with my opponents not even knowing basic opening principles, which was kind of a letdown. I wasn't letting that dampen my mood though, since I knew we would be tested heavily the next four rounds. Sachin however, was not too happy.

"You guys don't understand the situation I'm in right now. I'm here, watching your games, except instead of tense battles, I'm seeing you guys playing idiots that are making me feel like I'm amazing! Which we all know isn't true. Can you ask the pairing people to give us someone tough? So I can at least be interested in the games for more than five minutes?"

"Well, we'll be playing the 11th seed now, which is probably going to give us a good match, right? Like a few bad mistakes could easily cost us against this school." Summer responded.

"Who are they again?" Surya asked.

"James Madison University Preparatory High School." I responded. I may or may not have memorized the entire seeding list.

"So basically you're playing a bunch of nerds who decided to take up chess?" Sachin snarked.

"You don't need to sound so derogatory about them," I said while frowning.

"Hey, I was just trying to make a joke!"

"Whatever." Soon it was time to go up to the playing hall for the last round of the day. I was black, and was expecting a good fight from my opponent. After all, he was from the 11th best high school in the state, right?

Talk about expectations not being met. While this kid definitely put up more resistance than my first three opponents, I could tell he wasn't comfortable in his position out of the opening, while I was. These Caro Kann positions are really nice when you get everything that you want. This specific position was basically an equal endgame resulting straight from the opening, except me being more comfortable with the position led to me easily outplaying my opponent. I wasn't even the first one to finish, with Summer and Raj also having dispatched of their opponents. I noticed that some of the lower boards were actually pretty even, however, so maybe this team was more balanced across the eight boards. Not that it helps them when they have to play kids like Summer and Raj.

I decided to stick around and watch the games going on, unlike the previous three rounds, where sticking around would have been boring, as the games were already completely one-sided. I decided to watch Surya, who looked like the evenest game among the bottom boards. His position was completely locked up, but Surya did have a 20-minute edge on the clock. I wasn't really sure how Surya would win though, since with everything locked up there was no real way for him to make progress. As they made moves, however, I realized what Surya's plan was. He was going to play quickly and make a bunch of one move threats, causing problems for his opponent every move, basically playing against the bad clock situation, and eventually hope for a mistake once his opponent was extremely low on time. The plan worked, as eventually, like about 20 moves later, Surya got his opponent to be under a minute on the clock, and made a bishop sacrifice for two pawns that would open up the position, but with no time on the clock, his opponent would not be able to refute the sacrifice. By this time, we had won on every other board, and I left, knowing Surya would be finishing without any troubles now.

"Okay guys, today was an exceptionally good day, but we know the competition will become exponentially harder tomorrow. We will be playing the most elite teams now, as there are only have eight schools with a perfect score. However, being the only school to sweep every match today is definitely a good indicator of the type of chess we are playing right now. Sleep well, have a good breakfast, and be prepared to put even more effort tomorrow, otherwise, everything we did today is for naught." Mr. Wu was addressing us after we had finished dinner, which was at some obscure pizza place. As we walked back to the hotel room, Sachin seemed to be extremely excited about something.

"What has you so happy?" Surya asked.

"Let's just say, while you guys need to sleep early, I do not, therefore I'll be having fun the next couple hours, playing Minecraft."

"Seriously, Minecraft?"

"Well, what else is one supposed to do at a chess tournament?"

"Play chess?"

"Nah, I'm good." I just shook my head. Sachin was definitely a bit strange at times. But that's what made him Sachin I guess.

The next day I woke up feeling the tension. You know, the feeling that just washes over you when you know you have to put in all your effort into something? Probably tension isn't the best word, but that's what I'm going with. We were up against the 7th seed, Washington High School - the school North Central had destroyed in the last round of the Saturday tournament. I decided to text Dave, asking how the match was.

Dev: "You guys played Washington High School right? How were they?"

Dave: "Well, when we played them they were missing their best two players, so it led to us destroying them. However, you guys should probably be fine against them. I can actually send you what my board three played against the person you're playing now if you want, as he played with the same color you will be playing with."

Dev: "Thanks!"

Dave: "No Problem." I looked over the game. My upcoming opponent had played the Najdorf against e4, which didn't really help me... unless I decided to play e4 for this game.

Dev: "Hey Summer, do you think you can help me prep a line? My opponent plays the Najdorf against e4, and I have a line that he played, but I want to see where he could have improved, and what I should do against an improvement?"

Summer: "Uhh sure, send a picture of the notation and I'll tell you where he could have improved." 30 minutes later, I was confident in what was going to happen in this game.

It's a nice feeling when your opponent in chess walks right into your prep, isn't it? He's struggling and burning time off his clock while trying to find a move, while you can sit back in your seat or walk around, knowing that you know how to respond to his best moves, and if he doesn't play a move that you know, that he has made a mistake. That's the situation I'm in right now. 17 moves into the sharpest line in all of chess - the poisoned pawn variation of the Najdorf- and my opponent has burned over 35 minutes, while I'm playing my moves instantly. To my slight annoyance, however, my opponent did come up with the best response. It doesn't matter though, I know how to reply to that. I make my move and get up again. I get up, knowing that it would only frustrate me more in his situation if my opponent was leaving me at the board to suffer. A few more moves, and my opponent finally made a mistake. I sat down to try and find a refutation, and the first thing I noticed was that this position was just weird. It honestly made no sense at all. There were no obvious moves to start calculating. I guess this is why computers are so good, they just brute force everything, and don't have human instincts of what moves might be unnatural, or whatever. I started to try and do that, just brute force moves, and before I knew it, I had lost 30 minutes on my clock. I needed a better way to do this.

I decided to think about what the best moves were for him, and what purpose they might have served, and then see why this move doesn't live up to those ones. That's when I spotted it. The knockout punch that had been eluding me for 30 minutes. A beautiful finish to a game. A type of move that every chess player dreams of playing at least once in their career. The queen sacrifice.

I put some oomph into the move, to let my opponent know that he was dead. I just stared at him, watching the emotions go across his face. At first it was skepticism. Then understanding. Then a frantic search for a response. And then the look of helplessness. We've all been through it. When we know there is no way out of the hole we have dug for ourselves, and now I was seeing it on my opponent. And it gave me joy. *I was the reason for this!* This is what makes chess fun, after all. I know it sounds borderline sociopathic, but the extreme joy I was getting from watching him suffer wasn't really with malicious intent. I guess only someone who has been in the situation I'm in right now would get it. I watched as my opponent dejectedly accepted the queen sacrifice, knowing the imminent doom. I blitzed out the end of the game, not able to get the smile off my face. As he held his hand out in defeat, he flashed a smile as well.

"That really was a great sacrifice. You played well." And this is it, the reason why the game attracts so many people worldwide, and why it has done so for centuries. The fact that even when you're on the wrong end of a beautiful game, you can still enjoy it. And it's why the game will never lose its popularity, and instead will continue to live on, connecting people of all ages, all cultures, of any shape and size. I smiled back at my opponent, and told him where he could have improved, as well as some games in the line that we had been following until he erred.

I then checked the score, and saw we were up 30-5, with wins by Summer, Nicholas, me, and a loss by Rachel on board 8. I looked over to Surya and saw he was not pleased with the position. In fact, he was so upset he wasn't looking at the board, and was just shaking his head. However, we were better on most of the other boards, so it looked like a victory was certain. As I walked back down to the skittles room, Mr. Wu caught up to me.

"Good game, Dev. That was a really nice finish."

"Thanks."

"Was there a reason you were playing so fast? Because the position looked extremely tactical."

"It was all theory, so yeah I knew it, which is why I played fast."

"Ah ok. I just wanted to make sure you weren't just carelessly playing fast."

"Yeah, I get it. Once I was out of my preparation, I slowed down."

"Okay, anyway it really was a nice game, keep it up." That felt good. I got some other congratulations from kids I didn't really know, but who I'm guessing had seen my game. I wasn't surprised really, chess players have some sort of sixth sense where they can just sense when a game near them is exciting, and are just drawn to watching it. I've definitely been a victim of it. Anyway, I need to calm down, if I'm not careful I could get too excited and lose focus for my next game, which would be an extremely pivotal round, as it would decide if we would play for the state title in the last round or not.

In the skittles room, I just sat quietly, calming down my breathing, knowing that I would need to be back into normal condition before the next round. It took about 20 minutes, but I finally felt like I had reached an equilibrium in my body again, and had control of my emotions. I decided to play some blitz online as a warmup though, to make sure I was actually fine. In the middle of my game, however, Dave came over.

"Dude, that was a crazy win you had."

"Yeah, it was kind of cool wasn't it. Most of it was prep though, and I only had to think for the queen sac, so I guess it was really the computer that played well."

"Nah, that's your work ethic. And you've put everyone on notice, I know for a fact that people from Johns are preparing their board five for your next round."

"Wait... we're playing Johns?"

"Yeah... #1 versus #3, #2 versus #4 now." I had known that, but somehow it had slipped my mind.

"Shoot, I'm going to get murdered. The guy destroyed me last time."

"Yeah, but you're way better now. Everyone knows that as well, you're the one kid no one wants to play on board five."

"I think you're overselling me right now."

"Do you even know who your opponent was?"

"What?"

"The guy was a World Champion for kids eight years old and under, but stopped playing until he started high school. The kid is extremely talented. He should be a higher board, honestly, but he's around 1800 strength."

"Well just because he was good as a kid, doesn't mean he is now. And I got lucky with prep. So if people are really saying those things about me, they're just overhyping me."

"I wish I could have your calmness. Anyway, good luck, hopefully, we're playing for the championship."

"Okay, good luck to you guys too." It was now time to go up for the penultimate round, and I was suddenly extremely nervous. There was no way I could live up to all the supposed hype that was apparently around me right now.

"Are you okay?" It was Wei, who must have noticed my nervousness.

"Yeah, just a bit nervous."

"Most people would be extremely confident after a win like the one you just had." He chuckled after he said that.

"Yeah, but now I don't know how I can keep up the expectations. I mean, everyone knows about the win, so everyone's going to be watching me right now. And I got killed by this guy last time."

"Don't let that affect you. You've improved so much since you last played him. Just tune everything out and focus on the 32 pieces in front of you, and you'll be fine."

"Thanks, I'll keep that in mind." I really did feel better after hearing that. That feeling didn't last long though. Ethan Lee decided to make sure of that.

"Well well well, if it isn't the man of the hour. The prodigy himself. How does it feel? Are you ready to play another brilliancy?"

"Leave him alone, Ethan." It was Raj. "Don't listen to him, Dev. He's just scared that you're going to win, and wants to rattle you before your game." That didn't really help though, Ethan's words were affecting me too much, for some reason. Summer came over to me though, and whispered,

"Just look at your opponent. He's scared right now, nothing like how he was in November. You've got this, just stay calm and stay focused."

"Thanks... I guess." She was right though. He was nothing like the emotionless and intimidating kid he was when we last played. He actually looked worried. That's when I realized that I was white again. "Wait, Summer, aren't I supposed to alternate? Why am I white again?"

"They were also white last round, and when that happens, the higher seed alternates colors." Oh, well that works in my favor. I guess that's also how he was preparing for me then, he was expecting me to play e4. Which I wasn't going too. After all, I had only switched just because I had a line prepared. I could tell my opponent wasn't ready for the English either. It was slight, but I could see him wince when I made my first move. That's when I knew I was in the zone. All the games around me, all the small sounds of clocks being pressed, and even my own breathing just were tuned out. All I could think about was the board in front of me. And it just felt like every line I was calculating was accurate. It wasn't even like my last game, where I was blitzing out prep, this game I actually felt like I was the one making the moves. And I knew they were good moves as well. I watched as my pieces slowly gained space, pushing him back, then winning a pawn... and then another. Then I couldn't even find a move for him. He was in Zugzwang, as we chess players would say.

"Good game." My opponent said as he held out his hand. And just like that, everything was back to normal. The background noise was back, and I was noticing the events around me. And I had won my game. That's when I felt it. Sheer exhaustion. I had overworked myself, and now that the game was over, my body couldn't maintain the level it had been at before this moment. I looked around, and realized the match was similar to before. Surya and Rachel had lost again, but Summer and I had won, with Wei drawing. Max and Nicholas were losing though, so even though we were up 24.5 to 15.5 right now, if those games went as expected, we would be down 24.5 to 32.5. Meaning it was all down to Raj versus Ethan. Figures that the two former neighbors, and arch-rivals would be deciding who plays for the state title the next round. The game was even, but with every passing move, their clocks ticked down. There was a pretty large crowd around us, as people from all 128 teams participating had come to watch the pivotal game. This was what Henry had trained us for. I watched as Raj steered towards trades, looking for an endgame, exactly what we had been training over the last month. And it paid off. With fewer pieces on the board, and both players playing on instinct, Raj was quicker and playing better moves. The months of training, the hard work we had put in, challenging ourselves with whatever difficult position Henry had chosen for us, it was paying off now, as Raj sealed the game off, and brought us a 35.5-32.5 victory over Johns High School, the defending champions and favorites to win it all.

It goes to say that there was no way we would have been able to play a proper match against North Central after the emotional high we were in after our match against Johns. I got murdered by Dave, dropping a piece in the first 15 moves, not able to concentrate at all. My energy had deserted me. We lost in embarrassing fashion, 56-12, with Summer being the only win, completing her 7-0 sweep of the tournament and the first-place medal for her board. I had somehow still won first place on my board, with Raj and Wei also placing in the top ten for their boards. I didn't feel bad about the loss though, North Central had deserved to win it all, and we had definitely made a mark in the ego of the Johns kids. It was now time to return to school though, something I was disappointed about, knowing that the chess season is now over, and it would be my last time spending time with all the seniors, who had supported me throughout the entire year. Next year will definitely be strange without them, and while we probably wouldn't be competing for a state title anytime soon as we rebuild the team, my experience over the last two days was still amazing, especially as you can't complain about second place.

CHAPTER 28

FEBRUARY

Something changed after state. School seemed to slow down, and getting through the day felt like trekking through quicksand: no matter how hard you try you continue to sink. It didn't help that Allison Wang's smear campaign was beginning to take effect. It wasn't on the scale as it was at the beginning of the year, as over the last month I had been able to make some sort of impression on kids, but it was definitely the mindset of the majority of kids. I'm not sure exactly what was being said about me, but it must have been pretty bad if even Rakshini wouldn't want to speak about it. I don't get why this is all happening to me. Millions of kids go through four years of high school completely fine, yet I haven't even finished a full year and I've gone through so much drama and hate, it's almost as if the universe is conspiring against me. At this point, I've just given up, and just waiting for whatever stupid thing will be thrown at me next. Strangely enough, though, George was still not back to his old self, and at times seemed conflicted on how to act. I pushed those thoughts away, he clearly was still the same kid that he had been before.

"Dev? Are you even listening to what I'm saying?" It was Ms. Auguste, in the middle of Biology.

"Of course I am." I really wasn't, but I just needed to buy a couple of seconds so I could review what my eyes had been seeing but not comprehending the last couple minutes.

"What was I talking about, then?"

"You were just telling us why people use Chi-Square, and what the formula for it is: (Observed- Expected)^2/Expected." Phew, that was close. I could tell Ms. Auguste didn't believe that I was listening, but I had answered her correctly, so she couldn't really do much.

"Okay, maybe just act like you're listening then." And she went back to teaching the lesson. I could tell Summer was concerned though, probably because this was about the fifth time this had happened in the last week between both this class and English. I just didn't have the stamina to pull through the school days now, and tended to zone out a lot. A part of this feeling was probably because I didn't even have chess practices to look forward to now, and because of that, I had been restricted in how much time I was able to work on chess at home, as a result of another argument with my parents. Apparently getting an A- on a speaking grade in English was the direct result of me spending time on chess, and not because I can't talk in front of large groups.

"Okay, what the heck is wrong with you Dev?!" Called it.

"What's wrong with Dev?" Emily asked.

"Does this have to do with the fact that he's been caught not listening three times in Bio in the last week?" Sachin asked.

"And another two times in history" Surya added.

"Wait, it's not only in History?" Emily asked.

"It's every single class from what I can tell. So you better spit out what is wrong with you now Dev." Summer had a threatening tone, except I wasn't sure what the threat was. Or how to respond to that. You know how I'm apparently impulsive, right? Apparently that trait doesn't help me when four sets of eyes are staring at me expectantly and I have no idea what to say. "You don't know, do you."

"Uhh." I think that said it all.

"So it's either a mix of things or it's one thing that you don't understand."

"You know, I think Dev's right, Summer really can read his mind." Surya remarked.

"Scary stuff." Sachin added on.

"I don't know… I guess it's just the fact that the school days feel so long now."

"Yeah, I get that. But you don't see me zoning out of class."

"That's because you're so focused on making sure Dev is on task." Surya pointed out.

"I think Dev just needs to do something fun. You know, to get him back into a good mood." Emily spoke up.

"Like what?" Sachin asked.

"I don't know… maybe take him out for a movie? There's the winter dance? Maybe we can go to the city? Ice Skating maybe? We can think of something."

"Dev at a dance?! That would be hilarious. He would probably be that kid trying to become one with the wall." Sachin laughed.

"Yeah, so that's not going to work," Surya said a bit more seriously, but his face was giving away the fact that he was trying to hold back a laugh.

"Do you guys know any good movies?" Summer asked, trying to bring the conversation back on point.

"Is Rogue One still in theaters? It was good." Surya replied.

"Does Dev even know what Star Wars is?" Sachin snarked.

"That's the one with Spock right? Live long and prosper or whatever." What I was not expecting was a gasp of horror from Surya.

"Oh, I cannot believe you just said that."

"Did he seriously just insult *Star Wars* like that?"

"How dare he confuse the greatest franchise ever for the lesser version!"

"We definitely need to make him have a Star Wars marathon."

"I cannot believe he is so uncultured."

"Okay guys, can you stay focused? We are here to help Dev, not make fun of his uncultured life." Summer seemed exasperated at the antics of Sachin and Surya, while I was trying not to laugh at them.

"To be fair they do have a point… even I know Spock is from Star Trek and I haven't watched either franchise."

"How about no movies then."

"Ice Skating it is then!" Emily seemed excited, which I've learned is usually bad news for me.

"Oh, that would be funny, watching him try to skate." Sachin seemed to be living off jokes at my expense today.

"Uh, you guys realize I can't skate right?"

"That's what makes it the perfect choice! I will have laughing material for a good 50 years if we do it."

"I could teach you as well. I've been skating since the day I could walk." Emily said.

"Okay, how am I going to have fun though? Isn't that the whole point of this?"

"I think it would be a good idea… you would learn something new as well as be able to relax." Summer said after some thought. Was I really going to be dragged into this? It honestly seemed like the perfect way to embarrass me. Time to pull out the trump card.

"There's no way my parents are going to agree to this so…"

"I can just get Rakshi to convince them."

"Ooh, both your sisters could come as well! I still haven't met Lakshmi, she sounds like a lot of fun."

"I could care less about meeting the sisters, but if it means that this plan happens, then I'm for it."

"Sigh, I have no way out of this do I?"

"Nope!" Four voices said at the same time. Well, I guess I'll be able to spend time with my friends outside of school, if I'm looking at the bright side…

"You want us to do what?!"

"It's only a few hours on a Saturday…"

"Dev's grades are already slipping… and we gave him that weekend for chess state."

"Amma, you've got to be kidding me. With all the time he spends on research I'm shocked he can even finish his homework, so freaking out about English dropping to a 98 percent really makes no sense at all. And the kid needs some fun in life, we all know he was deprived of it before this year."

"He can have fun once he's 40 and retired with millions of dollars. The more fun he has now, the less fun he will be able to have when he actually has to work."

"Seriously? Dev is going into physics, the only way he's making that kind of money before he's 40 is if he gets a Nobel, or something like that. Let the kid enjoy his life now."

"He has the rest of his life to enjoy, he justs needs to focus on school for a couple more years, and then he can do whatever he wants."

"Are you out of your bloody mind? Like actually were you hit in the head? You've been so messed up the last couple of months, and I can't tolerate this anymore. If you truly believed the stuff you were saying, why didn't you raise Lakshmi or I like that?"

"You guys don't have the potential Dev has. He's a once in a generation, and I wish we never sent him to high school. We are only wasting his talent. I never should have listened to you about that!" Hold on. It was Rakshini's idea to send me to high school? Or at least she was the one to suggest that to Amma and Appa?

"Don't try and blame this on me... You both thought it was a good idea as well! As did the MIT admissions!"

"Yeah, I didn't think Dev would become a delinquent because of this. Or become so rebellious!"

"You don't even know what he's gone through at that school. There's been so much drama that he's had to deal with. You do realize the kid gets bullied for his intelligence right? He doesn't want to talk about it because he thinks it makes him sound weak, or some dumb thing like that, but it hurts him. And if I can see that, you definitely can as his mother!"

"The fact that he doesn't think he can tell us stuff is another bad consequence of this whole high school experiment!"

"You do realize that is completely your fault right? Instead of being supportive of him when he needed it most, you decided to criticize the choices he made in friends. The best part about it is that he couldn't have lucked himself into a better group of friends if he had tried. In fact, if he had tried to go out and find friends he probably would have made the kind of friends you are scared about. Instead by some divine intervention, he was sent people who actually support him and could care less about his genius!" The whole house was silent after that. Even Lakshmi, who had been blasting whatever episode of *My Little Pony* she was watching, had turned it off to listen.

"If they were as good friends as you say they are, they wouldn't have changed my Deva so much." Amma's voice was barely over a whisper. I had to strain to be able to hear her from my spot at the top of the stairs.

"It's called growing up." Rakshini had softened her voice as well. "It was bound to happen the moment he was thrust into the real world, you're lucky it's happening when he's still living here, otherwise it would have happened when he was across the country at MIT, and he would have returned unrecognizable to you."

"You don't know that. He probably would have been more focused on his research. Maybe he would have had a major breakthrough. He definitely wouldn't have gotten addicted to that chess game."

"He would have been surrounded by adult students, you should be lucky that his only "addiction" is chess, could have been much worse." Amma looked defeated. Looking at her now, it seemed like she had aged 20 years the last couple of months. I also realized that most of my anger at her was unwarranted. She was just concerned about me- sure she had a horrible way of showing it- and I shouldn't have been fueling her actions. She just felt like she was losing me, and had lashed out at what seemed like an obvious target to her.

"I guess you're right. He can go to this skating party thing." Without thinking, I went down the stairs and gave her a hug.

"Do you want me to ask if their parents can come? So you can get to know them? It might help you get to know my friends better."

"She already knows Sachin and Surya's parents, but yeah that would be a great idea... especially as she and Jenna didn't speak at all at Summer's house."

"Okay!" I ran back upstairs to tell everyone the good news, as well as the new plans. It was then that I also realized that I felt a lot lighter. The whole estrangement with my parents must have been eating at me more than I thought it was.

I really am a horrible skater, even after four hours of trying to balance myself on the ice. Despite all of Emily's efforts to teach me, I just wasn't getting it. Even Sachin and Surya had figured it out within an hour. Yet here I am, and hundreds of embarrassing falls later, I still can't do this. It didn't make me feel better now that Sachin had tons of video evidence, which I'm sure I wouldn't be allowed to forget about anytime soon. Not that I blame him, I would have done the same in his shoes. However, any embarrassment paled in comparison to the joy I felt in just being allowed to be around my friends, as well as the fact that Amma was clearly getting along with the other moms.

"Dev, I don't think it's possible for someone to be this bad at this. I'm sure even someone with the worst balance on Earth would have gotten this in the last 7000 attempts." Emily was doing a horrible job of containing a laugh.

"Whatever, I'm going to get this eventually."

"At this rate, eventually might be in a couple of hundred years."

"You're the teacher, so clearly you're the one doing something wrong."

"How did Sachin and Surya get it then?"

"Sheer dumb luck."

"No, you're just horrendous at this."

"I think that was obvious by now."

"Okay, I've got an idea. Just take my hand. And hold tight."

"What?"

"Just trust me." I grabbed ahold of both her hands, and the next thing I knew, I was being dragged across the rink.

"You know, I don't think this is going to help me learn how to skate."

"Try this!" I was suddenly on my own. And on my feet. And not crashing. "Whooo! Go Dev!!"

"You mean he finally did it? I thought the Earth would stop spinning before he started doing this by himself." Sachin called out from the other side. That's when it sunk in... I was actually doing this!

"WHOOOOOO!" I let out an uncharacteristic yell, but I couldn't help it, I had been frustrated so many times over the last four hours.

"Dev, watch out!" Emily yelled. I was too excited though, that I wasn't paying attention. And I rammed right into her, knocking us both into the ice. "Seriously? That's the thanks I get? After I spent the last four hours dealing with your inability to balance?" She was laughing as she said that, so clearly she was joking.

"Sorry, I really didn't mean to do that."

"It's cool, whatever. Just try not to do that again." I then tried to get back up, and realized I couldn't balance myself long enough to keep myself upright. "Seriously? Are be back to square one now?"

"Looks like it."

"Looks like his mini-run was a fluke." Summer had come over as well.

"Clearly."

"Can I get some help back up?"

"It's fitting, isn't it? You knocked me down, and now you need my help to get back up."

"I'm sure Summer would help me if you aren't willing."

"Nah, you're more fun to deal with this way."

"Ahh, this video might be the best one I've taken tonight!" Sachin yelled. "I thought it would be a celebratory video, but instead I got a collision, and then back to the usual by Dev!"

"I hate you all. And I'm never going skating again."

"Fine, I'll be nice." Emily put her hand out, allowing me to get back up. I immediately got off the rink, I am officially done with ice skating.

"Looks like you had fun." Rakshini greeted me, filled with mirth.

"Leave me alone."

"You were funny! Especially when you knocked that Emily girl down!" Lakshmi had run over to me, somehow still filled with energy after four hours of skating.

"Whatever." We all went out to eat after ice skating, and I honestly can't remember anything that happened during that meal which wasn't related to teasing my horrible skating skills.

The rest of February went by a lot quicker, as I was now a lot happier than I was after state, despite Allison and George's antics. Things were looking up, yet again, which could only mean that eventually, it would have to fall. After all, as Sir Isaac Newton proved when he discovered Gravity, all that goes up must come down. I just didn't realize how true that was to life as well. It was okay though, the ups are what make life tolerable, and surviving the downs are what make you stronger in life.

CHAPTER 29

EXTREMES

I f you could graph my feelings throughout the school year on a xy coordinate plane, the graph would be at its global minima right now. While previous time periods could be classified as local minima, what was happening right now trumped them all, and therefore was the global minima. Which was strange, because if I was being honest, February had been some sort of a global maximum. So it was a pretty steep decline to now. I guess it was also a pretty telling sign about how tumultuous this year had been if there were so many other events could be one extreme or another, either local minima or maxima. I guess, as the old soothsayer would say; *Beware the Ides of March.* Which is ironic, since it's actually coming up tomorrow, meaning that it was my birthday today. Not that I was making such a fuss about it, I hadn't mentioned it after the sleepover, so I was pretty confident it would pass by with no commotion, which was exactly what I was hoping for. At the same time, with all the drama surrounding me right now, I honestly wouldn't be opposed to a birthday celebration. And no, that is not me asking for one. Anyway, I should probably be focusing on the task at hand, my life is in danger right now. One moment of lost focus and it's all over for me.

"OW!" I didn't mean to yell, but what else would you do when you get hit by three dodgeballs at the same time? Seriously though, why is this a condoned activity in gym classes? Is the gym teacher seriously oblivious to the fact that I'm the main target for the opposing team, seeing as every round of the game starts with me getting nailed by at least two balls? I turned over to look at him and saw that he was happily playing a game on his phone- probably doodle jump. Well, he clearly cared about this job.

"Hey Shanmugan, are you even going to try and not get hit?" Some random guy from my team yelled as I walked off the court.

"What can you expect, all he knows to do is forge grades, that's not exactly a skill for dodgeball."

"Yeah, if he was actually a genius as he claims, he'd probably be able to calculate all the angles the balls are being thrown at and know where to be to not get hit."

"Or maybe he'd be able to actually hit someone, by calculating where to throw the ball." Yeah, my "teammates" were having a nice laugh about me. Nothing I'm not used too. I just ignored their taunts and stared at the clock. Thankfully, there would not be time for another game. I watched my team got pummelled for the fourth straight game, and was out of the gym as fast as I could go. I seriously hated that class. Which should be obvious from the fact that I barely average an A- in it. However, my parents don't care about that grade, so it's fine. I headed to Biology, excited to meet up with my friends for what was generally the highlight of my day. It's been six months and I still can barely swallow the fact that Biology, of all things, is my favorite period.

Next thing I knew, however, I was face to face with the floor. I must have tripped or something. I got up, noticing that there was a fairly large crowd to have spectated my trip. Whatever, they can think I'm clumsy or something, I could care less. It honestly would be the nicest thing said about me recently. I brushed the dust off my pants, and readjusted my backpack that had been slightly knocked off due to the fall. That's when I noticed that the crowd wasn't staring at me exactly, but instead at my back. So I decided to turn around, only to find myself face to face with Allison Wang. *Here we go again*, I thought.

"Took you long enough to notice me." I just scoffed, and turned around and continued towards the biology classroom. That's when I felt her hand on my backpack, making sure I wouldn't be going far. "Not so fast kiddo, it's been a while since we last chatted."

"I don't know about you, but I have a class I want to get to."

"Ah right. Biology. Excited to harass my little brother?

"You know, for someone that's supposedly smart, you don't listen very well. I never started anything with your brother."

"If you didn't start anything, I don't see why you had to apologize to him."

"If you don't have the common sense to figure out why, then I'm not going to tell you. Treat it as a challenging problem." She didn't seem to like that reply very well, seeing as I was back on the floor. However, before she could do anything else, she was distracted.

"What do you think you're doing to my brother? Are really stooping so low to physically dominate freshmen now? Is this how you get a self-esteem boost? By beating up on freshman?" It was Rakshini, being the protective older sister again. Speaking of which, I never did talk to her about how the whole high school thing is her idea.

"Always having someone to cover your back? When are you ever going to stand up for yourself?" Allison sneered at me.

"Ask your brother how his mouth felt after I decided to do something by myself." I responded before running off. If I was fast enough I could maybe get to Biology on time. As I turned a corner I could hear Rakshini's last words to Allison.

"Don't think you'll get away with touching my brother like that again you..." I didn't need to hear the last word, I had a pretty good idea of what it was.

"What took you so long?" Summer asked before I could even recover my breath. I had somehow actually managed to sprint my way to Biology on time.

"Had a run in with a special sister." Our code word for Allison.

"Ah... nothing bad?"

"Nothing I couldn't handle."

"Are you guys ever going to take up my offer on revenge?"

"No!" Summer said.

"Yes." I replied.

"Wait what?!" We stared at each other.

"I'm sick of this. We should show them we can stand up for ourselves."

"You're letting her get to you Dev... and if she has, then she's already won."

"It's true. Except for when I punched George, I've always needed someone to finish my fights for me."

"It shows that you aren't the instigator in any of this… that they're desperate for a reaction from you."

"I'm with Summer here, don't let them rile you up." Surya added.

"Fine. One more incident though, and I can't promise anything."

"Fine." Summer agreed. Which kind of surprised me. The rest of the period went by without commotion as we just continued to do stuff related to predicting genotypes or whatever. As we went to the library, I could feel like something was on everyone's mind though.

"So Dev, anything interesting coming up?" Emily asked as she sat down.

"What do you mean?"

"Oh, I don't know… just something special. Something you're looking forward too?"

"Spring Break?!"

"Nah, that's a bit far off."

"Does it not begin two Fridays from now?"

"It does, but I was thinking about something coming up a bit closer."

"The Ides of March?"

"Seriously? That's like not even a real thing, just some story."

"Uhh no, March 15th is actually called the Ides of March… but yeah the soothsayer stuff probably made up."

"That's not it."

"I honestly can't think of anything."

"So you mean all those seniors who have applied to MIT don't have something special today?" What was Sachin trying to say?

"That doesn't affect me at all…"

"So there's nothing else special happening today?" Surya asked. Ohhh… right.

"I hate all of you guys."

"Happy Birthday!" They all yelled, causing us to be on the receiving end of strange looks from other kids in the library.

"You do realize that I don't celebrate my birthday right? There are millions of others who celebrate it today as well, it's not even unique."

"So you mean we should tell Rakshini to cancel the plans?"

"I'm sorry what?!" Next thing I knew I was being dragged out of the library, and being led into Rakshini's car. "What are you guys' doing?!" I said as the five of us squished into the backseat.

"Going to Summer's house of course!"

"Why?"

"Because everyone's waiting for you to show up! Isn't really a birthday party if the birthday boy isn't there." I complained the entire car ride there, but even I wasn't buying it by the end of the drive.

"SURPRISE!" Lakshmi yelled as we entered the house.

"It wasn't really a surprise since I knew what was happening once I entered this house…"

"You didn't know about this before today, therefore it was a surprise!" I wasn't even going to bother arguing with her, she was adamant that she was correct.

"You ready for the cake cutting?" Uh oh, I knew where this was headed. The classic Indian birthday tradition of getting cake smeared on your face by a family member.

"Do we have to?"

"Oh come on, I've been waiting to do this for years!"

"Yes, I want to see this!" Sachin yelled.

"Fine." I already know that I'm going to regret this. Especially as Sachin has his phone out ready to record.

"What's wrong about cake cutting?" Emily seemed confused about the conversation that had just transpired.

"Just watch!" Sachin yelled. As people gathered around to watch the all important cake cutting, I braced myself for the horror show that was going to happen.

"I can't reach his face!" Lakshmi yelled as she held the first piece of cake in her hand.

"I'll help then." Rakshini then lifted her, allowing Lakshmi to cover my left cheek with cake frosting. Except Rakshini couldn't hold her for the entire duration, so I also ended up with cake on my shirt. Rakshini then cut out the next piece of cake and also smeared it. Honestly, I would have been hating my life at this moment if it weren't for the fact that this school year had brought up so many dumb and embarrassing moments, that this wouldn't even make the top ten list.

"Is this like common for you guys?" Emily asked.

"What do you mean?" Surya responded.

"Like assaulting the birthday kid with cake."

"Yeah, it happens all the time."

"Can I try then?"

"Wait if she does it, I want too as well!" Sachin yelled.

"So am I like in a dunk contest you find at carnivals now?"

"No, there will not be anymore cake smearing." Amma stepped in before Sachin and Emily got anymore ideas. As we ate cake, any thoughts of Allison or George were long gone, and instead for some reason everyone was using this as a way to tell embarrassing stories of me. Which of course lead to Rakshini dominating the conversation

"Ohh yeah, there was this one time when Dev began lecturing a friend and I about superfluidity or some nonsense like that, all because my friend spilled water on the floor. That was also the last time that friend came over. I probably have a story and a reason as to why none of my friends want to come over nowadays."

"Did I tell you guys that one time at the mall?" Everyone shook their head, while I just planted my face on the table, I knew what Emily was going to say next. "Okay, so we were looking at the newest phones in the apple store for fun, and I pointed out that they now had waterproof technology, which I thought was cool. And then Dev here replies with, 'So that means they're resistant to water?' " Yeah, that wasn't my greatest moment.

"He actually said that?" Surya was laughing the most at this story.

"Do you want to know my best Dev story?" Summer joined in on the 'fun'.

"Ooh boy, this is going to be good." Sachin exclaimed.

"So you guys know how he wore a suit on the first day?"

"That was a great prank by Rakshini, I wish I had a homeschooled sibling I could use that on." Sachin reminisced.

"Yeah, that's the thing. It wasn't a prank. He had spent four hours on google the night before trying to learn what to do on the first day of school!"

"SERIOUSLY?!!" Sachin and Surya yelled at the same time.

"Yeah… and to finish off Summer's story, when Summer found out, Dev was convinced that she was going to ditch him for me, for some reason."

"You can't be serious. What possessed you to get help from google?! When you could have asked Rakshini for help!" Emily said in between laughs.

"Okay, can we, like, change the topic now?" I said, hoping they would acquiesce. They did not.

"This is too entertaining." Sachin responded, with everyone else nodding in agreement. The next few hours continued similarly, except with funny stories being shared during a series of board games such as Monopoly. Despite the fact that I hate birthdays, hate celebrations, and abhor getting cake spread across my face, somehow I found myself enjoying this evening. I think it is also safe to say that we were at a new global maxima. At this point, I don't think I should even be graphing the highs and lows of my life, as at this point we were just on a sine curve that had a short period, and kept on increasing it's amplitude as x gets larger. Now if only we had the absolute value of this function, my life would be amazing. I guess that's just a fantasy and not really realistic to expect. And I guess maybe birthdays aren't as bad as I made them out to be. I will still argue that they are completely pointless to celebrate though.

CHAPTER 30

VACATION

E ven though it was under the guise of it being Rakshini's last Spring Break before college, I knew this was Amma trying to make things up with me. Even though I'm not sure going to Disney World in Florida is really something that would be enjoyable for me. Yet, here I am, in a car instead of going to school on the last Friday before Spring Break so we could get to Orlando before tomorrow. You see, we drive around everywhere because Lakshmi has an irrational fear of airplanes. Hopefully, she grows out of it soon though, it is tiring that every time we need to go somewhere, we have to take a road trip instead of a couple hour flight.

"THIS IS FUN!!" We were now in the period of the car ride where Laskshmi yells out of the window and the rest of us wish we were anywhere but in the car. "HEY LOOK WE ARE IN TENNESSEE NOW!" Sigh another 12 hours to go.

"How about we play a game?" Rakshini asked, clearly trying to get Lakshmi to stop yelling.

"Can it be the silent game? So I can try and nap?"

"NO I DON'T LIKE SILENCE!"

"Shocking, since I do."

"No, we won't play the silent game Dev. How about I name a country, and you have to name one that starts with the last letter of the country I said. First person to not know a country to say loses?"

"Can we do that with the elements on the Periodic Table?"

"No silly, you can't fit a table inside a car!" Nevermind, I forgot Lakshmi was still only in fifth grade, and clearly didn't even know what the Periodic Table was.

"Fine, countries it is." Do you know what's great about having a good memory? These games are extremely easy, since I knew every country and they didn't, so I'd outlast them eventually. We continued with games like that, with naming presidents, naming famous people in general, naming cities, and so on, until before we knew it, we were entering Florida. Somehow nine hours had just flown by. Well okay, maybe we hadn't done those games for the entire nine hours, since I did fall asleep for about three hours.

"IM BORED AGAIN! AND ME NO LIKE LOSING!" Lakshmi was clearly upset now.

"Okay, what do you want to do Lakshmi?"

"Let's name *My Little Pony* characters!"

"You aren't actually going to let her choose that are you?"

"She's been doing stuff that we outclass her in for hours now... we might as well give her some games to win."

"I don't like losing."

"Well too bad. Get over it."

"Okay! I'm going to start with Fluttershy!" The next hour was just torturous as we got introduced to way too many characters, and it was information that I wished I could unlearn. It also raised many questions for me. The main one being; 'How do people even enjoy this show?!' What happened to the classics, *Curious George, Cyberchase, Mr. Roger's Neighborhood*? Kids these days were clearly being ruined by these random shows about ponies. No wonder Lakshmi thought the Periodic Table was an actual table. A couple more hours, and we finally reached our hotel for the next week. I went straight to bed too tired from all the stuff I had been through in the car ride- mainly Lakshmi's antics.

Okay, Epcot is pretty cool. The American Adventure thing was pretty interesting, even though I knew most of the stuff it talked about, I liked how it presented American History in a way for the general public to understand. It was definitely a bit too patriotic, but what else could you really expect. I also liked the Impressions de France attraction, giving you a feel for the country that you probably couldn't really recreate again unless you actually went to France. Lakshmi was a bit bored, as she clearly had wanted more roller coasters, but she was satisfied when we went Racin' Around the World. I also thought the stores and food places that were a part of 'Around the World' were extremely creative, allowing you to feel like you really were traveling to different countries as you got to taste the different foods. I also definitely ate way too much, but it was worth it in order to get the full Epcot experience. I knew that the other three parks probably wouldn't be the same, but it was okay. Especially as instead of going to Hollywood Studios like Rakshini, Appa and Lakshmi were going to do, Amma and I would go to Kennedy Space Center and visit the stuff over there.

Visiting the space center was kind of like a childhood dream becoming a reality. Mainly because just like most kids, I had once dreamed of becoming an Astronaut. Seeing the history of the space program, and all of the memorabilia was pretty cool. Of course, Lakshmi argued that her day was better since she got to go on a bunch of rides, such as some Haunted Hotel one that she said was amazing. Rakshini, of course, asked me for anything new that I had learned, showing the stark contrast between my two siblings.

Day Three was the day that Lakshmi was most excited for: Magic Kingdom. Even Rakshini had reverted to her little girl mode and as a result, I was surrounded by two extremely giddy siblings for the entire day. I guess this was Disney Magic in action. Fitting since we were in Magic Kingdom. The rides themselves weren't bad, which is a compliment coming from a rollercoaster hater such as myself, but the sheer numbers of animated characters running around, as well as having to take pictures at the large castle because "that's the Disney experience" was definitely something I wasn't a fan of.

Universal Studios was next, and this was probably the highlight of the trip for me. Being a Harry Potter fan growing up, the area of the park dedicated to the Wizarding World was probably the highlight of the trip. Even though I have no idea how butterbeer is so appealing to the people in the books because if it tasted anything like the butterbeer I had today, it definitely left a lot on the table. The other themes were fine too, even though I'm not really familiar with most of the references the themes were about. I definitely had warmed up to the rides in this park, but don't expect me to suddenly become a roller coaster fanatic now.

Sea World was also pretty cool, but if I'm being honest it was really just a large aquarium with some rides as well. Not that I minded, since I found the sea creatures interesting, even though I wasn't too sure how ethical the captivity of the animals were- especially for their animal shows with the seals. Animal Kingdom, which we did the day after, was also fine, but the main highlight from that was the Expedition Everest ride, and seeing as that paled in comparison to most of the other rides I had been dragged to, it definitely was a disappointment. The safari was pretty interesting, but by this point I was also kind of tired of Florida and was ready to go back home.

"Do you want to know something that confused me the entire trip?" Lakshmi asked while we were on the car drive back home.

"Not really, but I feel like you're going to tell us no matter what." I replied.

"Why was Florida exactly the same as home?"

"What?!"

"It had blue skies, green grass, and black roads! How is that any different than home?"

"What were you expecting? The skies to turn purple because it's a different state?"

"YES!" Well, I wasn't expecting that.

"I honestly have no idea how to reply to that."

"Why is it a different state then? What makes them so special?!"

"Well you see, when we were still colonized by England..." I then went into a detailed explanation about how each colony had formed, and then the process of statehood that a region would need in order to join the United States. After I was done, which was about an hour later, I was expecting her to be understanding of why different states existed. Instead, I got,

"Well that was a nice bedtime story, if not a bit boring, but you still didn't explain what makes Florida different than New York, or from Alaska, or from Wyoming."

"I give up. Ask your teacher on Monday."

"EWWWWWWW! I HAVE TO GO TO SCHOOL ON MONDAY! CAN WE GO BACK TO FLORIDA?" I put my hands in my ears and tuned her out as I drifted off to sleep. I woke up as we pulled into the driveway of our home, which was at about 8 AM the next day.

Summer: "Are you back yet?"

Dev: "Yeah, just reached."

Sachin: "Perfect! Want to come over?"

Dev: "When?"

Sachin: "Now!"

Dev: "Seriously? I haven't even gotten out of the car yet!"

Surya: "That means you can get dropped off!"

Emily: "Guys, I think what Dev is trying to say is that he wants some rest after a 15 hour car ride."

Dev: "^^^"

Summer: "Okay, how about later today, at like 1?"

Dev: "Sure." So at 1:00, we all met up Sachin's house to enjoy the first days of spring weather that the year had to offer. It was pretty nice outside, so we decided to have a picnic in the backyard, and just talked about our Spring Break so far.

"So how was Disney?!" Emily asked.

"Overrated."

"Seriously??"

"You do realize you're talking to Dev right? He probably would have more fun designing roller coasters than actually riding one." Summer pointed out.

"That and Disney princesses are probably not something Dev is a fan of." I nodded my head emphatically at that.

"Whatever, he just doesn't understand the magic of Disney." Summer responded.

"Have you ever watched a Disney movie?" Emily asked.

"I haven't really watched movies in general. However, I do want to watch that new movie about those female NASA scientists who were also African Americn back in the 60s."

"Hidden Figures?" Surya asked.

"Yeah that one."

"We should watch that over the summer." Surya suggested.

"Only if you allow us to make Dev watch a Disney movie?"

"Does The Force Awakens count?" Sachin asked.

"NO! The Star Wars marathon is different than this." Emily said forcefully.

"Okay fine, I guess we can watch The Lion King or something."

"Then we have a deal." Sachin and Emily then shook on this deal, which confused me.

"Did you seriously make a deal about how you guys are going to control my summer?"

"No, we made a deal on how we are going to give you a life." Emily retaliated.

"You do realize I'm probably going to be traveling for half the summer, to go to physics conventions as well as present some research?"

"Perfect, your summer can be divided 50-50 between Dev things and normal people things!"

"Ugh." The rest of the break, or whatever was left of it anyway, went by fast as it didn't really live up to vacation, or hanging out with friends. However, on the last day of break, I went over to Rakshini's room to finally confront her about what I had heard a month ago.

"Was it really your idea to send me to High School?"

"How did you find out?"

"I overheard the argument you and Amma had for the ice skating thing."

"Oh... why bring this up a month later then?"

"Felt right." She just shook her head at that.

"Anyway to answer your question, yes it was my idea."

"Why?!"

"You would have died in college."

"What?"

"You barely could survive your first day of high school, now imagine that in a much larger area with kids four years older than you at the minimum. Then add in the fact that you would have to live on your own, meaning you would have to be able to coexist with a stranger? That's a recipe for disaster."

"Okay, I guess you are probably right about that. But the real reason I wanted to know was so that I could thank you."

"What?!"

"It was the right decision."

"Glad you think that."

"It's going to be so weird next year not seeing you in the hallways... or at home for that matter."

"Don't worry about it. I'll come home often."

"You'll say that now, but I bet the moment you enter the campus of Berkeley, you're going to never want to leave."

"How can I not visit when I have a younger brother that would be a deer in headlights without someone to guide him?"

"HEY!"

"It's true..."

"Okay, I have things to do."

"You probably don't!" She yelled as I left her room. She could really be frustrating at times. But I guess that's just a part of personality or something. Which got me thinking... how do personalities form? I would need to do research into that. Later, though, right now I had school to get ready for tomorrow morning.

CHAPTER 31

HURRICANE

I was in the eye of the hurricane. Not literally of course, but metaphorically, if the hurricane was the drama caused by George and Allison. The weeks after spring break had been shockingly quiet, which I found both calming and worrisome. After all, there was no way they would have just let me go right? On the bright side, I could feel the school year winding down. We were finishing up learning materials in most classes, and it felt like students and teachers alike were just ready to call it a year. If it weren't for the fact that I knew that Allison was still out to get me, I would have been ready to just relax and enjoy the nice weather that came with it being April. I know I should probably not let them cause so much worry, but I was.

"Dev? Are you listening at all?" Mr. Bakerman called me out in English.

"Yeah, Achilles was the guy who took a bath in the River Styx as a kid which made him invincible at every place except his heel, which was where his mother held him to put him in the Styx." We were beginning to read *The Odyssey*, meaning we were having a mini-unit on Greek Mythology.

"Very good, Dev! Now can anyone tell me how the Trojan War ended, and how the Trojan War affected the events of The Odyssey?" As the class went on, I tuned out, which was normal for me. Especially at this time in the school year when you can just feel summer approaching. While this time period for upperclassmen, such as Rakshini, meant AP Test cramming, for a kid like me who doesn't exactly need to take any AP Tests (well I'm taking the Physics C tests just for fun, mainly trying to see how fast I can finish it and get a perfect score), this time period is just painfully slow, which is probably how Tantalus feels being just out of reach from the hanging fruit, which in my case is the end of the school year.

The moment I knew that I wasn't out of trouble yet was when I walked by Allison after first period. She didn't say anything, but she gave me the classic "I'm watching you" symbol. I tried to ignore it, she was clearly trying to get into my head, but I just couldn't. I had to know what she was getting up to!

"She's just trying to mess with your mind, dude." Sachin said when I replayed the incident to him and Surya in lunch.

"I know, but it's just so unnerving. I just want to know what her plan is!"

"Start studying for finals? Maybe that'll take your mind off them." Surya offered.

"Like Dev needs to study for finals. He has like a 99 percent in every class." I neither confirmed nor denied that statement. I didn't need to.

"Yeah, maybe I'll do that even if it's just to distract myself." I didn't say anything the rest of the period as I mulled over the options I had, as well as reasonable ways to try and get Allison and George out of my head. I continued being lost in thought as I walked into History, as well as throughout the entire period. And the rest of the day. I'm pretty sure most of my teachers would have noticed the fact that I had entered Planet Dev, but none of them said anything, so the rest of the day went by in a blur.

I returned to Earth while I was in the library when I noticed that my friends were talking about me. Something about how Sachin was extremely tempted to slap me in order to get me out of whatever faze I'm in.

"Hey! I don't need to be slapped!"

"Seriously? That's what got you out of your thoughts?" Summer glared at me, which made me wonder what else they had tried.

"What? I care for my physical well being, and being slapped would not be ideal."

"I don't get how he even heard that seeing as he was completely out of it." Emily spoke up. Honestly? I'm not sure how I heard it either, I'm putting it on my survival instincts. My brain picked up a possible threat and reacted to it. Now, I don't know if that's true but that's going to be my theory for now. I returned to what I had been thinking about. Ah yes, how to ignore Allison. Now what I was going to do about that, no idea. Because deep down, I didn't really want to ignore her. I wanted to figure out all that there was to know, so I could predict what her plan was. That's when I felt it. A sting in my right cheek, as well as intense pain.

"There, now he won't be zoning out on us." Sachin said with a smug look.

"That hurt!"

"That was kind of the point." Surya replied.

"With friends like you guys, who needs enemies?" Do you want to know something else about Hurricanes? While the eye of the storm is where it's quiet, the most dangerous part of the Hurricane is the eyewall. And that's what surrounds the eye, meaning once you are in the eye, there is no escaping the destruction. You can only hope and pray for the best. That's all I could do now. Wait for the eyewall to hit and pray it's not as bad as I'm expecting.

Except, the eyewall never came. A week later, I'm still expecting Allison to do whatever she is planning, yet it doesn't happen. And with every passing day, I only become more paranoid. Carefully turning every corner in the hallway, to make sure I won't get ambushed. Changing the paths I take to my classes so I am less predictable in order to decrease the chances of an ambush. I had also taken to wearing glasses (with no actual prescription of course), as well as gotten a haircut in hopes that it would make me less recognizable. I had also gotten a new backpack. Yes, I'm aware that I might be going a bit overboard, but it was all in the name of safety. I guess I was kind of like someone who tried to fortify their house when a hurricane was coming, instead of just leaving the area, adamant that just a few extra protections are all that's needed to save the house from the heavy storm. Of course, it won't work, once a Hurricane has targeted an area, you better leave because there is no escaping complete and utter destruction. I don't have the option of running though, so all I can do is brace myself for landing. The landing of Hurricane Allison- which I'm aware was an actual Hurricane that hit Texas in 2001, but let's ignore that for the sake of the metaphor.

"She has to be waiting for the end of AP Tests! That's the only possible reason for her to not do anything yet!" I exclaimed during our library meetup.

"Seriously? Don't you think you're being a bit too paranoid?" Summer asked.

"Was that not obvious when he started wearing those disgusting glasses?" Emily replied.

"Or the buzz cut?" Surya remarked.

"Or when he bought a new backpack?" Sachin added.

"It was obvious, I just want to see if he realizes it!"

"Fair point, for all we know, Dev thinks he's acting normal." I looked at my watch, ignoring all of them. It was 3:15, meaning Harry was late. Or was he? I saw him enter the library and walk towards us.

"Hey!"

"Hi. Did you do it?"

"Yes." He then handed me a folder in his hand, which I then put in my backpack.

"Thanks."

"You still owe me."

"I know, but this was worth it." He looked skeptical, but shrugged and walked away. I turned back to my friends only to be met by four pairs of confused eyes.

"What was that all about?"

"Nothing important."

"You do realize I can tell when you're lying right?"

"Well looks like you've slipped."

"Seriously Dev? What's gotten into you!" Summer sounded kind of angry actually. Which made me stop and think about my next words.

"Self-preservation."

"What?"

"You asked what's gotten into me? I need to protect myself, and I will go as far as I need to do it."

"So you're going to cut us all off? You're friends? And you're going to rely on a guy you've spoken about 15 sentences with to do your dirty work?" Well, when she put it like that it sounded bad. "I don't get how we've known each other for nearly eight months and you still have trust issues with both me and everyone else here!"

"I wouldn't call it trust issues…"

"Then what is it?!" I noticed that the other three were just staring intently at the small argument we were having. Summer must have noticed them as well, as she dragged me out of the library. "There, since you apparently have a problem saying things in front of everyone, you can tell things to me alone. Oh and one more thing?" She then reached over to me and took my glasses off my face. "There, now I feel like I'm actually talking with Dev again."

"Uhh."

"So what's wrong? Why can't you trust us?"

"Because I know you guys wouldn't approve. So I'd rather keep things from you."

"What…?" She then reached into my backpack to pull out the folder Harry and given me. She opened it and gasped. "You've got to be kidding me!"

"Uhh…"

"Why were you having Harry stalk Allison?"

"Now I wouldn't use the word stalk… that has such a negative connotation. How about we go with… checked up on Allison." Summer just glared at me. "Okay fine it was stalking. Happy?"

"How can I be happy right now? Why wouldn't you talk to us? Or at least me? I thought we were good friends." She seemed… upset? What did I do to hurt her?

"You see, I really want to apologize right now, but I honestly don't know what I did to make you sad."

"You are actually so clueless sometimes." She said, even though it looked like she was trying hard to fight back tears.

"Which is why I need you to help me through when I'm clueless…"

"Probably the only reason why I put up with some of the dumb things you do."

"Okay yeah, stalking was a bad idea… and it was even worse that I didn't run it by you guys first." I then took the folder from Summer's hand, ripped it in half and threw the pieces in the nearest trash can. I didn't need any of that info anyway.

"So you're just going to forget about Allison now? I mean George hasn't spoken a word to you this semester, just like you guys agreed too! For all we know he got Allison to be off your case."

"I seriously doubt that."

"Well, that's what we're going to go with for now. Of course, there's a chance that's not the case but until proven otherwise she is completely innocent right now."

"Fine." We walked back to the library, and I was officially putting Hurricane Allison on a different trajectory, where our paths would not be meeting. I still needed to do one more thing though, before I could fully be satisfied that Allison was no longer a threat.

"Rakshini? Can I ask you something?" I knocked on her door after dinner, to make sure she wasn't busy. She probably was, because of all the AP Tests she needed to study for. However, she surprised me.

"Come in, I'm not doing anything." Well now that I was here, I wasn't sure how to actually word this without it sounding weird. "Did you come here just to check out my room? A room you've been in a million times?"

"No, uhh, I just had a question to ask."

"Well you haven't asked anything yet and I really don't have all day, so you better hurry up." Well, I guess it was now or never?

"Have you ever been in the eye of a hurricane?" Wait no, that's not what I meant to ask!

"I'm sorry what? In case you haven't realized, hurricanes don't affect this part of the country. Kind of hard since you know, we are a couple of thousand miles away from the ocean."

"No! That's not what I meant to ask!" Rakshini just burst out laughing. "Can you stop for a second? I really need to get an answer."

"Okay, you've got to admit, that was pretty funny. Only you would ask a question about hurricanes when you meant to ask something completely different." Well, she wasn't wrong. Still didn't mean I approved of her laughing.

"Whatever. What I meant to ask was that, have you ever been in a situation where you are expecting something bad to happen except it never happens? Which is like being in the eye of the hurricane, which is why I ended up asking that question."

"You're expecting Allison to do something?" What?! No! She wasn't supposed to realize what I was asking about!

"No! This is just a hypothetical scenario. Because I was thinking about hurricanes, and then related this scenario to one. Which then got me thinking about what I would do in a situation like that. Which is why I came to you for advice."

"Whatever, you mean Allison. And I'd just not think about it. Because unlike in an actual hurricane you have no idea if you're in 'trouble' or not."

"What if you are sure you're in trouble?"

"Still ignore. It's not any of your business what Allison is planning. If she's going to instigate something, then she's the one at fault, not you, and therefore you are fine. In fact, she probably wants you to be scared of her. So worrying about it only plays into her hands."

"So basically you're saying ignore the hurricane and hope for the best? If we're keeping up this extended metaphor?"

"Well the metaphor is flawed in the fact that you never got a warning, so you are just assuming you're in trouble. That and it's not like Allison is something worth freaking out over. She's just a complete idiot, and if you actually care what she's doing then you're just a bigger idiot."

"Hmm... okay."

"Is that all?"

"Well, I actually do have one more question... if you have time to answer of course."

"Ask away."

"Ok, suppose hypothetically a friend of you was extremely upset with you for a reason you don't know. They say they're fine after you apologize, but you don't think they are. What would you do?"

"Okay... what did you do to Summer now?"

"I never said it was Summer! I said hypothetically!"

"Oddly specific for a hypothetical situation. And I noticed you didn't deny either, which tells me more than what I need to know. And seriously you need to figure it out by yourself. Think of it as preparation for next year when you can't just come to me for help every time you screw up with one of your friends."

"Okay…" Well, that wasn't really helpful. I'll just google that later. But for now, all I know is that the coast is clear, with no hurricane in sight. Meaning I was never in the eye. And that I was never going to get blasted by the eyewall.

CHAPTER 32

BUILDUP

The final month of school. I could smell summer just around
the corner. At the same time, I felt kind of sad. High School
was honestly not that bad, and over the summer there was
a chance I wouldn't get to see my friends at all due to travels. It was
finals time, of course, so I was certain that the feud with the Wang
family was really just going to pass by with a whimper and not with a
bang. Which I was totally fine with, I was ready to put all the drama
behind me. I honestly don't get how the second semester just flew by
so fast. It's theoretically the same amount of days as the first semester,
yet it felt like it went by in a snap of my fingers. Maybe it was because
there wasn't as much drama. Sure, Allison had been kind of a pain in
March, but she had really been silent since Spring Break. I guess the
calm nature of the semester just made everything fly by so quickly. Or
maybe it's because once the weather gets nice, no one really wants to be
in the school and everyone's ready to get out of the building. Honestly,
the only class we were even doing anything in was Biology, as we still
had a unit in Ecology to finish before the final.

"Okay class, I know you guys don't want to be here, because honestly,
I don't either. But we do need to finish this unit before your final, so
if you can just give me your attention for one more week it would be
extremely appreciated." Ms. Auguste was calling for the attention of
our class, which was also what she had been doing for the last five
minutes. Let's just say being a teacher for the last period of the day,
this close to the end of the school year is probably not a fun job. People
finally started to quiet down though, letting Ms. Auguste talk about

the ecosystem and how all life forms depend on others, or something like that. Halfway through the period, she had finished and was letting us work on the homework. Even though I'm sure she was aware she was giving everyone free reign to do whatever they want. Which I'm guessing was the point, since 75 percent of the class had checked out during her lecture anyway. It's just that time of year, I guess. That's when I noticed a note being pushed onto my table. From directly behind me. That could only mean George Wang. Which shocked me a little.

Meet me in the English hallway after school today. 3:00. I showed the note to the others, to mixed responses. Sachin wanted to see what George wanted, Summer wanted no part in it and Surya was torn between his curiosity and practicality.

"I say we go." I said.

"You do realize it's probably nothing good, right?" Summer questioned.

"George hasn't done anything to us all semester. I think we should give him the benefit of the doubt. And also, what could really go wrong if it's on school property."

"I don't like it. But Dev has a point, it's not like we are meeting him in a dark alley or something." Surya thought out loud.

"Fine. We'll go." Summer relented. We texted Emily, telling her to go to the English hallway after school. She clearly wasn't a fan of this idea, but decided to come with us as well.

Rakshini: "You've got to be kidding me!" Rakshini was not so agreeing when I texted her.

Dev: "I don't see what's wrong. We are on school property right? Anything harmful they could try would have bad consequences."

Rakshini: "They clearly have a plan to do something…"

Dev: "Why are we assuming Allison has something to do with this? For all we know it's George who just wants to talk to me alone."

Rakshini: "You are really stupid if you believe that."

Dev: "I don't believe it, I'm just saying it's a possibility."

Rakshini: "Whatever."

Dev: "I'm going no matter what, so you can do whatever you want."

Rakshini: "You're digging your own grave here." I ignored that. I then turned to the others to discuss the plan.

"What plan?" Sachin seemed confused.

"Like how are we going to do this."

"We go up and see what he wants, we don't need to do anything else." Surya responded. I guess he was right. It's not like we called the meeting. Or had come up with the venue. So I guess all we could do now was just to wait for the day to end. I checked my watch. The time was 2:27. We still had 18 minutes until the period ended. And another 33 until we were supposed to meet George in the English hallway.

Do you know the feeling of when time slows down? That's what I'm experiencing right now. The last three minutes felt like three hours. I also started to get cold feet. Both figuratively and literally. My feet were suddenly just freezing. And I was having second thoughts about the meeting. What if it was going to be an ambush? I consoled myself though. I knew that they wouldn't try anything on school property.

I hate waiting. How is it not past 2:33?! This is actually awful. I've tried everything. Counting seconds, doing homework, trying to solve the current problem in my research... and it's only 2:33! It was like fate was toying with me, causing time to slow down for me, making me become extremely frustrated. What am I going to do for the next 12 minutes if it keeps taking this long for time to pass by?

And it's 2:36. I'm pretty sure I'm making it pretty obvious at about how frustrated I am now. My legs are shaking and I'm just facedown on the lab table, waiting for this to end. Why does this always happen whenever you're waiting expectantly for something? That's it, I need to do something. I got out of my seat and left the classroom, telling Ms. Auguste that I need to use the bathroom. As I exited the classroom, I realize I don't actually have a plan for what I want to do.

Dev: "Are you doing anything right now?"

Emily: "Well, just doing homework... so no I guess not. Why?"

Dev: "I'm outside your math classroom."

Emily: "WHAT?!"

Dev: "Time was too slow. So I got out of my classroom. Next thing I know, I'm here."

Emily: "ur impossible." I saw her get out of her seat though, so I guess I had accomplished something.

"Seriously Dev? It's 2:37, the bell is going to ring in eight minutes." She said as she walked out.

"I was bored! And every three minutes felt like three hours."

"So you just decide to walk to my math classroom?"

"Well to be fair, I didn't realize that's what I was doing until I was here."

"For someone as smart as you are, sometimes you just act really stupid."

"How is this dumb?"

"Okay, what's your plan then?"

"What plan?"

"For what you want to do for… seven minutes." The pause was so she could check the time. 2:38 PM.

"I don't know, I was hoping you'd think of something."

"Nice try. Go back to class. I'll see you after school." And with that she went back inside, leaving me just standing awkwardly outside. I guess I don't have anything better than to go back to Biology. Even though I might as well stop at a water fountain now that I'm here. By the time I got to my classroom, it was 2:41, and it looked like I might actually make it to the end of the period without wanting to throw something at the clock in the Biology classroom.

Finally, the bell rang! I was free! We decided to meet up with Emily in the library. After all, we did have 15 minutes until we actually had to meet George.

"Do you guys know that the idiot over here decided to come to my math classroom at like 2:40 for no reason?"

"Seriously Dev? That's why you just walked out of Bio?" Summer said, shaking her head. Sachin just burst out laughing.

"Yeah I get it, I'm weird, can we move on now? I believe we have a rendezvous with George now though, so we better be on our way."

"Did you just say 'we have a rendezvous' ?"

"Yeah? What's wrong with that, Sachin?"

"You could have just said that we have a meeting."

"This sounds so much cooler."

"Nerdier."

"Whatever." When we got to the English hallway, it was surprisingly empty. I had honestly expected George to be here early. We all decided to stand against the lockers in silence, there really wasn't much to say to each other right now. And we all were just waiting to see what this meeting was about. After all, this was the first thing George had said to us all semester, a thought that I still hadn't gotten out of my mind.

"Well if it isn't Devadas Shanmugan and his merry band of friends." Allison Wang said as she turned the corner into the hallway. None of us said anything, it was better to let her get everything she wanted off her mind. I heard footsteps behind her, expecting it to be George. It wasn't. It was a group of about 15 seniors. I was worried now, what exactly did she want to say? "You can't run, I have more people at the other end of the hallway. So we finally get our one on one confrontation. With no one to protect you except for your group of four puny freshmen." You know, I was starting to think that coming here was a bad idea. But where was George? I wasn't surprised by Allison being here, but I thought George actually would have shown up.

"What do you want to do?"

"I think it's time for you and me to have a little chat." A chat? That didn't sound too bad.

"About what?"

"What's your issue with my brother?"

"Honestly? I have no problem with him. We haven't even spoken a word to each other since the first day of the semester! Even before, he was just a cocky kid that didn't like it when things didn't go his way, which was my only issue with him."

"LIES!" Woah. I hadn't expected such a response. "Now, I'll ask you one more time. Why did you insult my brother on your first day of school, without knowing who he is!" What? What does she think happened?

"What are you talking about? I had a lab group and he wanted to join, but we already had four at a table! If that's an insult, then your brother is extremely sensitive, and that's his fault."

"No! You spurned him. You didn't think he was worthy. WHY! How were those bumbling buffoons worthy and not George Wang!" The bumbling buffoons comment was directed at Sachin and Surya.

"I don't know what he told you, but I'm being honest here. I met Sachin, Surya, and Summer all in previous classes, and we decided to be a lab group! There was no insult intended towards your brother at all!"

"You still are sticking to that story, are you? Then why did you offer that dumb bet? You clearly thought yourself intellectually superior to my brother and wanted to rub it in his face!" Is this seriously the type of rubbish George had spread about me at the beginning of the school year?

"Do you seriously blindly believe everything your brother says without any questions? No matter how absurd they are? Do you hold him to some sort of pedestal where he's basically a god to you? Do you even know him at all?!"

"YOU DARE!" Allison was furious now. She took a couple of steps towards me, making me feel extremely uncomfortable. She had crossed the boundary of my personal space, and I could feel her breath now. "I know my brother better than anyone else, and he would never lie to me! He is one of the nicest kids you'll ever meet, something you would have known if you hadn't decided he was not worthy enough to be your friend just on some random whim. He is nothing close to how you describe him as, and if it wasn't obvious who is right here, you should see how many people actually like you compared to him. Everyone sees through you Dev, everyone knows exactly how phony you are, and I'm going to ask this nicely once. I want you to make a public apology to my brother for everything you've said about him, and admit that you were wrong! Not another half-apology like you did last winter. I want you to do it in front of everyone. The fact that you already apologized once shows that you know how horribly you treated him. I mean you even brainwashed your Biology teacher to send him to his administrator!" Was she truly that blind to what kind of person her brother could be?

"Why don't you ask him again, what happened at the beginning of the school year. Maybe you'll get a different response. And it might open up your eyes to what kind of person your brother can be at times. He was the one bragging about how he is the son of Biologists and making it seem like it was his birthright to ace that class. He was the one that assumed his pompous attitude would make people want to be around him. And if you think for one second that any of his followers actually like him, you're wrong. They just didn't want to be on his bad side because they know exactly how vindictive he can be at times!"

"How do you spit out lies so confidently? I wouldn't be surprised if you were a sociopath or something because I'm pretty sure those are the only kinds of people that can lie without feeling any remorse at all."

"Or maybe it's because I'm telling the truth. Where is your brother anyway? Thought he would be showing up here since he did deliver the message."

"He doesn't need to hear the lies that you have been spitting out about him, so I told him to stay away."

"Or maybe you didn't want to see him look ashamed when I told the truth because deep down you know that I'm right about this."

"That's IT! I've tolerated your lies for long enough! It's time to teach you a lesson!" She reached out to me, pushed away Sachin who had tried to stop her, and the next thing I knew she was holding my neck. Did she seriously think she could get away with choking me? "Now, you're going to apologize, or else the next few minutes are going to be extremely painful for you."

"I... will... not... apologize... for... saying... the... truth!" I said, struggling to let the words come out. She then slapped me. And again. And again. My friends were being held back by her group of bodyguards, or whatever they were supposed to be. I would have to give in, or else risk something extremely bad happening. However, what happened next I could have not expected.

"LET HIM DOWN ALLY!" I knew that voice. Except... there was no way that it could be who I thought it was. Allison let me go, she clearly recognized the voice as well. We all turned to the other end of the hallway, to see George Wang standing there, all alone.

CHAPTER 33

GEORGE

We all were in shock. I don't think anyone moved for a good two minutes. You could hear a pin drop in the area, which is surprising as we were in the middle of the hallway. George then walked towards us, until he was right next to Allison and I. The seniors who had come with Allison had moved back, releasing my friends, clearly not sure what to do now. Summer ran over to me, I guess to make sure I was okay. I just nodded my head, letting her know I was fine now. I wasn't sure what to do now, what was George thinking when he told Allison to stop? And why? I could tell Allison was just as confused as I was, but she was still in shock, which was obvious from the fact that she couldn't form a coherent sentence yet. It took a few more minutes for her to finally spit out a full sentence.

"What's wrong? I was going to finally get Dev to apologize for all the stupid stuff he did to you first semester!"

"You were going to kill him if he didn't agree."

"Well, if he was smart he would have agreed before it went that far! I thought that's what you wanted? For him to finally admit that anything you might have done to him was fully deserved as he had started everything?"

"And I would have felt guilty forever, knowing that the apology should never have happened?"

"What?"

"Everything he told you was right. I was a jerk to him on the first day of school. Dev didn't deserve any of the nonsense I put him through. I should be lucky that he never tried to give me a taste of my own medicine, even though he had the opportunity to do so when I forfeited the bet. If I'm being honest, I was jealous of him. Of his intelligence. That he was so likable despite his social awkwardness. And that he can throw a much better punch than I can." He said the last part with a grin, which I couldn't help but return. "And what I was most jealous of? The fact that he had real friends. Not like me, who got his friends through my sister's popularity. Or because people were too scared of me to say anything against me. I was a Class A jerk, I knew it, and I've spent the last four months hating myself for it. For what it's worth, I'm sorry Dev, for everything I did to you."

"No problem."

"You lied to me?" That was all Allison could get out of her mouth.

"I knew you wouldn't approve of the kid I had become, so I had to. Or at least I thought I had to. If I was smart, I would have apologized to Dev the next day and never done anything else. I didn't think I needed to though. I thought I was popular and well-liked, so when I was a jerk to one person, it wouldn't be the end of the world. And I got some fun out of it. I thought it was funny at the time. Until the day after the first test. I was so ashamed about how you had embarrassed me in front of everyone that I wanted revenge. That's when I went too far. I knew it when I was doing it, but I was just so angry I thought I had no choice. Even then I was feeling bad about how I was acting, but I pushed those thoughts away. I thought it would make me seem weak if I just stopped everything I was doing." George was like a snowball at the top of a mountain now. As it rolls down, it gains in size and can't stop. That was him now, he had opened the floodgates to his mind and it was all pouring out now. "I know I should have told Allison to stop when she started harassing you this semester, but I didn't want to open up to her that I wasn't the kid she thought I was. I didn't deserve to have the bet called off, I should have been punished by you through that bet. I should have apologized to you earlier as well, I shouldn't have waited till now. I'm just a horrible human, and I know that now."

"George, it's fine. Really. You apologized, while it obviously doesn't make up for everything that happened, it's a start. And you clearly feel bad about it." Summer finally decided to step in to stop George's rant.

"You're telling me I choked a kid because you were jealous of him?" Allison was still recovering from the shock. And was starting to realize the ramifications of what George's words meant.

"Yeah… I really should have put an end to this earlier."

"YOU THINK?!" Allison was mad now, and this time George was the recipient. Out of the corner of my eye, I noticed that the seniors that had come here with Allison had all left, clearly noticing that their jobs were done. "How could you not tell me!? I thought we were always open with each other?"

"I made a mistake, okay? I'm sorry, and I'm aware of the huge mess I've made. I just haven't been able to make myself face the fact that everything isn't how I imagined it would be."

"You seriously need a better excuse than that…" Allison seemed disappointed now.

"Well, it's the only excuse I have. Not that I have much else to say. I royally screwed up and it almost became even worse. I know that no number of apologies will fix anything, but it's all I have now."

"I think you and I are going to have a long talk once we get home. Sorry kids, I didn't mean to hurt you, I just thought you had messed up my brother. Now it's clear that he's always been a rotten fruit." Well, that was a bit harsh.

"Don't be too hard on him, I mean we all make mistakes. He clearly learned some lessons this year, I don't think he needs you to reiterate all that to him now." No idea why I said that. I really shouldn't have. We parted ways and no one said anything for a while. I think we were all still processing what had just happened.

"Okay, I want to be clear… I'm not dreaming, am I?" Sachin was the first to speak up. And I honestly can say that similar thoughts were going through my mind. Surya decided to be humorous and lightly punched Sachin in the shoulder. "Okay, it looks like I'm not dreaming since I could feel that."

"So we all agree that what just happened was extremely weird?" Emily asked.

"Yes."

"Of course."

"In every possible way." Sachin, Surya, and Summer responded respectively.

"I guess it was. At the same time, I guess if we had realized that his overall silence the last semester has been because of remorse, then this would have been expected right?"

"No… because then we would have expected it earlier." Summer replied. I guess she was right.

"So what do we do now?" I asked after a few minutes of silence.

"We go back to the library and pretend that this never happened." Something I think we all agreed on as no one responded to that. I started thinking though, what had caused George to be the person he was the first semester? Was it the way he was raised? Was it influenced by his genetics in some way? And the scariest thought of them all. Would I have been a complete jerk as well if I had gone to public school my entire life? Would I have felt some sort of entitlement because of my intelligence, just like George had? I honestly didn't know the answer to that. I guess there was no point in dwelling in that line of thought though, the history isn't going to change itself, so I should only be focusing on the present.

I couldn't get the events with George out of my head. It was nearly 9:00 PM now, and it was still all I was thinking about. Especially since I was brought back to what I had written on that sheet of paper all those months ago. How was I so right about that? Maybe I was becoming like Summer and able to read minds? In all seriousness though, I felt bad. I should have reached out to George after that to make sure he was okay. Especially as it was clear something was wrong with him the entire semester. I would talk to him tomorrow. Make sure he was okay. Maybe even try and become friends with him? That thought sounded strange just thinking about it. I tried to imagine how I would have reacted to that thought at the beginning of the year. Yeah, definitely strange.

CHAPTER 34

CALMNESS

I n the weeks after *the incident*, as we were calling it now, it seemed as if the entire social hierarchy of our year group had shifted. I had reached out to George, and while I wouldn't say we were friends yet, we definitely were on friendlier terms. It was strange to think about, but I guess life is full of surprises. There was no way I would have thought I would have ever been on friendly terms with George Wang even only a couple of weeks back. It was now the Monday before finals, meaning every class period was filled with people signing yearbooks, talking about summer plans and everything. Under the guise of finals review of course. I myself didn't have a yearbook, but it seemed that I was getting asked to sign three to four yearbooks per period. These were mainly the kids that I had helped out in tutoring over the last semester. As for George, rumors fly around quickly, and let's just say his fall from the top of the food chain was swift. In fact, as of right now I was probably the only kid that even talked to him. Even my other friends were staying away from him for now, clearly the memories of how he had treated us still fresh in their minds.

"So how's it feel to finally be over with this year?" I asked George during Biology. I was making the most effort I could to be friendly with him.

"Relieved. A bit disappointing though. My parents are transferring me to a private school. Apparently being in a school with commoners is the reason why I was acting like how I was." That information came as a bit of a shock to me. I honestly hadn't expected that.

"Oh… I hope it works out well for you. It's going to be strange right? Transferring your sophomore year into a group of kids you've never met."

"Not more strange than how you must have felt at the beginning of the year. I honestly have no idea how you did it. From what I understand you had never been around kids your age before, and then suddenly thrust into the ocean of high school, with a bunch of sharks, such as myself, ready to take advantage of your awkwardness."

"Since when did you talk in metaphors? And to tell you the truth, I had an anxiety attack during first period on the first day. That's how I became friends with Summer. She dragged me out of the classroom and helped me through it."

"Sounds like a good friend… I hope I'll meet someone like that next year."

"I'm sure you will. It's your chance at a new beginning. No one will know who you are, you'll get to create whatever name for yourself that you want."

"Since when did you become an expert in social situations?"

"I'm just speaking from experience."

"Was that your thought process going into high school?"

"No, that's what I've learned should have been my thought process during the first few weeks." We both laughed at that.

"You know, I think I'll do just fine next year." I raised my eyebrows at that. Was he actually serious? "After all, I know what not to do from you!" I couldn't help but laugh at that.

"Yet somehow it still worked out fine for me."

"I guess it did… now I think your friends want to talk to you."

"Ok, talk to you later I guess."

"Yeah." I turned back to my lab table who were all staring at me as if I had two heads. Apparently it was so strange for them to see me and George on speaking terms. Then again, I guess it would be pretty weird if I were in their situation.

"I don't get you." Sachin said after a bit.

"I think it's nice of Dev to be talking to George. I don't get how Dev tries to see the best in everyone, but it's a quality that I'm envious of."

"Are you sure you don't have it? Because if you don't, why did you help me on day one." I asked.

"No that was me realizing that there was a fellow homeschooler who was completely lost in a large high school."

"Whatever." Now if you thought me talking to George was strange or weird, what happened on Tuesday was just... mind-blowing. It happened after gym, while I was on the way to Biology. I heard some voices that intrigued me.

"How does it feel to be at the bottom of the hierarchy now? Do you realize how much of a fool you look like now? I hope you suffer for all that you did. Lying to everyone just to gain popularity? People like you are better off dead." I didn't have to look to know who the voice was talking to. I followed the sound of the voices to see George Wang being pushed against a locker by some guy that looked like he was a wrestler of some sort.

"Leave him alone!"

"Ah, if it isn't the infamous Devadas Shanmugan. I haven't had the honor to personally meet you yet, but I've heard so much about you. Mainly from this loser though."

"Leave him alone, he doesn't need this right now."

"Oh really? I would have thought you would have enjoyed this. After all, it was your name that he dragged through the mud to make himself look good."

"I've moved on."

"I wonder how much he paid you to do so."

"Nothing. He made an honest mistake. And the last thing he needs is to get beaten up for a dumb mistake. Everyone makes mistakes at some point or another."

"And you're being a perfect example of a kid making a mistake right now."

"Am I? I'm just helping out someone in need. Because if there's one thing I've learned I can't stand, it's bullies. Like you." The kid started towards me, but before he could grab me, we were interrupted.

"What's going on here?" It was Ms. Auguste. She must have heard the commotion while walking from the science office to our classroom.

"Nothing, just some friendly horseplay." The wrestler kid replied smoothly.

"Actually, Dev here was stopping Mark from beating me up. And you were seeing the unfortunate reaction Mark had to it."

"Is this true Dev?"

"It is."

"Well if that's the case, I guess Mark and I have a meeting in the discipline office right now. And good job Dev, for not being a bystander." She walked off, with the Mark kid in tow, leaving George and I awkwardly standing in the hallway.

"Thanks, I guess." George said eventually.

"Don't worry about it. Consider it payback for what you did during *the incident.*"

"Except you had no obligation to actually help me."

"You didn't either. How about we both just move on now."

"Agreed." As we walked into Bio together, I could tell that we had immediately garnered the attention of the other kids in the class. "What? You've never seen two kids walk into a classroom together before? Mind your own business!" George said as we took our seats. I just smirked at my lab table in response to the looks they gave me. The rest of the period went by with no commotion, as we mainly did our last-minute cramming for the Biology final.

CHAPTER 35

SUMMER

This was it. The last day of school. Summer was here. I breezed through the one final I had that day, Biology, and before I knew it, it was over. The final, the school day, and the school year. I was officially done with my freshman year, and it felt pretty surreal. Kind of nostalgic as well, as I thought about all the great moments that had happened this year.

"Do you guys want to come over?" Sachin asked as we walked outside towards the busses.

"Sure!" We all responded. After some quick texts to our parents, we all got into Sachin's dad's car. This was it. Summer had begun. We were officially done with school for two and a half months. I thought I would feel bad about not going to school for a couple of months, but I was relieved. I looked to my left and right, to the new friends I had made and wondered if I would have made anything resembling this at MIT. The answer was obvious; no way! There was no way I would have been able to connect with any 18 years old kid. Let alone adults older than that. I knew that Rakshini had made the right decision when telling my parents to send me here. Not that I didn't know it before, this was just a confirmation of it.

"So what do y'all want to do?" Sachin said, as we all just sat around on the couch in his basement.

"I'm too tired to get off the couch, so let's just talk." Emily said.

"I agree, that Bio final was way too long!" Surya exclaimed.

"It wasn't that bad..."

"SHUT UP DEV!" Four voices said in unison. This was it. The moments I had been missing up until this year. The moments that had made me so angry at my parents for sheltering me for so long. It didn't matter now that I had been missing out though, because I had them now, and that's all that mattered. I realized how lucky I was to have made friends like this and just decided to enjoy the fact that I was here with them right now. I sat back on the couch and just listened to the conversation going on around me.

"Who would have thought that freshman year would actually end?" Surya was saying.

"I know right! It felt like it was going to drag on forever with all the drama!" Sachin responded animatedly.

"Next year is going to be way duller. You know, without having George Wang spreading hate on us, and us trying to deal with it."

"Or without Dev punching anyone!" Sachin added.

"Or the entire freshman class hating us." Emily added.

"I just realized... Rakshi graduated! I mean, I know, I was at the ceremony, but like the fact that she's moving out this summer. Off to Berkeley. Wow. Has it sunk in yet for you Dev?" Summer spoke up.

"Not really... thanks for putting it in the forefront of my mind though."

"No problem!" The conversation continued, mainly talking about the highlights of the year and what we were going to miss next year. Until Sachin decided to change the topic.

"So do you guys want to know the real reason why I called y'all over?"

"You actually had a reason to call us over? It wasn't improvised?" Surya retorted.

"Yeah... We can begin the Star Wars marathon!"

"YES!" Surya yelled.

"Do we have a say in this?" Summer asked.

"Nope! You guys can do your Disney marathon later!"

"Ugh, do you want to leave Summer?"

"I'm afraid the guys are going to force us to watch Star Wars with Dev."

"So... want to start with *The Phantom Menace?*"

228

"Oh come on Sachin, we all know how bad that movie is…"

"To be fair, they aren't true fans, so they might actually enjoy it."

"I guess. Go ahead." We ended up watching the entire prequel trilogy that day. It wasn't horrible, I guess, but I honestly couldn't understand how Sachin and Surya had such a fascination with the franchise. It was nice for a one time watch, but I couldn't imagine myself watching these movies again. However, there was one unexpected perk about watching all three movies today. We had forced the hands of our parents into a sleepover. After all, it was 10:00 PM by the time we had finished the movies, so at the end of the day, I couldn't complain about having to sit through these movies.

We ended up staying up all night. Mainly we played card games, but we also played some more classic games, such as Mafia, Hide and Seek (which is apparently really hard to do quietly as we were told multiple times to quiet down by Sachin's parents), and of course, played chess. By the time we were tired, it was 6:00 AM.

"So are we going to even sleep?" Emily asked as she fought back a yawn.

"I guess we can take a few hours nap now." Surya added. Which is how we all ended up asleep on the floor of the basement. I had a pretty good sleep, however, the way I woke up wasn't ideal. Apparently I had overslept the other four, so my 'punishment' was to get a mustache drawn onto my face with a sharpie. Which would have been unfortunate, if I hadn't woken up when Sachin had accidentally poked my eye with the sharpie cap. I threw a pillow at Sachin, which started a free for all pillow fight.

By the time we all left Sachin's house, it was 3:00 in the afternoon. A nice way to begin summer vacation if I may say so myself. Even if I had almost started summer vacation with a Sharpie Mustache. Hanging out with my friends is fun, and I wondered if I had somehow made friends before high school if it would have been like this. I couldn't imagine it. After all, I wasn't interested in making friends until I was told to do so as the reason I was going to high school. As I sat down in my room, I reflected on how my life has changed in the last year, in both the good and bad ways. Except I couldn't think of any bad.

CHAPTER 36

BEGINNINGS

Well, I guess my first year of high school is over. If you told me a year ago that I would have ended up enjoying high school, I would have called you a liar. And probably never have spoken to you again. I don't think I could have predicted anything that happened this year, and honestly, I prefer it this way. A year ago I was sitting in my room cribbing about the fact that I had to go a dumb high school for two years instead of MIT, but with a year down, I'm not even sure if I would be okay with leaving this place in a year. Sure the academics aren't anywhere close to my level, but with the amount of leniency I've been given with my classes, I still have more than enough free periods to continue my research and further studies. However, the main reason high school has become so appealing to me is the people I've met through it.

Not just my friends, but the teachers who had been super supportive of my 'unique case', and in the case of Mr. Turner actually helped me in furthering my own studies. And even the kids I wasn't friends with but I just saw every day and had created a bond of mutual respect with. I envied a lot of them, you know. How they get to live normal lives, and not be immediately judged by new people just because of some special talents they had. And how they just knew how to act around everyone else. Something that even after nine months of high school, I'm still not really comfortable with.

Another thing that has changed for the better because of high school is my relationship with my family. Or I guess it's more accurate to say that I actually have one now. This time last year my family was just a group of people I had to live with and paid for my extracurricular stuff. I mean, I didn't even ask Rakshini how to act on the first day of school because I saw her as nothing more than another child with the same parents. Now she's actually someone I would seek advice from whenever social nonsense goes over my head. Which is still pretty often. I've also spent a lot of time with Lakshmi, which has not only led to me realizing she can be fun - at times- but also worrying about the quality of life she is living. Especially with that addiction to *My Little Pony*. Amma and Appa have also become more of parental figures to me, I guess. Mainly because before this year, I didn't have problems to go to them for.

And then there are the changes in my personality as well. No longer am I a robotic, soulless, shell of a human (Rakshini's words, not mine) but I apparently actually can pass off as a normal kid now. Which I think should be some sort of accomplishment. Also, I apparently have something that resembles an actual life now, according to Emily, which is progress from back in January. I've apparently have grown a sense of humor as well, but my biggest improvement, according to Summer, is that I no longer randomly zone out when thinking about how to respond to something someone tells me. I have mastered the art of answering first and contemplating life later. I also now enjoy things outside of doing research, such as playing chess and just being around my friends. Sure it means that unlike before I can't spend my entire day on research, but you'd be hard-pressed to find anyone that thinks that's a negative development. I'm still not convinced that the trade-off between acting normal and going further into my studies and research is actually as good of a development as everyone says it is, but I'm not arguing with the masses.

And then there are the friends I've made these last nine months. While I had expected to make at least one friend in high school, after all, it was why I was sent here in the beginning, I couldn't imagine that I would end up with a group of friends as I have now. Sure, five people may not seem like a lot, but I think the bond we have created is just something amazing. If I wasn't living this life, I would be convinced it was something out of a novel, like the golden trio in Harry Potter. Sachin, who with his never ending sarcasm always able to lighten the mood of our group. Surya, with his calmness, and being able to make sure we never stray too far off task. Emily, who is always there to provide new takes on something, a different perspective if you will. Summer who acts somewhat like a mother to all of us, and that is meant in the most positive way possible because without her looking after us all, we probably would have done many more stupid things over the past year. Then there's me. I know it sounds kind of narcissistic to say I'm the glue that keeps us all together, but in reality I am the reason why they all met each other. Mainly because of my complete and utter cluelessness, leading to them having to work together to make sure I don't act like an idiot.

I guess what I'm trying to say here is that, if I had a chance to redo the last year, I wouldn't. Sure, there were some down moments, but this is life, you can't expect everything to be sunshine and roses. And this experiment? A major success. If I had a choice to go to MIT in the fall (which I do), I would choose high school. Every Single Time. Why? Because I see my whole life ahead of me. I don't need to fast track my life just because I can. I should enjoy what years I have left of childhood, and let college come to me when it should. I'm not ready to be an adult yet, and honestly, I can't see myself being ready for the foreseeable future. What I do know is this, life is only beginning for me, and I should grab any chances I have by the bull horns, because opportunities only come knocking once. As mainstream kids would say nowadays: YOLO. This is the end of freshman year, but a new chapter of my life is only beginning, and if this year was a preview for anything, it's that there is only more to come. But right now, I need to start packing, we have a long road trip, and many university physics departments to be visiting. And when I come back, Sophomore year will be upon us. Or, I guess as the Ancient Romans would say, the year of the Wise Fool.

THE END